THEO AND THE SECRET OF ELSHON

MELANIE ANSLEY

For Mom.
A thousand thanks for ten thousand reasons.

CHAPTER 1

The moonlight outside the narrow cave mouth had whittled down to a paw-sized disc, then to a whisker's edge. Then that too disappeared, leaving them drenched in darkness. The only clue that Theo wasn't alone in this maze of rock was the erratic flutter of wings before him and the soft padding of Indigo's and Brune's paws behind.

"Roach, I need light."

As good as a rabbit's eyes were, they were no match for total darkness. The gray-and-ginger bat who had guided them here had insisted on no flame until the cave mouth was out of sight.

"Shh," came a voice in Theo's ear, making him jump. The creature could be silent as old age. "A little further."

"It always is," Indigo muttered. Theo understood her apprehension. Rabbits weren't made for caves. Especially Indigo. The princess of Alvareth was accustomed to her homeland's open plains and high tundras.

"No fire," Roach hissed. A flap of his wings, and he was again off ahead of them.

Brune growled. The bear, though at home in caverns and used to all sorts of nocturnal winged creatures, didn't bother to hide his mistrust of Roach. Anyone who volunteered information as Roach had should be treated with "two pounds caution and three pounds suspicion," to use the bear's words.

But they had to follow the bat. After several moons of chasing dead ends and false leads across Mankahar, this was the best clue they'd found in locating the notorious word catcher, Orjo. Some said Orjo the Terrible, once the scourge of Mankahar, was dead. And if he was alive, he wouldn't want to be found.

But Theo and his companions had doggedly asked every gull, sea turtle, and albatross they came across for directions to the Land of Blue Elders, where Orjo was supposedly hiding. But no one had heard of it, and Theo was beginning to think that the information Lord Noshi had given him must be wrong. Then they had encountered Roach, a fishing bat, who overheard their conversation with a group of black-headed gulls.

Roach had told them his clan's cave held a secret—an ancient rock drawing with the Forbidden Language on it. His clan kept it hidden and let no one in, Roach had explained. A wise choice, as the symbols called the Forbidden Language were taboo, and the law of the land demanded death to anyone possessing materials with the symbols on them. All those who knew the Forbidden Language, the ones called omatjes, had been purged generations ago.

"Did you hear that?" Indigo asked.

The three of them stood still, ears primed in the darkness.

"Water," Brune answered quietly.

"No, behind us," the princess said.

Theo listened. Was that the faint clatter of bones? The cave entrance was like an open graveyard, littered with the remains of countless meals enjoyed by countless predators. Theo and his companions had tried to pick their way around them, but couldn't avoid sending fragments clicking, like some abacus of death.

"It's just the nursery," the bat's words sounded in Theo's other ear, nearly making him stumble. "My clan's pups live back there, near the mouth."

"Let's keep going," Brune urged.

Theo felt his way forward once more, following the elusive flutter of Roach's wings. The cave began to curve, and Theo hoped they would be able to find their way out.

"Here it is," Roach squeaked. "Fire now."

Theo rummaged for the bag of flints he kept at his left hip. On his right, he kept his priceless medicine pouch slung to his belt. He reached into the bag and gripped the familiar stones, the twist of hemp, and wood he kept there. He lit the hemp, then Indigo held out a femur wrapped in loose cloth. At least they'd had the foresight to bring a torch.

The cloth caught, smoldered, and flared. The tentative light reached out toward the cave walls and soon glowed against Indigo's white-furred face, the intricate swirls of blue tattoos inside her ears, and the sword in her paw. Then Brune's dark-brown muzzle, framed by the metal battle helmet he always wore, leapt into view. A leather harness crisscrossed his chest, the back scabbard holding Brune's battle-axe. Roach appeared last, twisting his head away at the light's touch.

"Sorry." Theo had probably temporarily blinded the bat. Roach scrabbled along the ceiling above them, then pointed with one dirty wing claw.

"The Cursed Wall."

Theo held up the torch and saw shapes and lines carved into the rock. Here and there, faded paint glowed in the fire light, and Theo recognized the unmistakable shapes of words caught in the stone. The Forbidden Language.

"By Aktu," Brune muttered. "It's a map."

Theo nodded. When had this been painted? Was it before Aktu's Language, the silent language that spoke through symbols, had become a death sentence? No one would dare paint such a thing now, even if they did somehow know the Forbidden Language. Like Theo.

"It is a rare treasure, no?" Roach whispered.

More than you can imagine, Theo answered silently. He cleared a film of moss and grime from the words, revealing a crude map of Mankahar. Theo recognized several lands named. There were the forests of Jaipri in the middle, the plains of Alvareth to the north, and the lakeside castle city of Ralgayan perched high atop its sheer cliff face to the east. And to the west, the map ended with the Sea of Petrified Waves, with just a blank space beyond called simply "The Forgotten Lands."

Homesickness struck. His lands. Where his native village of Willago lay. *No, not anymore. It was destroyed, remember?* His throat grew raw, especially at the next thought that came before he could stop it. *Because of you.*

"Does it show the Land of Blue Elders?" Indigo asked.

He shelved the painful memory and searched the map again. "No, I don't see anything."

"What are these?" Brune pointed to a cluster of irregular circles running like unstrung beads down the southern edge of Mankahar.

Theo held the torch closer. "Islands. Karbahar, Grish, Baldatha." He frowned. "No Land of Blue Elders."

"What about this one?" Indigo squeezed next to him and tapped one of the dots on the map. As usual, her closeness made Theo forget what he was doing. Just for a few breaths.

"She's right," Brune said. "Isn't that painted blue? What's it called?"

Theo wiped at the irregular circle with his paw and squinted. The torchlight caught the faint hint of blue dye, along with the faded words, and Theo grinned. "Isle of Blue Elders."

"Stripe me yellow and call me a bee, that must be it. Orjo's on an island." The bear laughed.

Theo stood and dusted his paws. "We still have to get there, remember."

"At least we know where 'there' is now," Indigo said.

Roach swung down from his rock perch above. "I give you our clan treasure, and now you pay us."

Theo frowned, looking from Brune to Indigo. The bat hadn't

mentioned payment. Indigo pulled a small ruby from her belt. It was the only jewel they had left, after using up everything Lord Noshi had given them in their hunt for Orjo.

She held it out, its facets blood red. "This is all we have."

The bat shook his head. "I don't want your rock."

"Then what do you want?" Brune growled.

The bat made a series of clicking sounds. "We want the blood of the omatje, the one who knows Aktu's language."

Theo went cold. Revealing himself as one who knew the Forbidden Language, an omatje, had been risky. But he hadn't expected this.

And now he could hear it.

The unmistakable scratch of claws along the cave roof grew louder, followed by the clatter of leather wings. Dozens, if not hundreds, of eyes gleamed from the walls and ceiling just beyond the torch's reach.

Indigo bristled. "This was all a trap."

Roach made several clicking sounds, swiveling his head toward her. "You must give us his blood. His blood can stop pacification. Like at the Battle of Ralgayan."

Brune cursed. "That tale has truly grown out of control."

"I changed Indigo's blood with mine, but it could have been anyone's blood. I read it in *The Miraculous Cures of Zo!*" Theo could see his words had little meaning. How could he explain to creatures that shunned the Forbidden Language that his knowledge had come from a book, not sorcery?

"The omatje's blood will stop pacification. Everyone knows." The bat licked his lips. "Many in our clan have been pacified, only his blood can save them."

The other bats gathered in crowds along the ceiling, on the walls, twittering their agreement.

"By Aktu," Brune growled.

"I am sorry," Roach said, sincere. And then they attacked.

CHAPTER 2

"**R**un!"

The bear's command was nearly drowned out by clattering wings and screeching assailants.

The close quarters kept Theo and his companions at a disadvantage. Brune couldn't pull his battle-axe free from his back harness, and Indigo barely had room to move her sword.

Countless tiny teeth tore at Theo, even as he tried to fend them off with his torch. Some instinct made him keep his arms up, protecting his eyes and head from the onslaught of fangs and claws.

"Get out of here!" Indigo shouted. They had to escape the confined space around the map wall. Without room to pull their weapons, they were defenseless. Brune's helmet offered his head some protection, and he held one burly arm over his eyes as he used the other to fight through a swarm of biting, slashing bats. But with only one torch, they were literally fighting blind, which only favored the enemy.

"We need fire!" Theo cried.

A hard clanging sounded against the walls as Indigo found enough room to swing her sword's flat side against the cave rock. Theo immediately noticed a change in the bats as they swirled away and tried to come back, disoriented by the sound.

"Hurry!" Indigo shouted. "Light something!"

Theo fought off the remaining bats around him, ignoring the pain in his torn paw as he gripped his torch. He yanked off his jerkin, exposing his chest and back. He lit the cloth and then whirled it around him like a slingshot, creating an arc of heat and fire. The flames singed the closest ring of bats, who yelped and veered away, and Theo immediately took advantage of the opening.

"Brune, keep them back! We need a bigger fire!" Theo began working his way toward the cave mouth, or at least, where he thought the cave mouth was. The jerkin would burn through within heartbeats, and when it was nothing but ash, the bats would close in again, like a river over a log. He could hear the snapping of Brune's jaws as the bear crushed his attackers in midair, or slammed them against the cave walls with his mallet-like paws. Indigo's sword hammered against the stone in a redoubled effort to confuse the bats. Even so, Theo knew there were too many. The enemy was an endless airborne stream, and his clothing was almost burned away.

Theo dropped the last of his jerkin, a tattered strip, and felt the onslaught immediately. They tore and bit into him, puncturing any exposed flesh and sucking hungrily on the resulting blood.

Brune swept them off Theo's back with one giant paw, then pulled the rabbit to him. "Get down!"

"What about you?"

But the bear brooked no argument. He grabbed the torch from Theo, curled his massive body around the rabbit to create a shelter of flesh and fur, and barked, "Your medicine bag! Burn it!"

Theo had forgotten about the satchel he carried everywhere. He upended the pouch that was still slung around his waist and found the bottles he was looking for—he always carried a supply of oils to make salves. He pulled these out now.

"Can you buy me a little time?" Theo shouted.

"What do you think I'm doing?" the bear bellowed back. A large bat tried to attack Brune near his neck, and the bear crushed it with one paw.

"I need some space, Brune!" It just might work, but he couldn't do it smothered in six hundred pounds of bear.

"Make it quick!" Brune stood and charged the wall of bats with his torch, Indigo resorting to using her sword more as a club than a blade.

Theo hastily tore off his shirt and ripped it into strips. He laid these in a lattice formation across the cave floor, creating a barrier. One bat struggled through Brune's and Indigo's defenses, and Theo had to rip it from where it locked its teeth on his ear. He threw it against the wall and heard a wing snap, then began pouring his oils on the strips of fabric. Warm blood trickled down his ear and onto his face.

"How much longer?" Indigo shouted.

"Almost there!" Theo threw open his medicine pouch and fumbled for the small packet of cinnamon. Nothing was labeled, but he knew his medicines by smell and feel and could have found them blind. Which he basically was. He pulled out the tightly wrapped cinnamon powder and ripped the cloth open.

"Brune! Torch!"

The bear tossed it to Theo, pulling a bat from his burly neck. Theo touched the nearly extinguished torch to the oiled clothes, and the cloth barrier came alive with flame. Smoke rose, thick, white, and pungent against the darkness.

"Run!"

Brune and Indigo didn't need encouragement. They hurtled toward Theo, the bats screeching in pursuit. The flames had grown higher now, and a thick wall of smoke was forming. Brune and Indigo charged through, coughing, but the bats who struggled past wavered and fell to the cave floor, disoriented.

Some, unable to stop the onrush behind them, plummeted into the flames and caught fire.

Brune used his heavy back paws to crush those that made it through, while Indigo hefted her sword and decapitated the others. Soon, the assault slowed to a trickle and then halted. The bear and rabbits stood, bloodied and winded. The flames still burned, and the air was thick with cinnamon, smoke, and the stink of singed fur. But they were alive.

"How did you ever live in caves?" Indigo asked Brune, touching a cut on her face and wincing.

"The bats were less bloodthirsty." The bear coughed from the smoke, then examined a series of bites on his forearm. "I hope you didn't use up everything in that medicine bag of yours." At Theo's expression the bear looked concerned. "You all right?"

"Why couldn't they believe me about my blood?" The rabbit's chest tightened with anger and futility. "This wouldn't have happened if the Forbidden Language wasn't taboo. If it was a common skill."

Brune slid down the wall and sat with a grunt. "You can't reverse over ten generations of thinking overnight, Theo. How you saved Indigo does seem like magic, even if you can explain it. Those bats wanted to believe there's a magic cure to pacification. And I can't blame them. Isn't that what we're looking for, too?"

"The Library of Elshon is more than just a magic solution," Theo said, stamping out the last of the flames.

A squeak made them turn, weapons ready. Huddled against an upper wall was a gray-and-tan bat, no bigger than Theo's fist.

Indigo's voice was soft. "We must be near the nursery."

Theo raised the torch and pointed beyond the small bat. "I think we're in it."

Dozens of small eyes, tucked into a recess in the cave ceiling, gleamed in the shivering light.

Brune glanced at the rabbit. "They've seen you're an omatje. That could be dangerous."

"You saying we kill their young, Brune?"

"I'm just saying letting them go means things are going to get stickier from now on."

"They'll tell others we were here," Indigo said, eyes still on the bats above. "Then Ornox will know where we are. It's a risk."

"So better to kill them?"

"Yes," Indigo said. "It's the hard choice a good queen would make." She looked at Theo. "But we're not going to, are we?"

"No, we're not." Theo held the flame up to the bat. "Go!"

They watched as the pup flew out the cave mouth and into the night, followed in a long stream by his siblings and nursery mates.

"This may end badly," Brune warned, but Theo knew he approved.

"A wise bear once told me, 'Why worry about bee stings when you haven't found the honey?'"

Brune grunted, his expression turning somber again. "We're not dealing with bees. We're dealing with Urzoks. And Ornox is one Urzok whose sting is far worse."

"Let's treat our wounds," Theo said, "then find out how to get to the Isle of Blue Elders."

CHAPTER 3

*L*ord Ornox of Vyad watched the shadows grow and stretch across the hall as the sun set, turning the wall opposite pink, then plum, before darkening to a blood red.

The man's feet ached from standing since noon, and old scars on his war-torn body itched from spending a day in his finest official garb. But he wouldn't give the imperial guards any details to pass on to the gossip mongers in the barracks. He knew that whatever discomfort he felt, outside appearances were what people saw. His chiseled nose and dark eyes made him magnetic yet menacing. A thick black-and-silver warrior's braid ran down to his waist, highlighting a broad back that was more bull than man. Only this last autumn, his hair had been free of silver. But what he had endured these last months would have crushed a lesser man, not just silvered his hair.

He focused on the grand hall around him, the gilded pillars and the mosaic floor of red and purple. He remembered the last time he had been here, when his plans for ruling Mankahar had seemed so imminent. He would defeat the Order that insisted on defying the empire, marry his daughter Agacheta to the emperor, and then rule from behind the throne if not on it.

But today, he stood here as a disgraced warlord, his daughter dead in what was now a notorious defeat at Ralgayan. Then, he had come as a powerful man to report his successes to his emperor. Today, he was kept waiting, like a lamb at spring slaughter, for the emperor to decide his fate.

The window from the hall here offered a view of the emperor's private chambers in the castle's innermost courtyard below, and Ornox studied it. The royal quarters sat atop a pyramid in the center of the courtyard, with a wide, stone staircase carved into the pyramid's north side. Two overhead hallways connected the chambers atop the pyramid to the castle's second level, where Ornox now waited. It was an unusual structure, designed by the first emperor hundreds of years ago, but its height and location made it easy to defend in case of attack. And it should have been his. The entire castle should have been his, if—

The doors to the royal audience hall opened to a brisk servant with a wiry beard. He bowed and motioned for Lord Ornox to follow him. The servant's silence, instead of greeting Lord Ornox with a recognition of his title, boded ill. Ornox kept his face impassive and followed the servant through the large doors, into a chamber with floor-to-ceiling windows overlooking a playing field. Beyond, the capital of Kalyun-eh spread into the distance, a jagged horizon of spires, bell towers, slate roofs, and manicured gardens. One side of the chamber was curtained with red silk, marking the emperor's private offices.

"Prostrate yourself before the emperor."

Ornox fought the urge to cuff the servant. He obediently prostrated himself facing the crimson curtain, forehead to ground, and forced himself to breathe in calm, measured breaths.

He heard the whisper of slippers as the servant bowed out, and then the curtain drew back.

"Get up, Ornox."

"Your Eminence, I—"

"I said get up."

Ornox rose to his feet. Beyond the now parted curtain, sitting at an ornate dining table made of elephant bone, was Dorgun, the emperor. A feast was laid on the table before him, and the emperor unhurriedly sipped his wine and swallowed a mouthful of meat. He was cloaked in expensive ebony silk and fine linen, and his face was more wizened than Ornox remembered. The ruler of Mankahar's most notable feature, however, was his deadened right eye. White as milk and rimmed in red, it couldn't possibly see but could still move.

Four men dressed in identical robes flanked the emperor. Everyone at court knew these advisors held the greatest sway with their ruler, and the one with the least height held the most sway of all. Ornox let his eyes rest on the shortest advisor—whose face looked like that of a boy of eight summers.

Brel was widely known as the Child because of his rare condition. The emperor's chief advisor hadn't grown a nail's breadth after his eighth year, and his skin had retained the pale-custard hue of a milk-fed youth. Only the eyes betrayed his age. Gray like a winter's sky and bloodshot, they had left innocence behind long ago—if they had ever known such a thing.

Ornox made himself look back at the emperor. Dorgun, high ruler of Mankahar, ran a manicured fingernail down the side of his temple, near his milky eye. To Ornox's mind, it was both ludicrous yet oddly chilling that such an ancient and sickly looking man could be ruler of this vast land. Everyone talked of the emperor's increasingly odd behavior—his wish to crown a rabbit his empress, his vagaries suggesting his mind was succumbing to age.

"Have you ever had snake meat?" the emperor asked, spearing a piece with his fork. "It's not for everyone, but I believe it sharpens the mind." He regarded the morsel. "Eat predators, and you will be one. Eat prey, and you grow fat as a lamb." He placed the piece of meat in his mouth, and Ornox watched the wrinkled throat work the food down.

"It seems you've become more prey than predator, Ornox. I

have to admit I'm greatly disappointed. You do know the most popular story being told around Kalyun-eh right now?"

Ornox said nothing. Of course he knew. Everyone knew.

"The story goes like this. There is a little rabbit, who defeated one of the empire's best warlords. He led a pitiful group of animals against a mighty imperial army, and won. Now this little rabbit is called ridiculous names like the Griffinrider, and the New Omatje, and such. You are familiar with this story?"

He burned at the emperor's blistering condescension, but kept his expression neutral. "My every day will be devoted to hunting this rabbit down."

"No," the emperor shook his head. "It won't."

"I understand the defeat was displeasing and a great failure, Your Eminence, but—"

"Displeasing?" Dorgun raised his eyebrows. They were painted on, to give the emperor a more youthful appearance. "I would be displeased if my cook burned my food. I would be displeased if my laundress ruined my clothes. I would hardly equate your defeat to either of those things."

Ornox knew not to defend himself. He was expected to listen.

"You were once a great warlord, a valuable asset, and now it seems you're a liability. We cannot let a rabbit make a fool of you, and by extension, me."

"I will make it up to you, Your Eminence, if you'll just—"

"I accept. You will make it up to us. The empire is pleased to receive your lands and your title as compensation."

Time slowed, stopped, as the preposterous words sank in. Ornox waited for some explanation, some laugh to betray this as a cruel joke. When only silence stretched between them, he spoke. "Your Eminence, while that is a natural reaction, may I humbly suggest—"

"No you may not," the emperor snapped. "Be grateful I haven't ordered your head and neck to part. You will hand over the seals and keys to Vyad today. Now, as a matter of fact."

Ornox looked over to the child-like advisor. He couldn't help it. The unnaturally young, custard-hued face stared back at him, and then the advisor stepped forward.

Ornox felt a trickle of relief. Brel would defend him. This was to teach him his place, something the emperor was fond of doing. Brel would intercede, pave the way for Dorgun to be magnanimous. It was a serving of humility Ornox had not expected, but it would have to be stomached.

The child-man held out a small hand, the dough-like fingers smelling of musk. Ornox looked at them, uncomprehending.

"Your seals and your keys, please." The advisor's voice was also that of a child's, completely at odds with his tone of command.

Ornox looked down at those pale-gray eyes, and felt his chest tighten. He reached into his belt pouch and pulled the stone seal, its familiar insignia a part of his family for generations, and let it drop into the outstretched hand. He might as well have given his right hand away. At the advisor's silent expectation, Ornox reached under his shirt and pulled a chain with a key on it over his head. Family lore claimed it once opened the side gate to the Vyad keep, but really the key to any great house was more symbolic than practical. It bestowed ownership, and with that a warlord's whole existence within the empire. Ornox felt more naked without these two items than if the emperor had stripped him of every last piece of clothing and displayed him in a square. One was to be without covering. The other was to be without identity, without heritage.

"You are no longer Lord of Vyad," the emperor said. "You may go."

* * *

ORNOX WAYLAID the Child just inside the castle gates leading to the outer courtyard, where the horses and carriages of visitors were brought for their owners.

When the senior advisor stepped from the southern gate, Ornox was ready. He had traded his distinctive official warlord garb for a simple monk's cloak and headscarf, then stepped into the Child's path as if he was an unusually forthright monk asking for alms. He smothered the thought that this was not too far off the truth.

"I have no alms—"

"A quick word then."

Ornox pulled his headscarf back just enough so the Child could see his face. The Child's eyes narrowed, and his lips flattened into a hard line of displeasure. This close, the heavy smell of musk was like a punch to Ornox's senses.

"You have some nerve." Brel's eyes flicked left, then right, wary.

Ornox resisted the urge to strangle the aberration before him. "I? You are the one who made me a sacrificial offering without raising a fat finger. If I deserve death for my defeat, what does a traitor to the emperor deserve?"

Brel's milky face grew mottled. "Careful, Lord Ornox. Remember who you are speaking to."

"I'm speaking to the one who will return my seal and keys."

"You think it's that easy? Your defeat is known far and wide, Ornox. The emperor cannot forgive such a humiliation. Be glad your head is not drying on Kalyun-eh's walls, and kindly leave."

Ornox went very still, feeling the anger within him curl on itself until it was white hot. "I do not forgive humiliations either, Brel. Remember that."

The gray eyes hardened. "Are you threatening me?"

"I'm saying you should choose your enemies carefully."

"I'm not your enemy, Ornox. But I can't help you. Not anymore."

A servant hurried over and pulled Brel aside. He whispered something to Brel, and in his hopes that the emperor had changed his mind, Ornox strained to hear. He made out the words "map" and "cargo" and felt the hard knot of disappointment settle back. Brel's pallid face, however, flushed with excitement.

"Brel, we're not fin—"

"Good day and good luck, monk."

With a last glance at Ornox, the Child strode away from him, into the sun dappled courtyard outside, leaving Ornox in the shadows of the entry hall.

CHAPTER 4

The Child was out of his sedan before it came to a full stop. He forced himself to walk, and not make an undignified run, through the side guardhouse to his manor.

There, a servant bundled in thick robes opened the side doors and took his master's cloak. Brel made his way to where he'd installed the man-operated elevator cage when he first took over the manor, as navigating stairs with his short legs was never enjoyable. The servant pulled a bell rope that rang on the second floor, and they heard the squeak of pulleys as the man above lowered the lift. It was a wooden cage, just big enough for three people, with a gate that latched shut and a track system on either side to keep the contraption steady.

Once it had landed on the first floor, the servant opened the waist-high wooden gate for Brel, who was inside and pulling the gate shut almost before his servant could do so. Another tug on the bell, and the lift heaved off the ground, rolling along the tracks on both sides as it ascended to the second floor.

There, the burly lift operator secured the ropes to a thick metal handle and opened the gate for his master. Brel strode out onto a hallway, and saw a tall, knife-thin man, with a pockmarked face and a long scar down one cheek, standing by a set of double doors at the end.

Brel again forced himself to keep to a brisk walk. Because his age didn't match his small body, he looked ridiculous running. And he didn't fancy looking ridiculous. Even if he was about to find something he had devoted most of his life to seeking—the Library of Elshon. If he found it, he would have answers, answers to questions no one had even thought to ask. Most importantly, he would be able to solve the one riddle that had dogged him his whole life. What was this terrible affliction he had that kept him from growing? Why him? Why this disease? Why did he perspire so much more than others that he always had to spend a small fortune on perfumes? He had long ago learned how to turn his deformity to his advantage, but to know his illness was to be master of it. And he needed to be master of it. Only then could he be master of everything else.

Soon he was before the doors, and the tall thin man.

"My greetings, Master Brel."

"You're sure he's an omatje, Caldrik?"

Caldrik nodded and opened one of the doors, following Brel in. This was Brel's ornate personal chapel, lit by a chandelier of bone and antler that hung from the high ceiling. Rows of padded benches lined the walls, with a statue of Emperor Dorgun on a dais in the center. It was a room both stately and somber, unyielding and intimidating. Which was, Brel knew, why Caldrik had brought their guest here for their first meeting.

Sitting on the far side, as if trying to get as far away as possible from the door and anything that might come through it, was the chapel's single occupant. A thin rabbit in a rough cloak.

The creature looked like he and death would not be strangers for much longer. Though he'd obviously been cared for, the old thing was still gaunt and haggard. One ear was severed at the three-quarter mark, and though it had now healed to an ugly stump, it was testament to a good deal of ill treatment. Despite this, his eyes were bright with defiance.

Brel made an admonishing sound. "Who did this to our guest? I said pressure, not torture."

"Agacheta cut his ear off, Master Brel."

"Ornox's daughter? Well good thing she's dead, or I'd kill her myself." Brel walked forward and sat next to the rabbit, who eyed him as one would a rabid dog.

"You'll be well treated here, if you choose. What's your name?"

The rabbit stayed silent.

"Answer him, rabbit, or I'll—"

"Hush, Caldrik," Brel said in his sing-song voice, then turned back to the rabbit. "My name is Brel. I am the most powerful man in Mankahar." He pointed toward the statue. "More powerful, you will find, than even the emperor. Now let me tell you something that I think will save us both a lot of time and pain. Are you listening?"

The rabbit scowled, watching him.

"I need someone who can catch and release words. An omatje. I don't care if it's you, or your grandson, the one called Theo. So if you don't tell me what I want to know, I will regretfully need to kill you and then hunt down Theo. But"—here the Child held up a finger for emphasis—"if you answer all my questions and do what I say, then I don't need Theo, and I won't go looking for him. Do you understand?" At the prisoner's wary silence, Brel continued. "I'll take it that you do. Now, let's start with your name."

The rabbit hesitated. "Father Oaks."

"Father?" Brel raised an eyebrow. "An omatje who is respected."

"What do ye want with me?"

The Child motioned at Caldrik, who pulled out a leather pouch from his robes. He opened it and withdrew a thin scroll of lambskin, which he handed to Brel.

The Child carefully unrolled the map until it lay soft and shining in his plump hands. He tilted it toward the candlelight so the rabbit could see better. Brel didn't need to see it, as he already knew it by heart from studying it every night since it had first come into his possession. There was an outline in the shape of Mankahar, with what looked like waves to the east. Clusters of half-moons or sharp peaks denoted the various ranges such as Mount Mahkah, the Blue Teeth, and the Purple Mountains, but most other landmarks were decipherable only through incomprehensible lines of caught words.

"Release the words, please," the Child said. "Starting up here."

Father Oaks glanced at the map, then said in his raspy voice, *"The secret of Elshon lies with Orjo."*

Brel clapped his hands together, his palms growing sweaty in his excitement. "Yes. Legend says Orjo's tomb in the Land of the Blue Elders marks the Library. And where does it say Orjo is?"

The rabbit frowned, searching over the map. "I don't see anything else about Orjo."

Brel tried to contain his frustration and leaned in closer toward the map. The rabbit recoiled.

"Just tell me everything it does say." Brel pointed. "This. What's this?"

Father Oaks bent in, squinting. "A bunch o' nonsense. Water, fire, air, an immortal, a feathered fish."

"Tell me about the immortal."

The old rabbit bent closer to the parchment. *"A once-great immortal's tomb, guarding secrets dark and deep."*

"'A once-great immortal.' That's Orjo." Brel took the map back onto his own lap, examining the spot with the words. A thin row of ridges ran in two jagged parallel lines, and the pieces began falling in place in his mind.

Caldrik frowned. "The secret refers to the Library, does it not?"

"It must. These are the Blue Teeth. Mountains that create a corridor." Brel tapped one knee. "Land of Blue Elders. Caldrik, what do you think of when you think of mountains?"

The other man thought on this. "Cold. Unyielding. Tall."

"Yes, tall and old." Brel bent over the map again. "Like elders towering over you. The Land of Blue Elders must be the Blue Teeth. That's why this line about an immortal is here. His tomb must be in the Blue Teeth."

"And Orjo's tomb marks the Library," Caldrik concluded. "Shall I prepare the men?"

"Yes. We leave at first light."

Caldrik bowed and left. Brel stared at the map, as if afraid it would disappear in his very hands. He drew a breath. "Father Oaks, thank you. You have no idea how happy you've made me."

"So ye've got what ye want. Will ye let me go now?"

Brel looked over at him, surprised. Then he beamed at the rabbit. "Oh no, Father Oaks. No. This is just the beginning."

CHAPTER 5

Over winter, rumors about the warlord had swirled and grown like snow in a storm, which meant it didn't take long for the manor to hum quietly with news that Ornox was almost here at the trading post of Nyatha. The maids whispered behind fluttering hands, while the stable boys and wranglers pulled out all their old theories as to what had really happened at Ralgayan last autumn.

"My brother was in the closest town up north. He says the warlord was so scared he fled."

"You believe that hogstool? About the griffin?"

"All I know is barely anyone left that battlefield alive, 'cept for Ornox. How do you explain that?"

"Even his daughter was killed."

"Aye, word is by a rabbit."

"That tale's even harder to swallow than the one 'bout a griffin. A rabbit? Kill a fighter like Ornox's daughter?"

"Some say he's not just a rabbit. There're those who say he's — Curse it. It's the master."

At this announcement, the maids scattered. And when they did, Pozzi ground his teeth in frustration.

It had been easy for the stout, piebald rabbit with the buckteeth to listen in on gossip. He'd learned that as a pet in the human household, it was best to speak as little as possible. That way, the humans—or Urzoks, to use the derogatory term used by non-humans—would forget that Pozzi understood their words and was storing every scrap of information they let fall, as a squirrel gathers every chipped or half-eaten acorn before winter.

And store he did. Whatever he heard, he made sure to remember so that he could repeat it to Keeva, and sometimes, to Walnut as well—though it was hard to know what to tell Walnut these days. The young brown rabbit had tasted more than his share of sorrow and seemed to take little interest in the talk about a far-off army called the Order that was fighting to free the animals of Mankahar.

"Pozzi! Where are you Pozzi?"

He turned and ran toward the little girl's voice. It was best to keep Hassah happy. She was, after all, the fragile barrier between the life they had now and the so-called life that every other rabbit at Nyatha led.

He dashed down the hall and nearly collided with a pair of leather boots.

"Watch it!"

Pozzi barely dodged the kick meant for his head. He knew the voice without seeing the face. Sarkus, the young son and heir of the master of Nyatha. Pozzi broke into a sprint and cursed as he heard the boy's footsteps pounding after him.

The rabbit raced around a corner and up a short flight of steps to the balcony that served as one of Hassah's favorite play areas. It offered a sweeping view over the fort of Nyatha. The manor and private quarters were on the north side, surrounded by a ring of gardens. The animal pens and stockades started on the south side, stretching to Nyatha's outer walls. Hassah and Keeva were sitting at a low table, playing at tea. Hassah's nurse Farriah sat by the balcony rail, stitching a blanket while she watched the stable hands below wrangle horses and mules.

Pozzi ducked behind Hassah just as the Nyatha bell rang out, a low boom that marked afternoon break for the farm hands and household staff.

Sarkus emerged onto the balcony, scowling.

"Hassah! What did Father say about your stupid pets?" Sarkus was in that twilight between childhood and adulthood. Where others his age seemed caught in an awkward pairing of gangly limbs and ill-fitting features, Sarkus had been blessed with youthful grace. He wore his thick, black hair cropped straight across his shoulders, and Pozzi had learned that the boy's smooth, wide face and tapered eyes were considered handsome.

Hassah looked up at her brother, defiant and intimidated all at once. Her wispy curls fell into eyes that were beautiful primarily because of their innocence. In Pozzi's opinion, the only beauty to be found among the humans was in their children.

"Next time I find them running around, I'll give 'em to the cobbler to make into boots."

Hassah pulled a face at her brother's retreating back.

"Come have willow tea with Lady Keeva and me, Pozzi."

Pozzi took a seat next to Keeva at the low table, where chipped cups and a teapot had been laid out.

Keeva's fur had returned to its famed lilac sheen that had captured so many hearts back home in Willago—including Pozzi's. Her once-stark ribs now had a healthy layer of flesh on them, thanks to Hassah's sharing of her meals. Seeing Keeva and being in the same room with her was the closest Pozzi felt to being home. Having been ripped from their village, they had endured a grueling trek over this harsh, foreign land. Some, like Walnut's mother, had not survived.

"Where's Walnut, Hassah?" Pozzi asked, nervousness returning. The young rabbit had become like a son to Pozzi and Keeva, the three of them forming an unspoken family unit.

Hassah made a face. "Naughty Walnut ate my apple bread. He has to stay in the cage."

Pozzi sighed with relief. Hassah, like any young creature only six summers old, had moods. So far, they were innocent enough, but Pozzi lived in constant fear that her moods would turn darker. Like those of her brother, Sarkus.

Pozzi joined Keeva at the table and snuck a glance at her. A nod of her head meant Hassah was in good spirits. A twitch of her whiskers warned that Hassah was temperamental, and to be cautious. A scratch at the ear told him that he should play prince to Hassah's princess. Today, however, Keeva simply stared ahead. Pozzi tried to catch her eye, but she was avoiding his gaze. A bad sign.

"Tea, Pozzi?" Hassah asked him, and the annoyed look on her face told Pozzi he'd already missed hearing the first offer.

"Yes please, Lady Hassah," Pozzi said, holding up his cup for her to fill.

"After tea, we'll choose your party clothes."

Pozzi threw another glance at Keeva, but her face remained carefully controlled, in what he now recognized was her scared expression. "A tea party?"

"No, silly! A real party, at the feast day." Hassah spooned so much honey into Pozzi's teacup that his teeth already ached. "There's going to be a big party, with lots of rabbits."

Pozzi's ears pricked at this. For the entire winter, he and Keeva had tried to glean news of their fellow villagers, including aunts, uncles, cousins, and friends—all who had come on the forced march with them, but who had been herded away to unknown parts of the Nyatha compound.

For reasons Pozzi still hadn't been able to puzzle out, Hassah's father Ghazan, master of Nyatha, had ordered that he, Keeva, and Walnut be brought into the master's own private household. Pozzi had only distant relatives as kin, but he knew Keeva suffered daily agonies wondering what had happened to her parents and siblings.

And perhaps she even missed her husband, Harlan, who had betrayed them all to save his own hide. Despite Pozzi's joy that the selfish bastard would likely never be seen again, he ached for what Keeva must feel. What was it like to know your husband had not only left you but actually convinced the whole village to board the wagons for Nyatha, telling them that they were being taken home? He must have known they were destined for the "farms" here. Marked for slaughter.

He forced his mind back to the present. "What sort of party?"

Hassah took a dainty sip of her tea. "A Passive Party. I have a new dress, so you must dress up too."

The honey turned to lead in Pozzi's mouth. A pacification party. That could mean only one thing. That was why Keeva couldn't look at him. He could tell by her glassy gaze that she was struggling not to cry.

His cup shook as he placed it on his saucer. "When's this, Lady Hassah?"

Dark brows furrowed the girl's face. She had never been good with telling dates. "Nurse Farriah, when is the Passive Party?"

"Pacification Party," the nursemaid corrected, biting off some thread. "Imperial Day."

"And we must all be up early." Hassah propped up an uncooperative doll that slouched on the seat opposite Pozzi.

Imperial Day. That was a week from now. He thought about asking whether they would be part of the pacification, but realized it would be pointless. She didn't seem upset. Which meant that if he, Keeva, and Walnut were destined for the cradles, where animals came out mindless and mute, Hassah didn't know about it. But it didn't mean that Ghazan's people couldn't come in and take them when Hassah was at her breakfast or bath.

How would they stomach watching a pacification? They'd both heard about the process but had never seen it. Animals passed in groups of fifty or more into specially made stone barns nicknamed the "cradles." Once in, the barn doors were shut, and trapdoors opened in the top, where a powder was liberally tossed in. Within a few heartbeats, all within the cradle would have lost their ability to speak and would emerge as soulless shells of their former selves. Most of these creatures, Pozzi knew, ended up as food for the Urzok tables, but sometimes, they were also used for sport, or labor; horses and oxen usually became Urzok transport, while goats and chickens often went to what Pozzi heard referred to as breeding pens. He knew the stories. Rows of cages where females were forced to bear young as quickly as they could, then killed when they could bear no more. He had never told Keeva about this and hoped she would never find out.

Pozzi realized that he had missed another of Hassah's questions.

"Pozzi, are your ears closed?" She was remarkably good at mimicking her nurse's expressions.

"So sorry, Lady Hassah," Pozzi apologized and hastened to pass a dish of sweet biscuits to Keeva. "I was just thinkin' 'bout what to wear."

* * *

HASSAH COULD NEVER STAY angry at her favorite pet for long and took Walnut out of his cage to bring him to her sewing lessons. Once they were gone from Hassah's room, Keeva let the flood of tears break.

"Pozzi, I can't watch that."

He hugged her awkwardly. Though it was not the first time he'd hugged her, he always felt strange about it. "We're not going to."

She rubbed at her swollen eyes, the fur on her tear-soaked cheeks crumpled from having been pressed against his shoulder. "Hassah will take us with her. She takes us nearly everywhere."

It was true. Hassah loved showing off her pet rabbits. Unlike the other household pets, who were pacified, Hassah's pets could talk and sing and dance on command.

"There has to be a way of stoppin' it," he said.

"Pozzi, don't be reckless. Think of Walnut."

"I am. How's he to watch somethin' like that?"

Keeva hopped on silent paws to the door to make sure no one was listening from the hall. "What can we possibly do? We don't even know where the prisoners are kept, and even if we did, how would we get past the staff? Hassah keeps us locked in here at night, and we can't leave the manor without her."

"There might be someone who knows where they are. Who could take us to them."

"Who?"

Pozzi motioned with his chin at the window. Keeva looked over, dubious. "The crows? Why would they help us?"

"They hate the humans, remember? 'Specially since Hassah's brother killed one of them. If it's a plan that'll put a thorn in Ghazan's side, the crows'll back it."

"If Ghazan finds out…"

"We'll have to make sure he won't." He didn't wait for an answer. Pozzi was already at the window, opening it wide. Hassah's room looked over the back orchards of the Nyatha manor, where apple and pear trees were already blooming with the warm breaths of spring. He and Keeva sometimes spent afternoons staring at the gardeners pruning the various plants, dreaming their separate dreams, but all revolving around their lost home of Willago.

He searched the eaves of the surrounding buildings. To his left, the manor stretched into the servant quarters, while to his right, the building branched into the main reception hall, meeting rooms, and dining halls. The smattering of crows that had set up their roosts here, much to the household maids' annoyance, made their homes in the high beams of the furthest building, where the shingles were loosest and where their human foes couldn't reach them. Usually, Pozzi could see one or two of them hanging about, though he only knew one of them by name. The one everyone knew by name.

"Hello!" It took a few cries before the snoozing old crow under the far eaves cracked one eye and searched for the voice. "Over here, sir!"

The pale-yellow eye focused on him, hostile.

"Beggin' pardon, but I seek Morrigan!"

The old crow eyed him a moment longer. "What for, rabbit?"

"I've a favor to ask."

"Crows don't do favors," the old bird cackled. "Crows trade."

Pozzi drew a breath. The crows were notoriously clannish, practical, and shrewd. "Fine. I'd like to trade."

Keeva frowned but stayed silent.

The old crow hobbled up onto both feet. Fluffing his neck feathers, he gave three caws, one low, then another two high. He cocked his head and listened. Soon, an answering call floated from over the chimneys, and the old crow nodded. "She'll be here shortly."

Morrigan appeared soon after. She swallowed a remnant of what she had been eating—innards from the kitchen slops, Pozzi guessed—and began to clean her jet-black feathers.

Morrigan was one of the largest crows in her muster. Ebony feathers shone a blue-black in the spring sun, and her claws were so wide they easily gripped a rain pipe without slipping. Everyone at Nyatha knew Morrigan, for the crows had absolute freedom, and if you wanted something done, the crows could do it. They just always had a price.

Pozzi waited. Crows, he had learned, were meticulous about cleanliness, so there was no point hurrying Morrigan. When she had finished removing the last speck from her chest and wings, Morrigan glided over to a water drain that protruded from the roof near Pozzi's window.

"What's this about, then?"

"I need your help. We want to free our fellow rabbits."

Morrigan regarded him, as if trying to gauge his sanity. "Let me explain something, rabbit. When they bring in the livestock, as the Urzoks call them, they're divided into groups. You follow?"

"Into healthy and sick, old and young, I know." He'd heard scraps of details, but he knew this was new for Keeva.

"Righto. But then there're ones for fur, and ones for meat. Then there're also the ones for games."

"So they're not all in one place," Keeva concluded.

Morrigan bobbed her head. "Righto. They've all been sorted into great big groups, so if you want to free your family, you're going to have to free everyone. That's not easy."

"If we do nothin', they're all going to be pacified Imperial Day."

The crow cocked her head. "If it's wanting to save your kind from pacification, maybe you don't need to free them. Maybe you just need to destroy the powder."

At first Pozzi was confused, but then he saw where Morrigan was heading. "You're sayin' the poison's kept in one place?"

Morrigan's eyes glinted. "Righto. And I might know how to get into the place. Light a flame, and it would all burn."

Pozzi glanced at Keeva's worried face. Fire definitely sounded reckless.

The crow fluffed her feathers. "You don't have to do it. You started this conversation, remember." She turned, preparing to fly.

"Wait!" Pozzi called out, and the crow stopped, eyeing him. "I can do fire."

Morrigan cawed in approval. "Very well. Then let's talk price."

"Isn't burnin' the pacification powder enough for you? That's a mighty blow to the Urzoks."

"We only care about one Urzok."

"Who?"

"Sarkus."

Keeva glanced at Pozzi. "What are you suggesting?" she asked Morrigan.

"I'll help you get to the pacification. But in return, we want Sarkus." The crow's eyes turned hard. "He burns our nests, shoots us with rocks and slings. We've lost several of ours to him. And a crow always gets revenge."

Pozzi hadn't expected this. "We can't kill him."

Morrigan tapped an impatient claw against the drainpipe. "What kind of crow revenge would death be? We won't kill him. We'll just teach him a little lesson. A crow lesson. But we need to get him in the open, unawares. Do that, and we'll take you to the powder."

Pozzi had no love for Sarkus. He knew the fates of Hassah's earlier pets—a duck that had ended up in a stew, a kitten drowned in Hassah's wash basin for her to find in the morning. For some reason, however, he and Keeva and Walnut had remained safe, and he had a feeling that Ghazan, the master, was protecting them. Why, he didn't know. But endangering Sarkus risked that protection.

"How will you punish him?"

Morrigan spread her wings. "That's not your business. Those are the terms." She crouched, preparing to fly. But Keeva's defeated expression made Pozzi grab at a wing feather.

"Wait!" he cried. "You have a deal."

Morrigan clacked her beak. "A crow never forgets a wrong. That includes broken promises. You follow?"

He wasn't sure how he'd deliver Sarkus, but anything was better than witnessing their family and friends going to the cradles. He had to take this a step at a time. "I follow."

Morrigan nodded. "The second night after you deliver Sarkus, meet me here when the moon is three-quarters. We'll take you to the cellars where the powder's kept."

CHAPTER 6

His men ate with unconcealed gusto, but Ornox had no appetite. The dining room felt small and close, which wasn't helped by the smoky fire in the hearth.

The fact that they were not in Nyatha's main dining hall was not lost on him. Ghazan, head of one of the empire's richest trading posts, didn't want it known that he had hosted Ornox, or that if word did spread, at least he hadn't hosted him in Nyatha's main hall for honored guests. Ornox had repeatedly asked the head servant who had shown them in when Ghazan would arrive, but had only received a hasty reassurance of "Soon, Master Ornox, soon."

He wasn't sure he could control himself to not stab the servant if he came back with the same reply next time. Having no title and no power was not an easy mantle for Ornox to wear.

How had it come to this? Only nine of his swordsmen, all sitting at this rough peasant table, had decided to follow their master in his darkest days. He looked at Yod, his most loyal assistant, who seemed to be made up entirely of edges—a sharp chin, pointy ears, tapered eyes, cheekbones that pressed out their corners and stretched the skin. Yod would go with him to the ends of Mankahar. The other eight, Ornox knew, stayed only because they were too old or too talentless to find employment elsewhere, but disguised their decisions as loyalty.

"I'm sorry for keeping you waiting."

He turned to see a portly man enter, the head servant nervously following like a stuck shadow. The master of Nyatha wore fine linen dyed a melon green, and the part of his collar that wasn't covered by his jowls bore the stitching of Nyatha's arms. A hand on the head of a lion.

"Have you eaten?" Ghazan motioned at the table. "I had my wife, Tansha, do pheasant, it's a—"

"I'm not interested in food," Ornox cut in. "Let's go to your solar to speak."

"Why don't we stay here? My solar hasn't been heated, and the spring evenings are still rather chilly."

Ornox recognized the lie as another sign that Ghazan did not want to receive Ornox anywhere considered official. The emperor had indeed made clear that the former warlord was thoroughly out of favor.

Ornox turned to Yod, who unlike the others had only eaten what he needed. Yod always kept one sharp eye on his master, ready to do any bidding.

Yod stood and motioned at the others. Though reluctant to leave their hot meals, his men obeyed, if only out of habit. But Ornox knew these days of obedience were numbered unless he could turn fortune around.

Ghazan spoke only when the last of them, including his own servant, had filed out and the only remaining sound was the pop of cones in the fire. "I'm sorry about your daughter, truly I am. But you cannot stay here."

"I don't intend to."

Ghazan's relief was palpable. "I'll have some food provisions drawn up for your men."

"I'm not after provisions, Ghazan. I'm after information."

"What makes you think I have information?"

"Agacheta told me you were the best merchant in the land.

You deal in everything that can make a profit, and that includes information. I need to find that rabbit Theo."

"I don't know where he is." At Ornox's stare, Ghazan held up his palms. "It's the truth. If I had that information, I would own two Nyathas, not one."

"I've lost my daughter, my lands, my title. Agacheta considered you a friend." That was a stretch, but Ghazan was his last hope in this nightmare that had become his life. "I demand you help me." He frowned, then forced himself to correct his words. "I'm asking you to help me."

Ghazan paced to the hearth and stood there, his back to the fire. "I have no idea where the rabbit is, Ornox, and truth be told, even if I did, I couldn't tell you."

Ornox frowned.

"Everyone is after that rabbit. You've heard the talk. His blood reverses pacification. He can summon a griffin. He's an omatje. The emperor will give a wagon of riches to whoever brings him the rabbit." Ghazan held out his hands to the fire, and a ruby glinted blood red in the light. "There are countless buyers who have paid good coin to know that information first. It'll be a bidding war, you know."

"I don't want him for coin. I want him for vengeance."

Ghazan nodded. "Understandable. But even vengeance has a price. Even if I had the goods, you couldn't afford to buy. I'm sorry."

"How about men? At least give me some men."

"Nyatha is a trading post, not a military camp."

"You could find me mercenaries."

"I rely on the emperor's favor, Ornox. If I supplied you with troops..." Ghazan turned away from the hearth, and something in Ornox's face seemed to sway him. "I am sorry for Agacheta's death though. Here. From one father to another."

The merchant reached into his vest and pulled out a felt pouch the color of young melon, the lion and the hand insignia stitched on it in gold thread. Ghazan held the pouch out to the former warlord.

"It's not much, but take it."

The grating sound of coin inside made Ornox's face burn hotter than the fire. "Charity? You're offering me, Ornox of Vyad, charity?"

"It's not charity," Ghazan said hastily, stepping forward. "I owed Agacheta some money. Take it."

A silence stretched until another cone popped in the fire, and with it, Ornox's suppressed rage. His fist lashed out, and the coins sprayed across the room.

When the clink of the coins faded to silence, Ghazan bowed, stiff. "Good night, Ornox. I'd appreciate you and your men leaving Nyatha by moonrise."

Ghazan left his guest standing by the fire, staring at nothing. He was still staring, unmoving, when Yod entered some moments later, taking in his master, the fire, and the winking pieces of gold on the floor.

Yod closed the door behind him, and then began picking up the coins and returning them to the pouch. He took his time, giving his master a chance to recover and think.

When Yod had finished collecting the coins, he silently tied the pouch and left it on the table next to Ornox, then slipped back out.

* * *

OUTSIDE, the night air had dropped low, promising frost by morning.

Ornox rocked with the gait of his horse. None of his men dared question why they had been turned away at nightfall, when host courtesy dictated guests be offered overnight shelter. No doubt his men missed the warmth of the kitchen, the comfort of a bed, and the promise of a hot breakfast. Instead, they were traveling on this deserted road out of Nyatha, toward the north where people didn't care as much what your reputation was in the southern capital of Kalyun-eh.

How low he had come, Ornox thought wryly. Lord of Vyad, once a warlord feared through the land, now reduced to traveling with spineless men.

But the real shame burned in the coin pouch hanging from his belt. Ghazan's coin pouch, which he had loathed to take but couldn't afford to leave.

He heard the sound of hoofbeats ahead. Travelers at night were rare. And this one was in a hurry. The half-moon above shed some light, but even before the rider came into view, Ornox sensed something odd.

The donkey was running full tilt, its rider a mere youth by his posture and the ease with which he rode—his bones clearly impervious to jolts. Strapped to the donkey's side was a cage cushioned with blankets.

"Halt!"

The youth pulled hard on his donkey and squinted through the dark at Ornox and his men.

"Where are you headed?" Ornox's voice carried authority that made people instinctively obey.

The youth stared at them, wary. The moonlight showed a face that couldn't have seen more than thirteen summers, and the garb looked like that of a cow herder. Ornox couldn't explain why he had stopped the rider, except that boys didn't ride donkeys at full gallop at night.

"Nyatha." The youth sat up straight, propped by the importance of his mission. "I got business."

"Trading is closed," Ornox answered. He looked over the donkey. "And where are your goods?"

The youth tensed, obviously unsure who they were but also too intimidated to ask. A fluttering in the cage drew Ornox's attention, and he made out the leathery flap of wings.

"I doubt you will get much for a single bat."

"I'm a bat with information." The bat's voice was high pitched, but clear.

"What kind of information does a fruit bat have? How to suck plums?"

A few snickers broke out from the soldiers.

"I know the whereabouts of Theo Griffinrider."

Ornox felt the world go still. "Where?"

The boy slapped the cage. "We agreed I'd do the talking, Roach." He looked around at the men, all silent shadows in the dark. His donkey let out a nervous bray, which made the youth stiffen.

"I will pay you for your information, boy."

The youth hesitated. "It's known Ghazan will pay well for information. It'd be a mighty fine price."

Ornox pulled the pouch from his belt, letting the coins make their telltale music. "I am Ghazan." He could sense the hesitation, but doubted this youth had ever seen the master of Nyatha.

"Beggin' yer pardon, but how do I know that?"

Ornox tossed the felt pouch toward the youth, who caught it. "If you have business with Nyatha, surely you know its crest of arms?"

The youth looked unsure.

"You can keep the contents in there now. And there's three times that if your information proves true."

The youth pulled a coin from the pouch and hefted it, then flicked it to test its sound. Satisfied, he turned to the cage. "Roach, tell Master Ghazan what you told me. About the rabbit and the Isle of Blue Elders."

CHAPTER 7

Seeing so much water still awed Theo, even though they had been traveling the coast for weeks.

"It's like it has no end, isn't it?" Indigo said next to him. Coming from the northern land-locked steppes, she shared his trepidation of this vast expanse before them.

And it truly did seem immortal. It exuded a salty, wet breath like that of a giant god, its skin changing from blue to black to turquoise to green, shifting with the light. It sighed and hushed on the sand, gurgled and roared amongst the rocks. From the shore, Theo felt he could look at it all day and never grow tired of its constant shifting moods. But now that they were faced with the prospect of crossing it, it seemed ominous and full of threat.

As he inhaled a lungful of salty air, Theo could almost hear his grandfather's voice, warning him about the dangers of going beyond his village's River Tithe. Of how those beyond that river boundary killed word catchers like him and his grandfather. Theo felt the familiar ache at the thought of Father Oaks, and whether he'd ever see him again.

"We won't get across by gawking," Brune grunted, shifting

the axe harness strapped to his back and glancing up the shore. "Let's find a way to cross the thing."

They were thirsty and foot sore after three days of travel down this rocky coast. Not for the first time, Theo thought how much easier this would have been if they had the pacified mares they'd ridden out from Ralgayan. But they'd been stolen soon after the group reached the more populated south, where horses fetched a high price.

Horses wouldn't have gotten them across water anyway, Theo comforted himself. So perhaps it was for the best.

Indigo watched the water rush over her feet. "I remember Orjo first telling me about ships on the sea." She watched the water pull back out. "We'll have to find one."

"The omatje who killed your mother and sister never gave his name," Theo reminded her. "You don't know it was Orjo."

"An omatje who is also a muskrat?" She looked skeptical. "It's no coincidence."

"The sooner we get going, the sooner we find out." Brune pointed. "And look. Aktu does indeed provide."

The rabbits turned to look and saw in the distance a trickle of smoke threading into the sky.

"There's bound to be fisherfolk with boats. They must know how to get to the Isle of the Blue Elders."

They began to walk, their paws sinking into the wet sand. Brune led the way, his thick legs soon leaving Theo and Indigo several paces behind. Theo glanced at her and could see the tell-tale twitch of her ears, the way one paw worried at her sword hilt. For Theo, Orjo was the key to the future. For Indigo, he reopened a painful past.

"I'm sorry."

"About what?"

"It's not easy meeting someone you think killed your family."

"I don't think it. I know it."

"He's the only one who can lead us to the Library of Elshon—"

"And you need the Library of Elshon to defeat the Urzok empire," Indigo finished. "Don't worry. I won't kill Orjo. No matter how much I want to."

She left him to join Brune. Theo realized after she had gone that he hadn't worked up the courage to ask his real question. Had she come on this journey with him solely for a chance at revenge? And if she had, why did that bother him so much?

You know why.

A deep, unspoken part of him wanted her to be here for him. Not because of some vendetta, not because it was the right thing to do according to her queendom's rule, as per her explanation when they'd left Ralgayan, but because she wanted to be with him. Just as he knew instinctively that he would go wherever she went, if he could.

The smoke led them to a ramshackle but tidy fisher's hut. Wooden racks outside held strips of blue-black seaweed, under which small, smoking fires burned.

"There's a boat under here!" Indigo lifted a long cloth that covered a filthy canoe, the length of three mares. Its sides were crusted with what looked like small, calcified snails.

"Hello?" Brune called out.

A head popped out from the hut. Wary eyes peered at them from a salt-lined sea otter's face, the whiskers sun bleached and the eyebrows bushy.

At the sight of the bear, the otter dove back into his hut. He reappeared a few breaths later, a long spear in his calloused paws. "Get gone! Find yourself another meal!"

Brune held up both paws, palms out. "We're just wanting directions, and to perhaps borrow the boat."

The otter's eyes narrowed. "I don't lend the boat to no one."

Indigo stepped forward. "What he means is hire, not lend." She drew out their ruby from one of her belt pockets. The otter's eyes softened from suspicion to excitement.

"I like your thinking." The otter turned the point of his spear away from Brune but kept it clasped tightly in one paw while reaching out with the other. Indigo casually pocketed the gem just when the otter could see its value.

"How familiar are you with the islands?"

The otter puffed air from his salty cheeks. "Born here, I was. There's little I don't know about these waters."

"We want to find the Isle of the Blue Elders," Indigo said. "You know it?"

The otter squinted, surprised. "Sure. Furthest island out."

"Have you been there?" Brune glanced over the waters toward the string of islands that walked off like a giant creature's pawprints toward the horizon.

The otter shrugged. "Me? Not on your life. No one's been on that island. Lore is it's unsafe."

The rabbits and bear looked at one another. "Unsafe how?" Theo asked.

The otter spat. "No one dares go near there, since everyone who does never comes back. Some say it's a dragon that lives there. I heard it once, roared like a herd of mating sea lions and belched smoke for days." He frowned at them. "Why do you folk want to go there, anyways?"

"We're looking for a special plant that grows there," Theo said. Theo, Indigo, and Brune had agreed that few would help them based on the truth, so they had devised a story for anyone who asked. "I'm a healer."

"Must be a very special plant," the otter remarked.

Indigo steered the conversation back. "So will you take us out there?"

The otter scowled, shifting his spear to the other paw. "You deaf, lass? Did I not just say no one dares go there? I like my head and body being attached, thank you. I won't set paw on that island for a boatload of those rubies."

"You won't have to set paw on the island," Theo reassured him. "Just take us there. We'll do the rest."

The otter looked at them, weighing Theo's words. "And the

boat doesn't touch shore neither. I drop you near the island, and you swim the rest, understood?"

Theo glanced at Brune and Indigo, who nodded.

"Understood," Theo agreed.

* * *

THE OTTER, having insisted his own boat was too small to carry Brune, led them to his cousin's down the shore, and though the boat offered more space, it looked about as watertight as a sieve.

"We'll take it," Brune said over Theo's and Indigo's misgivings.

The otter waved a paw dismissively. "Don't worry. We can caulk it up with a bit o' tar and some tree fiber, and she'll be good as when she last sailed."

Indigo eyed the boat's algae-eaten planks, dubious. "Which was when?"

"Not sure. Sometime before I was born."

With that reassurance he set Theo, Brune, and Indigo to sourcing fibers and helping fill the boat gaps. They set off midafternoon, when the "tide"—as the otter explained—was on its way out. Theo found it easy to set the otter talking about his greatest love, the sea. Soon, the creature was rattling off all he knew about the tidal times, the moon, navigation by stars, and all the best fishing spots for bewildering foods Theo and Indigo had no concept of oysters, eels, shrimp, catfish, limpets, and clams.

The otter had brought a stock of these foods and slurped regularly on a pile of shrimp he kept in a basket at the boat's stern. Brune gratefully shared the otter's one dried trout, but for the rabbits, there was little they were even willing to try except for the smoked seaweed the otter had stored. Theo chewed on his with determined politeness, but Indigo smoothly tossed hers overboard when the otter wasn't looking.

When night fell, they pulled down the sail, threw an anchor

over the side, and took turns sleeping. In truth, only the otter and Brune slept, for neither Indigo nor Theo could get used to the boat's rolling. While Indigo merely turned quiet at the discomfort, Theo managed to throw up his few bites of seaweed.

"Rabbits," the otter muttered. "Never meant to be on the sea."

Theo agreed. He would have given his right paw for some ginger to tame his stomach, but he'd lost most of his medicines in the bats' cave.

When morning dawned, the otter was up and hoisting the sail, guiding them straight east toward the rising sun. By noon, Theo could make out the silhouette of an island, its steep sides rising to what looked like a plateau. Like someone had taken a cleaver and sheared off the top of a mountain.

"It's not very big," Indigo commented as they drew closer. By midafternoon, they could see that the island was roughly a half day's walk from end to end. A white beach girded the island and led up to rocky outcroppings punctuated by the odd twisted shrub.

"This is where you get off," the otter said, heaving his anchor over the side of the boat.

Theo looked away from the shore, which was still several boat lengths away. "Just be here when we come back." Theo reached into his pocket and drew out the ruby, which had been halved.

The otter frowned. "This is half of what you promised!"

Indigo smiled. "The other half is for when you row us back."

The otter looked decidedly unhappy at this. "Which is when?"

Brune looked up at the island. "I'd say it'll take us two days, three at most to search the whole island."

"Two days," the otter grumbled. "If you're not back by then don't expect me to be here."

He helped them over the side. They shouldered their supplies —simple foods, a blanket, knives, and a sword each—and splashed their awkward way toward shore, holding their packs above their heads. Only Brune seemed unfazed by the water and pulled the rabbits onto his shoulders when at one point the sand dropped away beneath their paws.

The three of them emerged on the beach, soaked to the shoulders. Brune shook himself dry while Indigo wiped the excess seawater from her ears. Behind them, they could see the otter busily setting out fishing poles, whistling to himself.

"Doesn't look like a place that would be called Land of the Blue Elders," Brune grunted, surveying the tumble of rocks, sand, and scrub that lined the beach. "There's not much land, there's nothing blue. And I don't see any elders."

"We've only seen one side. Where should we start?" Theo asked.

Indigo shaded her eyes and looked up the hillside. "We'll get a better view from the top."

They set off across the sand. A stiffening breeze crept in off the sea, and the late-afternoon wind chilled the rabbits' wet fur. The ground sloped steadily upward, and as the sun dipped, they made their painstaking way up the hillside. Sand gradually gave way to more shrubs and large boulders, along with an abundance of plants that Theo had never seen before; spiky, hardy vegetation that clung to life in the cracks of rocks, or that spread out like grasping tentacles across the sandy soil where Theo would have thought nothing could maintain a grip, much less live.

The sun was low in the sky when they reached what they thought was the top of the island, and as they scrambled over the last outcropping, they paused.

The top wasn't a plateau or pinnacle as they had expected. Instead, the ground dropped sharply away from them, rushing downward into a steep, small crater that had been transformed into a valley. Here, the vegetation seemed completely changed, for the bowl of the crater had trapped rainwater, feeding a dense oasis of colorful plants. A hidden valley, completely invisible from the sea around it.

"It's an old volcano," Brune said, grudging wonder in his voice.

Theo had heard of these fire-breathing mountains described in one of the books his grandfather had kept, but never seen one.

"Don't they spout flame?" Indigo asked.

Theo pointed. "Not anymore, I don't think. Otherwise, those couldn't grow." Ringing the crater were cacti with bluish-white hair that grew so thick they looked furred. The wind played with the wispy manes, making the cacti look like wise, long-haired sages standing guard. Beyond them, where the sand gave way to rock and small pockets of verdant grass, the cacti grew sparser, replaced by water-dependent ferns. A small stream wound down from the far end to a pool at the crater's heart, and the gentle rush of a waterfall drifted up to their ears.

Indigo's gaze swept across the crater, taking in the cacti. "I guess this is the Land of the Blue Elders."

"He's here," Theo said.

"How can you be sure?" Brune scanned the island, clearly looking for threats.

"This is the only way a muskrat could survive out here—somewhere with plenty of water. And look." He pointed out several plants that had a precisely trimmed branch, or remnants of certain natural fertilizers around flowering cacti. "These are being cultivated. Someone lives here."

They began their descent into the crater, eyes and ears primed. They crossed paths with the occasional tiny lizard sunning on a boulder, or a roosting bird, but otherwise the island seemed uninhabited. It took them the good part of the day to reach the waterfall. Water rushed over a modest outcropping of rock and pounded into a wide, sun-drenched lake.

All three of them took long drinks at the water's edge, parched after the day's trek.

"Well," Indigo said, wiping her mouth, "if you were an omatje, where would you hide?"

Theo didn't bother to smile at the joke. It was as if Indigo felt that the more she pointed out he was an omatje, the less uncomfortable his taboo skill would feel to her. It was, to him, an awkward reminder that she still found him different. Which he was. The princess and the outcast.

"Somewhere I wouldn't be found." He searched the surrounding foliage, swiveling his short gray ears. He could hear nothing unusual, yet he had the strange feeling that they were being watched. He glanced at the sky, already a deep russet from the setting sun. "It'll be dark soon. We have to make camp."

Indigo nodded. "Might as well be near the water."

"True," Brune said. "Though we could find somewhere more…hidden."

Theo shook his head, scanning the rocks and slopes around them. "There's nowhere hidden on this island. Not with Orjo. If he's here, he knows we're here."

They gathered what edible tubers and plants they could find. Dandelion leaves, bush mint, and cactus flowers. They built a fire, not only for warmth but in the hopes of drawing Orjo out, of showing him they weren't trying to hide. Here, on Orjo's turf, there didn't seem any way to hunt down the elusive muskrat. They would have to wait for the notorious beast to hunt them.

CHAPTER 8

The cool of early spring had ripened, hinting at summer days to come, and Keeva, as they had planned, had persuaded Hassah to play blind ball in the main courtyard. It was a popular spot for children and maids alike in the morning, as the east-facing courtyard warmed quickly, and the fountain in its center provided a stone seat for sitting.

Hassah squealed as a blindfolded Keeva tried to throw a soft ball to tag her and Walnut, who dodged and darted. Whoever was blindfolded could win by hitting the other players with the ball, while the players had to avoid the ball and tag the "blind" player. Pozzi had begged off, blaming a sore leg, but really he was too nervous to play.

Keeva threw the ball, catching Hassah on the arm. The girl pouted for some time at losing, but then Keeva distracted her by running off shouting, "Catch me, slow foot!"

As Pozzi predicted, Hassah's nurse, Farriah, chose not to join in, preferring to take position on a shady stool and gossip with the passing maids who worked in the main house.

As the shrieks and patter of feet continued, Pozzi kept glancing at the hallway door.

Where was he?

Sarkus, he knew, had lessons all morning, with a short break just after the laundresses took the day's linens away for washing. The boy emerged almost every day around this time.

Except for today.

Pozzi glanced up at the rooftops, squinting against the sun. He couldn't see the crows, but he knew they were there. They had to be. Pozzi and the villagers were running out of time. The Imperial Day celebrations and the mass pacification were only three days from now.

He batted at a fly. The squeak of a wheel made him turn toward the outer courtyard where deliveries were made, but he immediately wished he hadn't. A burly man with a braided beard and thick boots was pushing a cart piled high with fresh pelts. His sleeves were rolled up and red with caked blood. Pozzi tried to keep his breakfast down. Even bloodied and thrown into a cart like scraps, he could see those were rabbit skins, a cloud of flies buzzing above in a frenzy.

"Where are you?" Hassah giggled, clutching her soft ball as she peeped beneath her blindfold.

Pozzi searched for Walnut and Keeva and was relieved to see they were so intent on their game that they hadn't noticed the cart or its contents.

Pozzi made his way closer to the wide archway that separated the main courtyard from the outer delivery yard. In the outer yard, the burly man motioned to someone. Pozzi heard the snorting of a horse and the sound of a wagon door being lowered.

"That the lot?" A wagon driver walked into view, surveying the cart's contents.

"Aye," the burly pelt worker replied as he threw the pelts into the wagon. "Last of the day. And good thing. Gettin' hotter n' a smelt out here."

The wagon driver grunted in agreement.

The pelt worker slapped the side of the wagon and returned to his now-empty cart. "See ya next week then, Kayden."

"It'll be fun!"

Keeva's voice made Pozzi rush back, remembering only just in time that he was supposed to have a sore foot.

In the courtyard, Sarkus had emerged from the house. He was headed for the cistern, where fish were kept for table. Keeva was following as closely as she dared. Hassah stood at the fountain, cradling Walnut, her blindfold pushed up onto her forehead.

"I'm not playing some silly game." Sarkus sat down on the cistern brick and began hunting for stones.

"I don't want you to play anyway!" Hassah scowled. For all her denials, she clearly looked up to her indifferent brother and craved his attention.

"I know! Maybe we could play for a prize," Keeva suggested, as if the thought was new.

Hassah lit up, while Sarkus looked mildly interested. The youth banged on the cistern, making the fish scatter. "What kind of prize?"

"How 'bout this soldier?" Pozzi came forward, pulling a little warrior figurine from his pocket. He had been carving it over the last few days in preparation for today, whittling a man with a sword from one of Hassah's discarded wooden clogs.

Sarkus glanced at it, then turned back to sorting through rocks. "I'm too old for those kinds of stupid toys." He picked up a smooth pebble and hefted it, then pulled out his slingshot.

Keeva glanced at Pozzi, worried. They had to get him to play. Whatever the cost.

"I bet even a fat, lame old rabbit like me can tag you three times blindfolded."

The youth's eyes narrowed dangerously. "You're full of hogstool."

Pozzi held out his paw to Hassah for the blindfold and the ball. "Maybe. Or maybe you're too scared to find out?"

The dare pushed Sarkus to his feet, his face hard with indignation. "I'm not scared."

Pozzi took the blindfold and tied it over his eyes, then held out his paws and felt Hassah place the ball in them. "Ready?"

"You couldn't hit me even if you—"

Pozzi swung his arm toward the voice. He was rewarded with a solid smack as the ball connected. "One point."

"Pozzi got you!" Hassah taunted.

"Shut your mouth!"

Pozzi lifted his blindfold to retrieve the ball. "Just luck, Sarkus. You'll do better next time."

The boy smirked. "Be quiet and put the blindfold on, rabbit."

Pozzi pulled the cloth back over his eyes and gripped the ball. He raised his arm as if to throw. Sarkus moved, the sound like thunder on a still day to Pozzi's ears. The rabbit threw toward the fountain, and though he didn't hear the ball, Walnut's shriek of laughter told him he'd succeeded.

"Two points." He lifted the blindfold in time to see Hassah giggle, then cry out as Sarkus yanked her hair.

"Ow! That hurt."

"Then shut your hole, girl." Sarkus scooped up the ball and sent it hurtling toward Pozzi, the force of it nearly bruising his paws. "Again. I was letting you win, you know."

Pozzi pulled the blindfold down again and waited. He pulled his arm back, but Sarkus refused to fall for it a second time. The rabbit took a deep breath, waiting. The scuff of a shoe on stone alerted Pozzi, and he spun, throwing the ball. He heard it hit home.

"You lose, Sarkus!" Hassah shouted.

Pozzi could sense the frustration rolling off Sarkus like heat and felt his pulse race at the boy's next words.

"He's cheating! Let me see the blindfold."

Sarkus snatched the cloth from the rabbit's paws, examining its thickness. Pozzi glanced up at the surrounding eaves. *Where are you, Morrigan?*

"If you think I'm cheatin', why don't you be the blind one?" At

Sarkus's hesitation, Pozzi shrugged. "Unless you're too slow to tag a fat old rabbit."

Sarkus glared at him, then tied the cloth around his head, covering his eyes. "You better run, rabbit."

But Pozzi didn't move. He had spied the queen of the crows sitting atop one of the roof gutters.

"Bring me the ball! Did you hear me?"

But no one heard him.

For just then, the Nyatha bell rang out, whitewashing all other sounds. It drowned out the nurse's chatter with the kitchen maids, the splash of the fish in the cistern. It also drowned out the wing beats of the crows who dropped like black stones from the bell tower, swooping as one silent cloud upon the blindfolded boy. It went on ringing as the birds' beaks found flesh, and the pealing muffled Sarkus's screams as he tore the blindfold off and tried to protect his face.

Hassah ran to defend her brother, but the nurse didn't realize anything was wrong until the last note of the bell had faded away. By then, not a crow was in sight, leaving the wailing boy with bloodied face and hands, rolling on the cobblestones.

CHAPTER 9

*D*igging up tombs was a dirty business, Brel conceded, watching the five men working in a practiced rhythm. Their grunts of exertion punctuated each shovelful of earth that flew up from the deepening hole.

But this tomb was worth it. This tomb was priceless.

Brel pushed the damp, silvering hair from his forehead with impatient fingers and took the map out again from where he kept it in his inner breast pocket. He ran his finger over the pattern of lines that he couldn't read but that he had known by heart. "The secret of Elshon lies with Orjo."

If anyone knew the legends about Orjo, or any omatje for that matter, it was Brel. Orjo the Terrible, Orjo the Immortal, who couldn't be killed—until he was. And buried at the site of the Library, according to legends.

Caldrik approached, holding a lantern.

"Our diggers should be hitting the coffin soon, Master Brel."

Brel folded the map and carefully returned it to his inner breast pocket. "Let me know when they reach it."

Brel walked toward a cluster of tents some fifty paces away, their insides aglow in the night like giant fireflies. As he walked, he pushed again at the stubborn lock of hair that had fallen, smearing his face with the signature blue dirt here in the Blue Teeth.

Named for the blue cliffs that stood like sentinels overlooking a dried-up ravine, the Blue Teeth was home only to a few gnarled trees and some dozen equally gnarled monks who insisted on a spare existence at the northernmost ridge. Here at the base of the cliff, the Teeth really did look like disapproving elders, standing watch as Brel's men uncovered its secrets.

He reached his private tent, guarded by two personal soldiers, and pushed the flap aside. In the rush of leaving, he hadn't been able to travel with his usual luxury, and he surveyed the basic amenities. A collapsible bed frame with furs and leather pillows, a bear skin, a wash basin, and his collection of musks. In one corner, sat Father Oaks, looking much better than when Brel had first met him. It had been uncomfortable to look at the ugly battered creature, and Brel had given his cooks and servants strict orders to provide plenty of hearty stews and medical care.

"I wish you could enjoy this as much as I am." Brel rinsed his hands in the basin of water, then liberally applied a splash of musk from the bottle he kept in a sleeve pocket.

The old rabbit grunted.

"You have to look at the bigger picture, Father Oaks." Brel rummaged for a small wooden box and opened it. "This Library will change Mankahar. Bring back knowledge and powers that we've long forgotten were ever possible." He scooped out a small amount of wax and smoothed it into his hair, testing to see whether it stayed. Satisfied, he turned and smiled at the rabbit.

"I know you dislike me. But I have a great deal of respect for you. And together, we are going to unlock powers we can't even imagine."

The rabbit remained stony.

"Don't be too hard on yourself, Father Oaks." Brel put a comforting hand on the rabbit's shoulder. "You want to save your grandson. I want to rule Mankahar. We both get what we want, and I think we can make a wonderful partnership."

"Ye and I have nothing in common," Father Oaks said.

Brel regarded him for a moment before squatting until he was eye level to the old creature. "May I offer some humble advice? Because of this disease of mine, I was teased and tormented as a young boy. I was angry then, but I learned. I learned to make the best of it. I learned to find out where others were weak, and I made those my strengths." He stood. "I know you didn't choose to be here, to work for me. But you can waste your days cursing your fate, or you can accept a comfortable life in my service."

"Until ye've no use fer me."

Brel smiled. "You will die of old age before we sort through a tenth of the Library."

Caldrik burst in through the tent flap. "Master Brel, you'd better come."

Brel's hands broke out in fresh sweat, and he followed Caldrik back to the tomb site.

More torches had been brought, and Brel grabbed one from the nearest soldier. The hole was now a yawning pit, and the digging crew had worked ropes under what looked like a child's coffin.

By Blackhide. It was here. Brel could barely keep from jumping into the grave himself.

"Keep digging!" Brel commanded once the coffin had been hauled up. "The Library will be under Orjo's body."

He barely registered the men's exhaustion as he swept the blue earth from the wood coffin and looked for markings. There were none, just the signs of time and rot. He motioned for Caldrik.

"Open it."

Caldrik and a soldier stepped forward, hefting metal bars, and wedged the ends under the coffin lid.

He'd waited so long, worked so hard, and followed so many

false leads to find this library, this well of mysterious untold power.

The secret of Elshon lies with Orjo, in the Land of the Blue Elders. If Orjo lay within this coffin, then the Library was underneath.

The splintering of wood made Brel lean forward. He grasped the lantern Caldrik held out, trying to steady the flame as he peered into the exposed coffin.

And saw a pile of rocks.

Caldrik reached in and pulled a rock from the top, then another. Brel felt numb disbelief, before a hard little ball of rage formed in his gut.

"This is not Orjo's grave." Caldrik said, matter of fact.

"No." Through his anger and disappointment and confusion, Brel was now sure of one thing. There was only one creature who would create such a decoy, and only one reason why he would do it. "Orjo's alive."

CHAPTER 10

$\mathcal{M}$orning on the island dawned cool and overcast. A northern breeze herded fat, white clouds across the top of the crater, though within the valley, the air lay still and flat. A flock of tiny birds swooped and fluttered over the waterfall, their chatter almost as loud as the cascade.

Indigo, who was last to keep watch overnight, woke Theo and then Brune. The bear scratched at his shaggy neck and stretched. "If Orjo is here, at least he had the decency to not kill us in our sleep." Indigo's dark expression made Brune wince. "Sorry, Princess."

Theo decided to change the focus as quickly as possible, before Indigo could dwell on how her mother and sister had died. "Let's eat and then get moving. We have an entire island to search, and only two sunsets before the otter leaves us here."

"We may not have to search the whole island," Indigo commented, looking up at the waterfall. "Anyone living here would want to be close to a water supply."

Brune nodded. "Let's follow the water upstream then. Work our way down."

They had no trouble finding a quick meal of cactus flower, water reeds, and wild tomatoes before setting off for the waterfall's source. They circled away from the lake edge until they found a rough, nearly vertical path that twisted its way up the rocky side of the waterfall. The sun climbed with them, and soon, the three of them were panting with the heat and effort.

They let the water guide them, following the streams that fed into the waterfall, searching as they went for any signs of a den, a hut. And though there were hints of habitation—old remnants of a fire pit, a discarded piece of frayed rope near the base of a tree—there was no sign of the muskrat himself.

The clearest proof that the island was inhabited came at dusk, when they reached the end of the island that overlooked the eastern sea. Here, rough waves slapped the cliff sides, and gulls screeched as they fished off the rocks, but what made Theo even more convinced that Orjo was here was the sight of a lean-to built against a large boulder.

"It's been used recently," Brune commented, looking at a small ring of stones that marked a fire pit.

"And maintained." Indigo stepped inside the lean-to. The walls were made from tall, straight branches lashed together with sturdy rope, most of their side branches hacked off. The odd knot or branch left in the wood had knives hanging from them, as well as a bag of flints.

Theo followed her in and looked around. "So he spends the night here at times." He paused, considering. "Which means he doesn't usually live near here."

Brune nodded. "He's likely on the other side of the island."

"But the water ends at the waterfall," Indigo reasoned. "Unless there's another stream or lake we haven't found."

Theo looked back the way they had come. "He has to be near the falls. It's the biggest source of water on the island."

Indigo frowned. "But there was no sign of a den, a hut."

"We must have missed something," Theo said. "We have to search again."

Indigo glanced out at the setting sun. "We can't make it back now. Might as well shelter here."

Though Theo chafed at this delay, he knew she was right. They ate the few hard berries, dandelion leaves, and wood sorrel Brune had foraged, then bedded down, Brune sleeping outdoors as the meager shelter was far too cramped for a bear.

Theo slept fitfully even when it wasn't his turn to keep watch, and he rose before the last star faded. He gathered a breakfast for everyone while Brune and Indigo packed their few things, and they set off for the waterfall once more, trekking all morning and then retracing their path down the winding rock face until they stood at the lake's edge.

"I still don't see anything that could be a den," Theo said, scanning the area.

Brune waded into the lake, gauging its depth. "You think he's underwater? Even muskrats need to breathe."

They searched the waterfall, the surrounding greenery, and the rock outcroppings above them. Nothing but birds and insects and lizards stirred. There was definitely no muskrat.

"Maybe he's got a hole beneath one of these rocks." Brune circled one of the giant rocks that hunkered on the lake shore.

"If he does, the hole's well hidden," Indigo commented. "I don't see anything."

Brune grunted in agreement.

"Where did the birds go?" Theo asked.

The princess glanced up at the flitting birds. "Which birds?"

Theo pointed toward the wall of foliage next to the waterfall. "I could have sworn some of the birds disappeared into the rock."

He picked his way over the slick stones toward the waterfall, ignoring the bright little birds that swooped and called. The moss on either side of the pounding water looked like a dense, impenetrable carpet.

He stepped onto a round stone close to the moss and reached out to touch it. Just as he did, however, a bird wriggled out from within it, surprising him and making him lose his footing. It screeched at him and took to the sky just as Theo managed to regain his balance. He grabbed for the moss to steady himself, but his paw went right through it. It wasn't anchored on rock, but hung free, like a curtain.

He parted the curtain of moss, revealing a wide ledge behind the waterfall. In front of him was a rock wall, set deep behind the cascade, with ledges where some of the birds sat and squawked at his intrusion. A narrow opening in the rock, no wider than an arm across but at least double Brune's height, led to a cave beyond.

"In here!" He called over the roar of the water. Indigo entered first, followed by Brune.

The princess took in the cave, and him. "You all right?"

"I think there's a series of caves back here."

Brune nodded. "I'll get our packs."

Theo and Indigo made their way into the passage, to the cave beyond. Here, the walls opened up to a cramped space about ten paces across. A large, gaping hole in the cave floor emitted an eerie light, which shimmered and slid along the walls.

Brune, pulling their packs behind him, squeezed through the passage and joined them. "Any sign of the bastard?"

A voice floated up from below. "If we're going to be insulting each other, let's do it face to face."

Theo peered down into the hole, but could see no one.

"Orjo?"

"You won't find out by staying up there."

The three of them looked at each other. Indigo moved to go first, but Theo shook his head.

"I'll go first," he whispered.

"What if he attacks you?"

"I don't think he will. There must be some honor among fellow omatjes. Right?"

Indigo looked to Brune, who seemed dubious but nodded. Theo sat at the lip of the hole and jumped into the underground cave. Once he'd found his feet and stood, Theo froze. Not with fear, but with wonder.

Fangs of crystal hung from the ceiling, aglow like a choppy sea of iridescent blue and green. The colors ran the length of the cave and down its walls, as if an artist had flung magic paint made of light that had frozen as it dripped from the ceiling. The rippling water at Theo's feet reflected the cave crystals, making Theo feel like he was wading in a pool of stars. As if here, underground, all the stars of the night had come to hide their mysteries.

Indigo landed in the water behind him and took in the sight.

"What? Never seen glow fungus before?" the voice asked.

Theo squinted. The chamber stretched back into the volcano's heart for fifty paces or so, with the odd glimmering rock formation jutting through the water. On one of the rocks at the far end sat a muskrat, wrapped in a faded cinnamon-colored robe and holding an open book. The wizened creature's mahogany fur sprouted like a mane around his head, almost engulfing the tuft-like ears buried on either side of his face. Two ancient eyes above a crooked muzzle looked Theo and his companion over.

"I'd say welcome, but I try to be honest when I can," the muskrat said.

This was Orjo? The feared scourge of Mankahar? A look at Indigo, the tension in her body and the recognition in her eyes, confirmed that this was, at least, the same omatje she'd met so many years ago.

"Now which one of you called me a bastard?"

"I did."

Brune jumped down through the hole, sending the ankle-deep water flying. He stood, his head nearly touching the stone teeth of the cave ceiling.

"I am Brune of Hegg. This is—"

"I know who he is," Orjo interrupted. "Theo the Griffinrider. The omatje whose blood can reverse pacification."

"That's an exaggeration," Theo said.

"Of course it is. You're lucky you didn't kill someone. Not all blood is changeable you know."

Theo tried to digest this. "You've read the *Miraculous Cures of Zo*?"

"Read it? I know the healer who wrote it. Very basic stuff, really. If ignorance was gold, Mankahar would be rich beyond its dreams." He looked Indigo up and down, noting her tattooed ears. "And what's a royal of Alvareth doing here?"

Theo stepped forward. "We need you to take us to the Library of Elshon."

Orjo gave him a condescending smile. "Why would I do anything other than tell you to get off my island?"

"Because," Theo said, "it might save Mankahar."

Orjo laughed, a dry, piercing bark that shook him all over and seemed to split his face in two. "Then the answer's definitely no."

"Finding the Library could bring back the Forbidden Language," Theo argued. "Omatjes like us wouldn't have to live in fear. Or in exile."

"There aren't any omatjes like us left." The exile sounded bitter. "We'll die out soon and good riddance."

"You can't mean that." Theo hated how naive he sounded. He could accept those words from someone else. Expect them, even. Just not from another omatje.

The muskrat snapped his book shut and slid it inside his robe, against his chest. "What happens to Mankahar has nothing to do with me."

"Aktu's balance affects all of us," Brune said. "Even those living on islands."

"Have you ever thought that this is Aktu's will?" Orjo's expression was that of a teacher pointing out the obvious to a slow pupil. "That this is part of her plan, to make all creatures slaves to the Urzoks?"

"Then it's also Aktu's will that we resist." Indigo's paw shifted on her sword hilt. As if she felt she could fight every battle, even verbal ones, with a physical weapon.

Orjo chuckled. "Ah, how luxurious it must be to have faith."

"How empty life must be to have none," Brune replied.

"We aren't leaving until you take us to Elshon."

Orjo regarded Theo, cool. "Then we are at what's called an impasse. Which usually can only be broken one of two ways."

Brune glanced at Theo. "We're not after a fight."

"Too bad. That's usually the easier option." Orjo sighed and stood up off his rock. "I guess it's option two."

"Which is?" Theo asked.

"We drink and talk it through, like civil folk."

CHAPTER 11

The muskrat walked with an unhurried stride, but with a surprising litheness. His tail, Theo noticed, bore many scars, some obviously from blades and others from fire or other injuries. Orjo the Terrible had, evidently, survived terrible things.

Orjo led them around the subterranean lake, into a dark tunnel that curved upward before ending at a door woven of thick, dried reed whose color matched the surrounding rock. If the muskrat hadn't pushed against it, Theo might have walked right by it. The exile pushed the door aside and motioned for them to follow.

Theo went first, trying to avoid Indigo's and Brune's unease rubbing off on him. They entered a cave so large its ceiling arched several heads above Brune's. Bowls of glow fungus, the same stuff as grew on the cave walls, sat in high sconces, lighting the space as well as any lamps. Theo saw a rock chamber that was clearly well lived in; woven mats lay on the floor, while almost every table and chair was covered in thin, white squares of paper, lines of caught words marching across most of them. While Theo looked around in wonder, Brune and Indigo were clearly ill at ease being surrounded by the taboo symbols.

"Did you make this? The paper I mean?" Theo picked up a sheet.

"Careful with that." Despite his harsh tone, Theo detected a note of pride in Orjo's voice. "Of course I made it. And the ink."

The muskrat took off his cloak and hung it on a peg, then crossed the room to a cupboard and pulled out cups, a bottle, and a kettle. "This cactus liquor is my own recipe. I'd offer you last year's vintage, which was better, but I'm afraid I finished it."

He passed the bottle to Brune, who sniffed cautiously and grimaced.

"Don't judge a brew by its smell." Orjo poured the liquid into three cups and placed them on what seemed to be both a dining and work table.

"None for me, thank you," Indigo said.

The muskrat smiled, but his eyes were serious. "I don't trust anyone who doesn't drink with me." He waited, expectant. "That's the deal. You want to discuss the Library, you drink."

Indigo regarded him, cold.

"I'll take that as yes." Orjo moved piles of papers until he had excavated a stool, a chipped toolbox, and two buckets. He turned the buckets upside down to convert them into seats and motioned to Indigo and Theo.

At their looks of hesitation, he shrugged. "I don't get company often." He sat down on the stool and motioned once more for them to take their places. "I know what you're thinking. What if it's poisoned?" He took a deep drink from his cup and refilled. "I promise you the worst thing this brew will give you is a nasty headache and foul breath."

Indigo looked to Brune, who sat down warily on the toolbox. She followed suit, sitting on one of the buckets.

The muskrat cocked an eyebrow at Theo. "You too, Griffin-rider. You want me to take you to the Library, we'll have to start by being open with each other. As the bard Calgornan said, 'Wine in a man is like water in a boat. Pour it in to see if he leaks or floats.'"

Theo lowered himself onto the remaining bucket.

"There now! I suppose we should toast." Orjo raised his cup. "Last to drain has manure for brains." At their stiff expressions, he sighed. "Mankahar is losing its sense of fun along with its freedom, is it? You'll never get me to take you to the Library if you don't drink."

Brune and Indigo each took cautious sips, while Theo couldn't get beyond the smell. He pretended to drink, but kept his lips closed. Even so, he immediately wiped an arm across his mouth. Indigo made a guttural sound and nearly spat it back up.

"It tastes better once your tongue goes numb," Orjo said, refilling their cups. "That's the way. Now, who else knows you're here?"

"No one," Theo said.

"The sea bats," Brune blurted. He looked surprised, then grimaced, as if trying to get the taste of the drink out of his mouth.

Orjo drained his cup again. "Good. Anyone else?"

"An otter rowed us here in his boat." Indigo frowned, as if confused by her own words.

The muskrat chuckled at her expression. "Like I said, brew loosens the tongue, doesn't it? So it sounds like you've exposed my whereabouts, and more than once. Doesn't make me want to help you."

"Even if it meant defeating the Urzoks?" Indigo pushed her cup away.

"That's a noble cause. But I've found noble causes tend to be bad for your health."

"The stories say you're immortal," the bear growled.

"I can live forever, if that's what you mean. But that's assuming something like a blade, let's say, doesn't find its way into my neck." Orjo raised his cup. "To life! And longevity."

At his expectant look, Brune downed his drink, and Indigo reluctantly pulled her cup back for a sip.

"How did you become immortal?"

"That's a long story." Orjo brushed Theo's question away. "And I'm doing the asking here. Tell me about you, Griffinrider."

"I never rode the griffin."

Orjo made a sour face. "Some free advice, from one legend to another? Never spoil your reputation with truth, lad."

"So your advice is to lie." Theo sniffed his cup. It definitely didn't smell like any liquor he'd known.

The muskrat put his eye to the bottle, then shook it and listened. "There's a difference between lying and letting others believe what they want to believe. And I've enjoyed all the stories about you."

Orjo stood, teetered unsteadily, and half walked, half groped his way to the cupboard, where he began to rummage for another bottle.

"You're not the one who has to survive the stories." Theo thought back to the bats. The exaggerations about him were almost more dangerous than the Urzoks themselves.

"True! My favorite is the children's song." Orjo pushed aside a jar, then pulled out what looked like another bottle of liquor. Not satisfied, he put it back and kept searching. "Aha!" He pulled out a third bottle and returned to the table. "Have you heard the children's song? No? The gulls sing it once in a while when they pass through here, it goes like this:

> *The omatje's riding now*
> *Riding now, riding now*
> *Theo the Omatje's riding now*
> *On his wings of flame.*
>
> *Hide your gold and lock the door*
> *Lock the door, lock the door*
> *Hide your gold and lock the door*
> *For Theo the omatje rides tonight.*

"Infantile," Orjo said, setting the bottle on the table and fishing out a knife from his pocket. "But catchy."

"We need you to find the..." Indigo frowned, as if trying to herd her thoughts. "Library. And then I can kill you."

Theo and Brune stared at her. She glared at Orjo. "There's something in this brew!"

"I told you, brew makes conversation flow." Orjo leaned forward. "So you want me to take you to the Library, and then kill me. Is that your plan?"

"No!"

"Yes."

Theo had never seen Indigo drunk. She had the occasional cup of ale, he knew, but she was too keen on control to ever let it get any edge on her. But she clearly had no control of her words and seemed to know it.

"Well, Theo," Orjo commented. "Seems you don't know your own friends' intentions. Doesn't make me trust you."

"Orjo, no one is killing anyone! We just want to find the Library," Theo insisted.

Now Brune was swaying a little, eyes glazed. Theo had a sudden, random memory of his best friend Pozzi from Willago, who'd always argued that drinking brew was like sport. You got better at it with practice. How practiced was Orjo? Could he possibly outdrink a bear ten times his weight?

Pop.

Orjo had managed to work the wood cork out of the bottle and began refilling the cups. "The cups don't lie, Theo."

The cups.

Theo cursed his stupidity, and snatched the drink from Indigo's paw. But it was too late. She slumped over the table. Brune stared at her, blinking.

"The cups..." The bear managed a slur of words and tried to stand, but his legs wouldn't cooperate. Bottles and sheaves of paper flew as the giant crashed into the wall, then slid to the ground, blinking.

"You poisoned them!" Theo scrambled to his feet and put a paw to Indigo's nose. She was breathing. Brune tried to push himself up on the toolbox, but only managed to knock it over before succumbing to the brew and lying still.

Orjo calmly poured himself another serving. "I said the brew wasn't poisoned. And it wasn't."

"What do you call this then?"

The muskrat smiled. "A very simple truth tonic that I dipped the cups in. I needed to know who you told about my island. But if you manage to kill me, they'll wake up with nothing but nasty headaches and the thirst of a four-humped camel."

Theo clumsily freed Indigo's sword from her scabbard, trying to keep his paws from shaking. "And if I don't?"

The muskrat wiped his lips with his sleeve and stood. His smile, unlike his stance, was disturbingly sober. "Then I kill all of you."

<h1 style="text-align:center">CHAPTER 12</h1>

He knew he should have probably waited, bided his time to see Orjo's first move, but instinct told Theo that his only advantage now was surprise.

He scrambled onto the table and rushed, sword gripped and raised as Indigo had drilled him. He wasn't the best sword fighter by a long shot, as she kept teasing him, but he wasn't defenseless. That, and Orjo's inebriation, were all he had.

The muskrat proved much quicker than Theo expected. He sidestepped the rabbit, letting the sword bite hard into the table top, then refilled his cup with more liquor.

"Your fighting skills have been greatly exaggerated, lad," Orjo said, downing his drink. Theo freed his sword from the table and clambered down.

"I just want you to take me to the Library," Theo said, putting the table between Orjo and himself. There was going to be no surprising the muskrat. It would all be defense.

Orjo chuckled. "I don't see how that benefits me at all."

Theo saw the cups hurtling toward him and managed to dodge both, but the muskrat had upturned his stool and now charged him with it like a battering ram. The stool took Theo square in the chest, and he crashed back into a shelf of pots, which fell and shattered around him. Several stings lashed his arm. Before he could find his feet, he felt a solid blow across the face. The muskrat's stool. Orjo then slammed it down over Theo's torso and sat on it, pinning all of Theo's limbs between the stool legs.

Theo tried to grasp the sword that had fallen out of reach, but the muskrat deftly kicked it into the far corner.

"You are no fighter, Griffinrider," Orjo said, his voice quiet with pity. He bent down and picked up a shard of pottery that had a very nasty-looking edge. "If it's any comfort, there is no joy in taking your life."

"And my friends?" Theo protested. "They only came because of me."

"Then they made poor choices," Orjo replied, gripping the pottery piece and preparing to strike.

A distant sound of voices, then splashing from the subterranean lake, and in an instant, Orjo was off him. The muskrat rushed to the entry, peering out the reed mat.

Theo immediately scrambled out from under the stool and went to Indigo. She was still breathing. So was Brune.

The voices grew louder, and now he could hear the clang of metal and the splash of heavy boots.

"Urzoks!" Orjo cursed, letting the curtain fall and giving Theo a murderous look. "You led them here."

Had he? But how? The otter couldn't have gotten back in time to alert anyone this quickly. Brune stirred, his shoulder twitching. Theo shook Indigo and was rewarded with a groan.

Orjo crossed the room and pushed at a chest of drawers, sending it toppling. Behind the drawers was a pantry-like recess. Except that instead of food, there were shelves neatly packed with quivers of arrows and a bow.

"You can't kill all of them by yourself," Theo argued as Orjo slung the quivers over his shoulder and grabbed the bow.

"No," Orjo said, "but I can escape while they're busy killing you."

The muskrat touched one ear in salute, then disappeared into a back room.

There must be an escape route. Theo had to follow and take Indigo and Brune with him.

The splashing of the Urzoks was closer now. They sounded as if they were almost around the lake. Soon they would find the curtain leading to Orjo's den.

"Brune!" Surely the bear's weight meant the drug had less effect on him than on Indigo's strong but small frame. "Wake up, Brune!"

The bear grunted but lapsed back into a half stupor. Theo looked around. The bottle of cactus brew was still on the table and had miraculously not spilled. He grasped it by the neck and flung the contents into the bear's face. Brune spluttered and rolled into a defensive position, then clutched his head.

"By Aktu, there's a beehive trying to get out of my skull," the bear groaned.

"Help me carry Indigo," Theo said. "We have to leave."

Brune seemed to hear the Urzok voices as well and shook his head to clear it. "Where's that water rat, rot his hide?"

"He's gone through a back way. We have to follow before we're trapped."

Brune found his helmet and clamped it on, wincing at the pain, then scooped the inert Indigo up in his paws. Theo rushed in the direction Orjo had taken, and Brune followed.

In the back room, Theo found no sign of Orjo or of an escape route. The space looked like a storage area, only ten paces square. Unlike the rest of the den, it had wooden floorboards, and the walls were lined with cupboards and chests as tall or taller than Theo.

"I saw him come in here," Theo said, checking the walls for hidden doors.

"There." Brune nodded toward a small hole in the floor, just next to a chest. "That hole. Too smooth to be a worm hole. Has to be a trapdoor."

Theo tried to move the chest, but it wouldn't budge. "How did he move this by himself?"

He could hear Urzok footfalls just outside Orjo's curtain now. It wouldn't take them long to discover the entrance. Orjo was good at creating camouflage, but not that good. Theo stopped, struck by this thought, and started examining the chest.

"Here, I can lift it," Brune said.

Theo held up a paw, then tapped the chest. A hollow echo answered him. The chest was empty, a decoy. He slipped his paw into the false worm hole next to the chest and heaved. The floorboard underneath lifted easily, empty chest and all.

"Hurry!" Theo motioned for Brune to get in with Indigo. It was a squeeze, but the bear managed it, lifting Indigo after him. Theo followed, easing the trapdoor shut behind them.

Underneath, they found themselves in a cave with shelves of foodstuffs along one side, and a long tunnel leading off into darkness on the other, the space barely big enough for Brune to crawl through.

"I don't like my chances of getting stuck in there," the bear growled.

"I know," Theo said, "but we can't fight off all those Urzoks."

Just then, footsteps rang out in the room above them.

"Flip everything!"

Indigo stirred, and Brune clamped a paw over her mouth. This woke her, and she struggled until her eyes found Theo's. He motioned for her to be quiet.

The footsteps above paused.

"D' you hear that?"

There was the sound of several chests being violently flung open, then the boards creaked directly over their heads. Theo, Brune, and Indigo remained frozen, barely daring to breathe in case the Urzoks heard.

"Anything?"

"Nah. Empty."

The footsteps went back into the other room, and Theo

looked to Indigo. She nodded and motioned for them to get moving.

Brune squirmed his way through the narrow, dripping passage, trying to be as silent as possible. Indigo leaned against the wall as she walked, gingerly touching her head. Theo brought up the rear, glancing behind them as the light faded along with the noises from the den.

The tunnel floor was dank and slippery with moss, and even after his eyes adjusted, Theo could barely make out Indigo ahead of him. As used to burrows as he was, this lightless, airless space began to close in on him and make him feel like they were crawling deeper into a tight coffin. Brune must have felt even worse. Theo thought back to the cave with the bats and tried to keep his unease at bay. He was starting to hate caves.

As if smelling his hesitation, Brune whispered from up ahead, "Keep going. I sense light."

Theo kept close behind Indigo, her familiar scents of pine and cedar guiding him more than sight as the darkness here was almost absolute. He could hear the sounds of stone breaking within Orjo's cave behind them. The Urzoks really were leaving nothing unturned, destroying the den in their quest to find them. How long before they discovered the trapdoor?

The floor began to slope downward. What if they were burrowing deeper into the earth, instead of up? But if Orjo had escaped this way, it must lead out, mustn't it?

Brune's bulk up ahead made it impossible to go much faster, as the bear had to clamber on elbows just to get through. Theo could hear the distinct thud of boots above and behind them, and then excited shouts. They had discovered the trapdoor.

"We have to hurry!" Theo whispered.

"I don't see any light, Brune!" Indigo added.

"It's worse than that," Brune panted, and then Theo noticed it too. The sound of water. "I think this leads to an underwater cave."

"We have to go back."

"We can't. Just follow my voice," Brune said. "You said it yourself, Orjo would have had an exit."

The tunnel continued to slope until Theo felt the cool rush of water against his paws.

"What do we do now? I can't swim."

"We have to," Indigo said.

"She's right." They heard the splash of water as the bear waded in. "Wait here. I'll see where this leads."

There was another splash as the giant dove beneath the surface.

They waited, the moments stretching interminably, with just the sound of the water and the shouts of the pursuing soldiers for company.

"They're almost here," Theo said.

He heard Indigo unbuckling her sword belt.

"What are you doing?"

"If they get here before Brune returns, we should hide underwater," the princess said. "It's so dark they may not be able to see us, even with lanterns. It's our only chance."

Theo was about to protest when he felt a current against his legs, a splash of water, and Brune emerged, gasping.

"There's a passage," the bear said. "It goes up and leads to light. But you'll have to swim underwater for a slow count to ten."

Panic swelled in Theo. "I can't do this."

"Yes you can," Indigo pressed her sword belt against his paw. "Hold on to this and kick with your back legs."

"Let your ears do the feeling," Brune said. "At ten breaths, you'll hit a hole in the ceiling. That's where we climb."

Before he could refuse, or ask what they would do if he couldn't find the hole, Indigo had looped her sword strap around his paw.

Theo inhaled until he thought his chest would crack. And then he jumped in after Indigo and Brune.

The water over his head felt like a vice, and Theo understood fully the terror of a watery grave. He kicked with his hind paws, gripping the sword strap, and remembered what Brune had said about letting his ears do the finding. He forced them to unfurl, and cold water rushed in, muting everything but the sound of the blood in his chest. Jagged rock scraped him on his right, and he had to remember not to open his mouth.

He was forgetting something. What was it? In the panic of being surrounded by cold water, he could barely string his thoughts together. *Count!* An impossible ask. His lungs were protesting even now.

One.

His shoulder scraped a wall.

Two.

The echo of boots on rock reverberated through the water.

Three.

His heartbeat filled his ears. His lungs felt singed.

Four.

He tried to focus on the strap he was gripping and the movement of water in front as Indigo pulled them forward.

Five.

He could do this. He was halfway there, not long now and—

The strap slipped from his paw.

He scrabbled, but found nothing except icy water. In his panic, he opened his eyes, which was a mistake. The bizarre sensation of water against them, and the cold blackness that surrounded him, gave his panic claws. Instinct made him open his mouth to breathe—

Suddenly his ears hit air, and a large paw grasped him by the shoulder, bruising in its strength. Brune hauled him out of the water and shoved him against something, something rough and scratchy. His paws wrapped around it, and even sodden and terrified, he recognized it for what it was. A rope ladder.

He could have laughed in relief.

"Up here!" Indigo called.

He looked and saw the faintest halo of light above them.

He didn't need her to tell him to climb. He began pulling himself up like some desperate monkey, feeling the ladder rung by rung. He could hear the slapping of the water below, along with the shudder of Brune's weight close behind, but he was so glad to be out of that dark, cold water that he could have sung in delight.

The joy died in his throat when he reached the top, however. Indigo was pushing against something.

He raised his paws to help her and hit calloused wood. A door. But it seemed impossible to budge.

"He must have locked it from the outside," Brune growled. "Let me." He squeezed up as close as he could to the rabbits without crushing them. There was not enough room in the tight well for them to trade places with the bear, which meant Brune couldn't bring his shoulder against the door.

The bear pushed, grunting with the exertion. He then braced his feet, one against the wall, one against the ladder rung, and pounded with his balled-up paw. The wood splintered, but held.

Cursing, the bear switched paws and gave the door several powerful punches. His paw broke through, and soon, Brune had cracked a hole big enough for the rabbits to crawl out.

"Hurry! They're close."

No sooner had Theo cleared the broken ledge of the door and emerged into the welcome sunlight, however, than something whistled past him, burying itself in one of the broken door pieces.

"Stay down!" Theo warned Indigo, who was still in the well. He dropped flat to the ground, then looked up and saw Orjo nocking an arrow to his bow, two dead Urzok soldiers sprawled nearby.

"I'll give you credit, Griffinrider. You're hard to kill," the muskrat said. "But this is where we part." Orjo raised his bow and took aim.

"We can help you," Theo called out, standing up.

"What are you doing?" Indigo hissed from inside the tunnel mouth. "Get down!"

Theo glanced at her but didn't move. He could see what she couldn't—the bow trembled in Orjo's paw. And the side of his robe was black with blood.

"You need help. You missed your mark from ten paces," Theo said.

"That was a warning shot," the muskrat snapped. "This next one will have you through that naive little heart of yours."

Theo could hear shouts below. The Urzoks had found the ladder and were climbing.

"Not with that cut in your side," Theo said, taking a step toward Orjo. "That's a lot of blood. Soon, you won't be able to stand, and what then?" He let this sink in for a heartbeat. Two. The bear was splintering the rest of the tunnel door open, clearly deciding that the threat down there was greater than the one out here.

"You need us!" Theo insisted.

The muskrat's eyes narrowed, and Theo realized he had said the wrong thing. "I need no one."

And with that, Orjo let the arrow fly.

The arrow skidded off a rock several paces from where Theo stood. Orjo slumped against his bow between the two Urzok bodies, winded.

Theo rushed to support the muskrat, who gave up all pretense of pushing him away. Behind him, Theo heard Indigo and Brune clamber out of the well.

"Here!" Theo called out, taking the bow from Orjo's grasp and tossing it to Indigo. She caught it in one paw and swept up the arrow that had missed Theo, before rushing back to the well.

"You hold 'em off. I'll block the tunnel." Brune unsheathed his axe and began hacking at the base of a nearby tree.

Theo ripped Orjo's robe open to see the damage. A deep cut, one that would require as much sewing skill as healer's skill. If he could find thread and needle.

He heard a curse of pain cut through the sounds of Brune's hacking and knew that one of Indigo's arrows had found a soldier climbing out.

Theo ripped the sodden sleeve from Orjo's arm and pressed it to the wound, drawing a hiss from the muskrat.

"Press on it, like this." Theo moved the muskrat's paw to the gash. A loud groan made him look up.

"Stand away, Indigo!"

The princess leapt aside as the felled tree came down, its trunk crashing over the well hole and covering it. They heard a shout and a splash as a soldier fell back into the underground cavern.

"That should do it," Brune grunted, returning his axe to its holster on his back. "Now, which way off this horrible island?"

* * *

THE PATH down to the northeastern beach was steep and not really made for easy descent, but the muskrat insisted it was the only way.

"There's a boat I keep on this side. In a cove."

From the top of the island, they hadn't been able to see any sign of the otter.

"Think the otter's fled?" Theo asked.

"Most likely." Indigo scanned the waters. "Either way, we need another way off this island."

"So you going to wait here for your otter friend, or you going to take my boat?" Orjo snapped.

Brune carried the injured omatje and followed the two rabbits as they negotiated the best way down the hill. They kept their ears and eyes tuned for signs of other Urzoks, but it seemed the invaders had decided to focus their efforts on the western side of the island.

When they reached the bottom of the steep path and stood on a narrow, pebbly beach, Orjo pointed toward a shallow cave where the tide was seeping in. There, moored to a piece of jutting rock, was a long boat with a curved prow, its small sails folded and tied to its sides like a roosting sparrow.

They clambered aboard, taking care with the injured muskrat. Theo helped Brune ease Orjo down against the bow while Indigo pulled out oars from beneath a seat.

"Do you think we can sneak past them? The Urzoks I mean." Indigo glanced up as if one might appear any moment.

The muskrat shook his head and motioned at the sails. "Not a chance. But we won't need to." Orjo pointed at a wooden box strapped under the prow. "As a matter of fact, we want them to get nice and close."

Theo pulled the box out into the open and threw up the lid. Inside was a meticulously organized assortment of survival supplies: medicines, food, flints.

"Not that. Behind it," Orjo rasped.

Theo looked. Tucked in behind the box, under the prow, was a built-in wooden shelf, its contents held back with a tightly woven hemp netting. Inside the netting were what looked like four white orbs. Theo saw they were actually round balls of clay with flat bottoms. Each one had a twist of rope the length of his paw jutting out of a hole.

"What are these?" Theo reached out for one.

"My very own little griffin," the muskrat chuckled, before wincing as the boat heaved.

Brune pushed the boat into the incoming tide. He gave one final shove, freeing the boat from the sand's grip, then pulled up the rope holding the vessel to the rock and climbed in.

Orjo gasped in pain as the boat rocked violently with the bear's weight. "You'll sink us!"

Brune tossed down the rope and took a seat, his mallet-like paws gripping the two oars. "You're welcome to do the rowing yourself if you'd prefer."

The bear heaved at the oars, and they began sliding out of the cove. Soon the boat was in open water. Indigo began unstrapping the sail, while Theo rummaged in the medicine section of the box. He found the thinnest hook he could, along with what looked like a long piece of cured fish gut for thread.

"We're going to need fire," the muskrat said.

Theo began searching again. "We can use liquor to clean the hook. It's faster."

"Forget the hook. I'm talking about those." Orjo pointed to the orbs beneath the prow.

They rounded the corner to the main bay, and the Urzok ship slid into view. It was a longship, with identical ends so that it could move forward or backward at will. It sat low in the bay's shallow waters, like some sleek mahogany crocodile.

As the boat slid out from the inlet and into the open bay, Indigo pulled the last of the sail up the mast and secured it. The bear put down his oars to help her push the mast into its stand in the middle of the boat, and as soon as it was in place, the sail arched with the wind. They all steadied themselves as the vessel lurched forward.

They hadn't gone far before shouts arose from the longship, and the Urzoks aboard began preparing for pursuit. They cast off their single anchor, and the ship began gliding toward the muskrat's craft.

"They're gaining," Indigo said, glancing at Orjo.

"Trust me," Orjo said. "We want them close."

This wouldn't be a problem, Theo noted. The Urzoks were bearing down on them with worrying speed. Indigo pulled an arrow from her quiver and began sighting. Orjo pointed at the orbs in the prow.

"Flints! We need the flints."

"Why?"

"Just pass me those, and get me some fire!" Orjo rasped.

Theo pulled all the orbs out of their netting, placing them by Orjo, then fished out the flints from the supply box.

"Light that lamp over there!" Orjo pointed to a seafarer's lantern stored under the bow, which Theo pulled out. He hurriedly began striking the flints near the lamp's oil-soaked wick.

"There're too many of them!" Indigo sighted along the arrow shaft, the bow drawn.

"Don't waste arrows." Orjo motioned for the lamp, now lit,

and Theo held it out. "That's it, now let's just get them a little closer..."

"How close do you need, rat?" Brune grunted. "I can count their whiskers." One of the Urzoks was whirling a grappling line over his head, ready to hook it to the smaller boat so they could reel in their prey like a trout on a line.

"Your throwing arm as good as your bow arm, lass?" Orjo held the ball out toward Indigo. At her hesitation, he barked, "Light it and aim for the ship's middle."

Indigo put down the bow and arrow, took the orb, and let Theo light it with the lamp. She drew back her arm and hurled. It arced up and over at the same time that the Urzok threw the grappling hook. The two missiles passed each other midair, the grappling hook landing in the boat and scraping along the bottom before catching against Brune's seat.

The boat jerked as the rope went taut, and then a great clap of thunder from the longship rent the air.

"By Aktu!" Brune instinctively held up an arm to protect himself from the flying splinters. Indigo dropped to the boat floor. Pieces of wood and sail sprayed them like rain, while the Urzoks began shouting. Theo heard the crackle of fire and saw that the longship mast and sail had erupted in flames.

"Good shot!" Orjo crowed. "Again!" He pushed another clay ball into Theo's paws. "Quickly. If you destroy their hull, we'll send them to the sea bottom."

Theo was about to ask what was in the clay balls, but a tug on the grappling rope interrupted him. One of the Urzoks was trying to pull them in.

Indigo lit the next ball, then threw.

At impact, another deafening wall of sound and flame erupted. The boat rocked from the force, while Orjo laughed and groaned in turns. The Urzok who had been pulling them toward the ship had toppled into the water, rope forgotten.

"Sorcery," the bear grunted.

Indigo dislodged the grappling hook from Brune's bench and

heaved it overboard. Now freed, the boat slipped away as Brune renewed his pulling on the oars.

"What was in those?" The princess watched the longship sink below the water's surface, the remaining soldiers disappearing with it.

"Black Snow. Alchemists used to make it all the time, but the art was lost. I'd been saving it for a rainy day." The muskrat managed to chuckle before gasping. He drew a pained breath and shivered despite the warm day.

"Cold?" Theo asked.

"Freezing."

"That's because you've lost a lot of blood," the rabbit explained. "If I don't start sewing that closed soon, you'll grow sleepy and die."

The muskrat grimaced. "There's a point in there somewhere, I'm sure."

"I'll make sure you live, if you take us to the Library."

At Orjo's silence, Brune growled, "You heard the rabbit. What's it to be?"

"Well, I don't fancy dying."

Theo drew out a bottle of blackish liquid from the medicine box and pulled out its cork. The strong smell of fermented cactus stung his nostrils, and Theo poured a generous amount on the hook.

"This might hurt a little."

"Don't lie."

"This will be agonizing."

Orjo grasped the liquor from him. "That's better. Let's get started then."

CHAPTER 14

From behind the waterfall, Ornox leapt out into the sun-drenched pool, sheathing his sword.

As he splashed his way toward shore, he scanned the surrounding area for Yod. No muskrat worth his fur would live in a den with only one entrance, and while five of his men were chasing the quarry into that dark subterranean lake, he would make sure he was waiting when they came out.

He climbed the hill leading up to the lip of the isle rim and stopped to look up. He spied the hunting hawks he'd bought circling, watching for any hint of a creature resembling Theo. Or the infamous Orjo.

It was hard to believe anyone could have survived the Purges, when the first emperor had wiped out all traces of the Forbidden Language. Even someone as powerful and wily as the fabled Orjo would have struggled to escape the net. There were too many bounty hunters, too many informants, and too few places to hide from the empire. Then again, the fact that Theo existed proved that omatjes had somehow persisted.

And the important thing was to find this Theo. Killing Theo and avenging his only child was worth any price, which was why he had sold his last piece of Vyad jewelry, a gem-encrusted ring, in exchange for the warship that had brought them here. To the supposed Land of Blue Elders that Theo wanted to find, according to the bat Roach.

"Lord Ornox!"

Yod's voice pulled Ornox's thoughts back to the task at hand. His servant was clambering down the hillside, breath ragged.

"Torgin and Mulkk are dead, my lord." He gestured. "Found them up near the northeastern side. We're following the animals' tracks and should corner them soon."

The warlord looked up, shading his eyes. The hawks were trained to perform a midair swoop if they sighted their quarry. The one on the eastern side of the island was still spiraling, while the other—

"Where's the western hawk, Yod?"

Yod followed his master's gaze, a frown gathering his eyebrows.

A giant roar ripped the air behind them, unnatural and deafening. Ornox instinctively dropped to the ground and couldn't stop the thought that tore through his head.

The Griffin!

Shouts bellowed out, followed by the smell of smoke and the bizarre whiff of rotting eggs.

That beast of nightmares. It had found him...

He heard the distant cackle of flames, panicked shouting, and he sprinted to the rim of the island, where his remaining soldiers had also taken cover. He looked over the edge, and saw that his longboat was now no longer docked where he had left it, but a few lengths out, one end in flames.

There was no Griffin, so how in Blackhide's name had his ship caught fire?

A small fishing boat pulled into view on the far side of the longship, with a bear at the oars and a white rabbit at the stern. Another rabbit was in the middle, tending to what looked like another furred beast. A muskrat.

As Ornox and Yod watched, the white rabbit's arm moved, as

if she was throwing something, and then another roar sounded. The longship's stern split from the main hull, and the mast began tilting, slow and inevitable, into the sea.

"By Blackhide's beard…" Yod muttered.

Ornox could see only two men swimming to shore, abandoning the crackling mass that was all that was left of his ship.

And then the mast fell into the sea with a resigned groaning of wood, taking its tangle of sails with it.

"What do we do now, Lord Ornox?"

The warlord watched the last of the hull disappear, his mind churning with what he had just seen. "Search the cave. Find the magic that sank our ship."

* * *

HE MADE both surviving soldiers tell him in detail what had happened on the longship, hearing their stories separately so as to make sure they didn't muddy each other's accounts. He heard their descriptions of the round, white missiles from the fishing boat that had exploded on impact.

When he was satisfied he had every detail his men could offer, he called to Yod and bade him follow into the muskrat's cave. Such a valuable weapon had to be obtained personally, not entrusted to a bunch of ragtag soldiers, as he had to admit his force was.

Yod followed his master into the muskrat's den. The warlord could tell his servant was trying to hide his unease. The Forbidden Language was everywhere. It covered strange, thin pieces of bark-like squares, its black tracings like the mad web of some otherworldly spider. Pots and bowls bore trapped words, and Ornox knew that few places in Mankahar, if any, had so much of the Forbidden Language.

"I thought you were strongly made, Yod. If not, you can leave me now."

"Sorry, my lord." Yod seemed to gather himself, then reached out to sweep a mess of the thin bark squares off a shelf. Ornox gripped his servant's arm midair. "Search, but destroy nothing. Let nothing fall or break. If those men are right, it creates fire on impact."

Yod nodded and continued, more gently this time.

Ornox surveyed the room. Shallow bowls of the luminescent fungus that grew in the lagoon lit up the interior, revealing a space that was cluttered and claustrophobic despite the high ceilings. Overturned furniture lay broken or abandoned, and signs of fighting and ransacking were everywhere. If this weapon exploded on impact, it was a wonder this cave hadn't been destroyed by fire when his men had come through.

Where would such a weapon be kept? Somewhere out of the way. Somewhere hidden. Somewhere it couldn't accidentally fall on anything. Ornox searched through cupboards and chests, then moved into a simply furnished bedroom. He overturned the bed pallet, opened the one storage box, and was rewarded when he pushed aside a cloak hanging on a peg.

Hidden by the peg was a shelf cut into the wall, with three rows of white clay balls. Each had what looked like a wick, about the length of a finger, protruding from a hole in the top.

Ornox pulled one out and hefted it. He put it to his nose. There was that strange metallic smell, along with the hint of smoke. It reminded him of the griffin, the memory sending a shock through him.

Yod entered, and took in the orbs in his master's hands. "What should we do with them, my lord?"

Yes. What was the next move? He wasn't sure what he held in his hands, but he knew it was powerful. Valuable. And if he played his hand right, it might win him everything.

"Take all of these. We're going to go see an old friend."

CHAPTER 15

The room had been freshly cleaned and aired, but even so, the smell of medicine and oil lingered like a persistent stain.

Pozzi followed Hassah in—or rather, he was led in, since she gripped his paw with tight, nervous fingers. Pozzi himself was just as reluctant to enter. The nurse's lecture to Hassah before they came had not been reassuring.

"Remember, child, he's still your brother. No matter what he looks like. He's your same flesh and blood."

And with that, she had handed the girl a basket covered in a cloth and sent them through the door.

A large, single bed had been pushed up opposite the window so that the occupant had a view outside. Not that Sarkus was looking at much now—his head was turned away from them, propped up on a small avalanche of pillows. Hassah's mother sat in a chair next to the bed, blowing on a bowl of stew. Her eyes were puffy with tears, and guilt chewed at Pozzi.

"Come Hassah, sit." Tansha rose and guided her daughter down onto the chair, still holding the bowl. "Sarkus, your sister's here. She's brought something to cheer you."

Sarkus kept his face away. "I don't want it."

Hassah looked to her mother, who motioned at the basket. Hassah lifted the cloth, and for a few breaths, the smell of medicine and oil retreated, beaten back by the aroma of cinnamon and cloves and apple.

"It's your favorite."

"I said I don't want any."

Hassah again looked at her mother. "Can I have one?"

Tansha frowned her disapproval, then sat on the bed, bowl in hand. "Cook made them extra soft. They won't hurt your mouth any."

Pozzi swallowed. He had been able to convince himself over the past two days that Sarkus's wounds might not be as bad as he imagined. The boy had been whisked away once the head cook and guards had arrived, and Pozzi had hoped the blood had made things look worse than they were. But Morrigan had wanted revenge. A crow's revenge.

"Won't you speak to your sister, Sarkus?"

The boy didn't answer.

"You've no need to hide from your family, my son."

Sarkus turned his head. "Is that so?"

Pozzi managed to stifle his reaction in time, but Hassah couldn't. Swollen red and purple marks covered Sarkus's once flawless face, and one side drooped away from his skull, like candle wax melting off its holder. A wound above the right eyelid had puckered the flesh there, making one eye look unnaturally large and ghoulish.

Hassah's frightened gasp drew a slap from Tansha. "Mind yourself, girl."

Hassah began to cry.

"He did this!"

It took Pozzi a moment to realize that Sarkus's finger was pointed at him, the hot anger almost palpable.

Tansha put down the stew and pulled Hassah to her feet. "Go now."

Hassah gripped her basket and took Pozzi by the paw, tears streaming.

"That's right. Get out!" Sarkus shouted.

Tansha tried to mollify her son as Hassah and Pozzi rushed from the room into the safety of the hallway where the nurse waited.

"There, child. It's all right."

"Why is mama angry with me?" Hassah's lip trembled. "It wasn't my fault! Or Pozzi's."

"Of course it wasn't. Your mama and Sarkus are angry with everyone right now," Farriah reassured her. "Don't worry. Things will be better in time."

They walked toward Hassah's room, the girl holding Pozzi's paw. Pozzi could still feel the sting of the boy's venom and trembled at the image of that face. Did Sarkus know Pozzi's role in the crows' attack? If he did, and he told his father, their protection as Hassah's pets would surely be over.

* * *

Despite what the household referred to as "the young master's accident," Ghazan insisted preparations for Imperial Day continue as planned. The Nyatha manor had been swept, scrubbed, and dusted until even the door handles shone. Ribbons and pear flowers had been woven into wreaths and hung over lintels to attract good luck. The grounds buzzed with increased traffic as fur traders, cattle farmers, meat sellers, and slavers arrived, all eager for spring trading, feasting, and gossip.

These preparations only made Pozzi more nervous, and even Walnut's bright chatter couldn't keep his thoughts away from Sarkus's deformed face and the upcoming night. He didn't even know if going near the stuff would affect him. But he had to go. For Keeva. For Walnut. The little brown-colored rabbit that he and Keeva had, without realizing it, come to treat as their child was probably one of the main reasons they hadn't lost themselves to despair.

"Pozzi, you look sad."

Hassah's words nearly made him drop the blanket he was unfolding. He, Keeva, and Walnut slept in a glorified cage. It had ornately carved slats, but those slats closed and locked every night. Hassah had one key, and Farriah had the other.

"It's nothin', Hassah," he said, eyeing the girl's nurse who was busy folding away clothes. He knew she was eager to tuck Hassah in and blow out the candles, then hurry off to a much anticipated ale with the kitchen hands and grooms. She wouldn't be back to her room, which adjoined Hassah's, until late, tipsy with watery wine. But despite her distraction with household chores, Farriah's ears were always tuned to her charge.

Hassah leaned in close, her nose practically pressing the bars. Pozzi could see the key to the cage on a thin chain she wore around her neck. "My mama always says it's nothing when she and Papa fight," she whispered. "I know she's lying."

The girl could be clever, if often self-absorbed. "I'll tell you later," he whispered back, his eyes flicking to the nurse.

Excited by the sharing of a secret, Hassah grinned before meekly following all her nurse's ministrations for bed, sitting through the brushing of hair and the washing of face with unusual patience.

When the candles had been snuffed and Farriah's footsteps had receded down the hall, Hassah threw off her blankets and padded over to the cage. She squatted down so she was eye level with the rabbit.

"Tell me, why are you sad, Pozzi?"

"I'm sad because I'd like to sleep in a real bed. Just once."

Hassah frowned. "Papa says you stay in your crate at night. It's the rules."

"I know." Pozzi let out a heavy sigh of defeat. "It's just

that...your favorite toys get to sleep in your bed. Yet you never let us sleep there."

Hassah chewed on this for a while, and Pozzi worried he had misjudged his ability to sway her. She could be wayward, but she almost always followed her father's rules. He could see the edge of the rising moon through the window behind her. The crows would arrive when the moon was three-quarters. He didn't have much time.

"You're not to tell anyone! Promise?" She held up a finger in her best stern expression.

"I swear on your gilded tea set." Hassah's most-valued possession was a gift her father had brought back from his travels to the empire's capital, Kalyun-eh.

Hassah fished the key from inside her night clothes, then unlocked the crate to let Pozzi out. She closed the door on Keeva and Walnut, who had lain down to sleep. Pozzi knew that Keeva only pretended. She was tense as a drum.

Hassah hugged him tight and carried him to her bed, placing him on the far side before clambering up after him. She pulled him down next to her and wrapped a soft but surprisingly strong arm around him, using her other arm to pull the blanket up.

"Good night, Pozzi."

He hoped she couldn't feel his heart hammering like a crazed thing in the dark.

* * *

THE MOON WAS NEARLY three-quarters high. Even with the curtains drawn, Pozzi could see it had already cleared the window top. He shifted, hair by hair, from under Hassah's arm. He searched for the chain with the key on it, but the girl was lying in such a way that it was directly under her.

He was about to try tugging on the chain when he heard a tapping on the cage. He looked over.

93

"Forget the key!" Keeva whispered. "Just go!"

He looked back at the sleeping girl, frustrated. Keeva was right. He'd never get it without waking Hassah. He slid off the bed and to the ground on silent paws.

"Be careful," Keeva warned.

He had no idea what was ahead, whether Morrigan would even keep her agreement. And even if he found the pacification powder, would he be able to set fire to it all?

He crept to the window, found the latch, and eased it open, careful to press on the hinge to prevent its telltale squeak.

He resisted the urge to look back at Keeva, then stepped out into the bracing spring night.

The rooftop was empty. The moon was definitely three-quarters. He waited, and then waited some more.

Morrigan had broken her word.

He was about to turn back when dark shapes swept up and over the chimneys on his right.

He recognized Morrigan by her size, but the others were strangers. Swarthy, hulking things, five in all, their feathers catching the moonlight like blackened glass.

"Ready?" Morrigan asked.

"You didn't tell me what you were going to do to Sarkus." Even now the image of the boy's disfigured face made Pozzi flush in anger.

"We said we were going to teach him a lesson. A crow lesson. And we did." She cocked her head. "Do you want to destroy the pacification cellars or not?"

Pozzi took a breath, then nodded. As guilty as he felt, nothing was going to undo the damage to Sarkus's face. "Which way down?"

Morrigan motioned at one of the five crows, who pulled out a grayish-looking lump from a fissure in the chimney. He shook it out, and Pozzi saw it was a tattered kerchief.

"The workmen who fix the chimneys are lazy brats,"

Morrigan explained. "Half the time, they fix up cracks with strips of cloth to save on mortar and clay."

The crows unfolded their find with their beaks, and each of the five took an end.

"Climb on," Morrigan said. "And try to keep still. You follow?"

Pozzi felt queasy, but there was no time to think of other options. He obediently stepped into the middle of the kerchief, its thin fabric doing nothing to reassure him.

As if reading his mind, Morrigan said, "It's a short trip."

Without waiting for an answer, she leapt over the roof edge. The five crows took flight, the snap of their wings and the scratching of their claws on the roof shingle deafening to Pozzi's ears. The roof slid away, and suddenly there was nothing—nothing but cold, racing air. His feet kicked in a panicked spasm, but one of the crows clutched his leg with a claw to steady him.

He forced himself to look over the edge, for this was his one chance to get a lay of the Nyatha compound, to see the entirety of his prison and understand its geography. He saw the manor they'd left behind before they swept downhill, over the rooftops of squat buildings and pens that he had but glimpsed every day from Hassah's window. Shapes shifted beneath them—the backs of cattle, the humped mounds of closely pressed sheep. Here and there, a light blazed from some window, and Pozzi knew many of these were guard posts. There were also rows upon rows of wagons, and even at this hour, some of them were being swept out by young hands, the manure and piss of hundreds of animals being cleaned to make way for new ones.

"Hold your breath." Morrigan's warning came too late.

The smell of blood, mingled with sweat and terror, slammed into him.

The slaughterhouses. He had heard of them, but he'd never been this close. Here at Nyatha, the animals were brought to be pacified, and then once they lost their reason and speech, they were bred, sold to traders, or slaughtered for the household's use.

Without warning, the crows banked, and the smell mercifully waned. They were descending. Before he could orient himself, a hard surface met him with a bone-aching thump, and the crows were pulling the kerchief from around him.

They had landed near a long, squat building. The roof was sloped, like the manor, but had no chimneys. Around the perimeter was a high wall, its top spiked with wooden stakes. A strip of dusty ground encircled the building. Two lanterns flickered over the gate, where Pozzi could make out a small barracks.

"This is it," Morrigan said, quiet.

"Where they keep the pacification powder?"

The crow nodded. "There's an old disused cellar entrance around the corner, but it's too tight to fly in. Go in that way, you follow? If you start the fire there, it'll take to the foundations."

"Did you bring it?"

One of the crows hobbled forward and dropped a small hemp bag at his feet.

Pozzi scooped it up and peered inside, but it was so dark, he could only just make out the contents.

"It's all there," Morrigan said. "Oil mixed with the strongest liquor we could steal. Set of flints. Spare rags."

"Thank you."

"We'll be waiting nearby. Be back by dawn, because we won't wait. You follow?"

And with that, they were gone, rushing into the safety of the trees.

Pozzi looked around, heart loud enough to drown thunder. He forced himself to calm down, then listened for any sounds of prowling sentries, or worse, dogs. When the way was clear, he dashed across and pressed himself against the side of the building. He skirted along it, looking for the cellar door Morrigan had mentioned.

He had almost made an entire round of the building, and was

worried about having to slip by the guards, when he tripped over a raised piece of wood. It took him a moment to make out that the wood was wide, with iron handles.

The cellar doors.

He felt the planks of wood, then realized it wasn't a set of cellar doors, but rather a single door on one side, with the other side, where a door should be, covered by crossed slats hammered into it to temporarily cover the hole. He had tripped over one of the slats that protruded from the edge.

Pozzi peered into the cellar and made out a staircase. He pulled at the slats, but the nails held fast. The door was so large that he could budge it even less than the slats. He would have to squeeze through the slats.

He dropped his pouch of supplies inside. He'd never been thin, even on the journey here when they'd been half starved. Big boned and bigger hearted, his mother had called him. Expelling his breath and pulling in his stomach, he shoved his head and shoulders between two of the slats and began clawing his way in.

He was less than halfway through when he realized that the opening was much narrower than he'd thought. He wriggled back out, trying to see if any of the other holes were wider. They weren't.

"Skin the rabbit," he muttered to himself, taking off his jacket. It was an expression Hassah's nurse sometimes used when she pulled the girl's dress over her head before a bath. The phrase had an even darker humor to it now.

He shoved the jacket through the opening to the other side, worried that even here, a discarded jacket might alert someone to his presence. Pushing all the air from his lungs and pulling in his ample belly, he squeezed himself back into the opening. There, he was halfway. Now he just had to...he felt himself catch. His hindquarters were stuck. He pulled forward, then tried to push back. But no matter how he struggled, he couldn't seem to move. He was trapped.

Something crunched. Footsteps. Followed by another.

"...pigs are where the coin is. But the old man won't hear it."

Pozzi froze. The footfalls were close, much too close to not notice the cellar doors.

The footfalls continued.

"That's what I'll do when I've saved enough."

The second guard still didn't reply, and then the footsteps stopped.

Pozzi stayed still, praying they hadn't seen him in the dark. But no, he could see the flicker of a lantern.

Hands grabbed his hind legs and yanked. His back stung from the scraping, and then there was nothing but blinding hot light. Once his pupils had adjusted, he saw dark, black eyes, hair braided and graying beneath a broad hat. Everything else was shrouded in darkness.

Pozzi opened his mouth to speak, but the guard's words stopped him.

"Must have escaped from the Hutches. If we return him, we can squeeze some coin from those minders."

The Hutches! He could speak, tell them he was Lady Hassah's pet, and they would return him. But then Hassah would never trust him again. And he'd never have a chance at stopping the pacification.

So he kept quiet.

"Look. He's shaking like a leaf," the first guard smiled, revealing several chipped teeth. "He's well fed too. I bet the lads at the Hutches were keeping him for a special occasion. Come on. He'll likely fetch us some real grog."

The guard's companion didn't reply, and for the first time, Pozzi noticed that the second guard was only a little older than Sarkus—a short, slight figure with cropped copper hair and hazel eyes. Pozzi realized the short guard was not a boy, but a girl.

But then the two set off toward the Hutches, and Pozzi only had thoughts of panic at what waited for him there.

CHAPTER 16

At their approach, a figure stepped from the gatehouse.

"No deliveries this late."

"We found one o' yours over by the pacification warehouse."

The guard shoved Pozzi out to catch the light from the sentry's lantern. The short, copper-haired guard kept silent, watching.

"Blackhide rot it," the gatehouse sentry said. "That's the third escape this week. That Nade is going to get us all in hot oil."

There was a lengthy conversation about how Nade should be punished, before the sentry rummaged for a few coins and tossed them at Pozzi's captor. The guard caught the coins, and the sentry took Pozzi by the scruff.

The two guards headed off, the copper-haired one giving Pozzi one last glance before they melted into the darkness, and then Pozzi was alone with the sentry. His new guardian fumbled for his keys before tucking Pozzi tightly under one arm.

They entered a low door, and Pozzi's head went light at the smell of filth and close bodies. Inside, it was dark and dank smelling, with only a single lantern hanging from a nearby rusty hook. His captor lifted it. The feeble light showed a straw-littered floor, and they were walking between rows of metal pens, each one crammed with rabbits.

Pozzi squirmed, trying to find a familiar face.

The sentry tightened his grip. "Settle down, troublemaker."

Pozzi felt genuine panic. If he was trapped here for the night, then it was over. Any surviving villagers would go to the cradles, and he'd never see Keeva or Walnut again. What had he been thinking?

He struggled, but it was too late. The sentry's irritability had fanned to anger now, and his grip on Pozzi turned painful. They passed rows of pens and were outside again, on the far end of the Hutches. They were in a large yard awash in moonlight, with a staked fence dividing the space in two. On the other side of the yard was an iron cage with narrow bars, its door padlocked.

"Nice and easy," the sentry said, unlocking the padlock with one of his keys and easing the hatch open. He shoved Pozzi inside, muttering, "Fastest way out of this place," then closed the door and locked the padlock.

The sentry banged loudly on the bars before heading back toward the main building.

Pozzi gripped the cage. A noise behind him made him freeze.

Something was breathing.

Something large.

He didn't want to look, but he had to. A shadow unfolded in the corner. The only color visible came from yellow eyes bright with hunger.

Something white. The wolf—Pozzi, even through his fear, had now realized it was a wolf—licked its muzzle. There was the rattle of metal links as the wolf advanced. Was it chained? Pozzi felt little relief as he doubted that would help him much.

"I thank Aktu for this offering…" the wolf murmured.

"I'm not an offerin'."

The wolf stopped in his tracks, regarding him.

"You're not pacified."

Pozzi took an instinctive step away, and something clattered.

Bones. Bones littered the cage, he realized. He thought of his bones joining them.

"Please, let me out."

The sound of scraping metal stopped. "I'm not here by choice either, rabbit. But I haven't eaten for two days."

"I need to get in there." Pozzi pointed at the Hutches. "I came to save them, and I can help you, I—" He realized how foolish the words sounded as soon as they were out of his mouth. What bargain could he make? He literally did not even have the shirt off his back.

The wolf gave a low, throaty laugh. "Tell me, rabbit, who are you going to save, exactly? And how?"

Pozzi bristled at the wolf's tone. "I'm going to free my fellow villagers."

The wolf didn't answer immediately, as if thinking. Then he said, "What's your name?"

"Pozzi."

"Aktu be with you, Pozzi. I am Argasar, last of the Black-moons. So tell me how you think you're going to free your villagers."

Pozzi gauged the bones lying around. None was big enough for a weapon. "At home, I was taught never to trust wolves."

"Ah. But you are not at home, are you? In Nyatha, we don't have the luxury of choosing our friends. So, would you rather talk or be eaten?"

So Pozzi told him. Of the pacification warehouse. Of how he had planned to set it on fire. He told Argasar of how his friends, whom he hadn't seen for several months, would be pacified within days.

"And how is it that you ended up in my cage?"

Pozzi told him of how he, Keeva, and Walnut lived with Hassah, the master's daughter, and that he had to get back before dawn if they were to not risk their own lives.

The wolf paced the cage, as if thinking.

"I can help you," Argasar said after some moments, voice soft. "But I will need your absolute trust."

Pozzi's fur prickled. Trusting a wolf went against all instincts. He'd already made a pact with the crow, and that had taught him that no one helped another for nothing. Back in Willago, maybe. But not here, not in Mankahar.

"You're a prisoner, Argasar. Like meself. How would you help?"

"I can create a distraction. If you were to free your fellow villagers, how do you plan to get them out without being detected? Whereas if I were loose amongst them, you can bet the Urzoks will come after me first, since they don't want to risk losing their precious livestock. While their attention is diverted, you'd have your chance to get them out."

"How do I know you won't just eat us?"

"Give up a chance at freedom for a meal? Then I deserve to die here." The wolf began pacing again, his chain grating against the cage floor. "Besides, how will you even get out of this cage without my help?"

The wolf was right. Pozzi had lost precious time, and if he was going to help his fellow villagers, he'd have to escape. Soon.

"What do you want me to do?"

CHAPTER 17

The sentry came running, just as Argasar had predicted. Pozzi did his best to act as Argasar had coached him, especially when the sentry shined the lantern on him to get a better look. The rabbit bared his teeth, letting his stored-up saliva spill out in long strings, and tried not to gag at the taste of blood in his mouth.

"What in Blackhide's name..." the sentry muttered.

Still facing the cage door, Pozzi backed up against Argasar's prone body. The man angled the lantern against the bars for a better look, but Pozzi stayed in place. Argasar lay with his mouth open, blood trickling from his muzzle, more smeared on his neck.

The lantern light blinded Pozzi, but he heard the scratch of key against lock, then the squeal of the door.

"Here rabbit, here now, let's have a look at you..."

Pozzi hated the idea of moving toward that hand, which the sentry had now gloved, but he knew he had to. The pacified animals were all used to being fed by the Urzoks and would have an instinct that an outstretched hand meant food.

"That's it, you little vermin. Here now..."

A gloved hand closed on his neck, and suddenly he was blinded as the sentry shoved the lantern close in his face.

"What pox is this, you little troublemaker?"

The sentry turned his attention to Argasar and moved the lantern over him. He took a step closer, squinting at the wolf's gaping mouth.

He put the lantern down, then reached out and poked the wolf's gums.

Argasar was on the Urzok so fast that Pozzi's captor didn't loosen his grip at first. Both of them hit the floor, hard. The sentry's cries faded as Argasar found the man's throat, and a sharp crack sounded.

Pozzi looked up to see Argasar standing over the sentry, his muzzle truly bloodied now, his eyes shining.

"Are you all right?"

Pozzi nodded, unable to look away from the sentry's staring eyes. He had never seen an Urzok killed.

"Then get his keys," the wolf said. "We're saving your village from pacification tonight, aren't we?"

* * *

"Was that the first time you killed a human?"

"Human?" Argasar repeated. He was standing behind Pozzi, who was focused on trying to open the Hutches gate. He was working his way through all the sentry's keys from his keyring. "You are domesticated."

Pozzi paused as he switched to another key. "You did it like it was natural."

"It was self-defense."

Pozzi shook his head. "We could've threatened him. Forced him to lead us out."

The wolf's voice turned cold. "I got us out. And unlike you, I was being farmed for my fur."

Argasar was right. He had gotten them out. And Pozzi should be grateful. He had no love for the humans—or Urzoks. Well, perhaps he wouldn't want to see Hassah harmed, but otherwise, the lot of them were nothing but misery as far as Pozzi was concerned. So why had it bothered him so much to see Argasar kill that sentry?

The lock still did not budge. Pozzi switched to another key. Only three left. One of these had to work.

"There are usually five Urzoks on duty," the wolf said quietly. "I'll go in first and distract them. When you hear shouting, follow."

Pozzi nodded, though the idea of the Urzok camp being roused by shouts terrified him. The lock clicked, and the gate swung open with a drawn-out creak.

"Well done, rabbit." Then the wolf was gone, a great white ghost slipping into the Hutches.

Pozzi waited, heart pounding, ears primed. He could see the faint outline of Nyatha's walls, the first telltale sign of dawn. Time was short.

A clang of metal rang out, then a surprised voice. Pozzi waited until more shouts arose, followed by a smattering of numerous feet running toward the far side of the building.

Now.

He slipped past the door where Argasar had gone. He saw again the vast, open space, piled high with cages that marched in tidy rows down the length of the building. Inside those cages, dark masses of rabbits huddled against each other, with little room to move.

He ran to the nearest cage. Several pairs of cloudy yellow eyes peered at him from matted fur. He forced the latch holding the cage shut, and the side of the cage sprang open.

"Run!" he hissed. He was already onto the next cage when he noticed that no one inside the first one moved. "Are you deaf? Run!"

Pozzi hit the side of the cage, and this seemed to shake the rabbits out of their shock. They bolted out of the cages. Shouts and growls from the far end reminded him that he didn't have time to linger; he had to find his villagers.

More lights were being lit as outside sentries joined the fray, and Pozzi could see better now. He suddenly realized that there was a system as to how the rabbits were sorted—every cage held a particular color, forming rows of whites, tans, blacks, and grays.

There was only one reason to sort them by color. They were destined to be skinned and made into clothing.

Pozzi's stomach went cold at the enormity of what Morrigan had pointed out. He would have to spring all the cages if he was to guarantee his villagers' freedom. But would he have time?

Argasar's growls grew more vicious, and the Urzoks began shouting instructions to one another, trying to corner the wolf on the north side. Pozzi shrank into the shadows twice as feet ran by him in the semidarkness, a flash of metal twisting the light as knives were drawn and chains were wrapped around fists.

Pozzi slid between the cages, unlatching all that he found and searching the shadows for familiar faces. He found none. He could feel the desperation rising in him now as rabbits started flooding from their cages, blinking in disbelief at their newfound space. There were lanky hares, short-whiskered northern rabbits with snowy coats, long-eared jackrabbits from the prairies, and dozens of red-eyed albinos.

They tumbled out in a confused and ever-expanding pool, some running for the first exit they saw, others following tight on Pozzi's heel, and only when one of them spoke did he understand why.

"Aren't you leading us out?"

Before he could scream at them in frustration and point toward the door, there was a resounding crash of glass. Soon, the unmistakable smell of smoke charged the air with panic.

"Fire!"

Though the flames had barely touched the straw, it was enough. Piles of stored hay and rabbit feed made prime tinder, and soon, the far wall crackled. Angry cries to trap the wolf turned to urgent cries for water.

Almost as one, the rabbits seemed to smell the fire in front of them and turned to run in the opposite direction. Pozzi found himself struggling against a tide of rabbits determined to flee, but he knew there were still hundreds of cages left unopened. And he hadn't come across a single rabbit he recognized. The thickening smoke didn't help his breathing or his vision.

Someone grabbed him by the scruff. Argasar.

"You're going in the wrong direction, rabbit!"

Pozzi struggled, but the wolf only bit harder into his neck, until Pozzi felt his skin break.

"Listen to me! Get out now, you can't save them all."

The presence of the wolf inflamed the rabbits' fear, and they flooded out of the structure like a swarm of bees escaping a smoking hive.

"West! To the west!" Argasar barked, dropping Pozzi. He added, "There is a cattle exit at the west, not very well guarded. Rabbits can get under the fence easy. Get them out and then run. The lucky ones will make the forests of Redwood in the north."

"I can't leave," Pozzi said. "I have t' go back!"

Argasar flicked his ears back. "Suit yourself. If you change your mind, head to Redwood Forest."

And then he was gone, running over and above the rabbits toward the west, shouting his rally cry for them to follow him to freedom. Most followed. Some who did not ran in different directions and disappeared into the laneways of the Urzok grounds. Even now, Pozzi could see reinforcements arriving, Urzoks pulling on drenched cloaks and hauling buckets of water to douse the flames.

As dawn broke and the yard turned into a mad sea of Urzoks, beasts, trampled mud, and clanging bells, Pozzi fought against the tide again, dodging boots and claws and swinging pails in his fight to find his way back to the manor. He couldn't tell whether the tears running down his soot-covered face were from the smoke or his own sense of defeat at not having found a single familiar face from his village. Were he, Keeva, and Walnut the only rabbits from Willago left alive?

"Flints, knives, foodstuffs. We can get rid of the rest." Indigo held up the half-empty supply box.

They had made it to the mainland, pulling up against a sandy stretch dotted with volcanic rocks. After hauling the boat ashore they had unloaded Orjo onto the beach, along with everything they thought could be of use from the boat.

"We'll need the medicines." Theo sorted through the packets and vials. It was a basic selection, but better than nothing. He came across a small green vial whose scent was unfamiliar.

"Truth tonic," Orjo explained.

Brune and Indigo gave him dark looks.

"What? As you know, it's very useful for getting information," the muskrat insisted. "There's also a coin pouch in there."

Indigo found the cloth pouch with its coins and added it to their pile to keep.

"What about this?" Theo lifted a packet that was tightly wrapped in oilcloth. It was resting underneath the medicines and was the last item to be pulled out.

"That's coming with us too."

Theo unwrapped it, revealing an old book with a well-worn cover.

"It's extra weight," Brune argued.

"It's priceless," Orjo snapped. "Where I go, it goes."

Theo released the words on the book's cover. *Songs of Calgornan*. He remembered Orjo quoting the name. "Who's Calgornan?"

The muskrat sighed. "An omatje who doesn't know Calgornan. The greatest bard who ever lived, lad. That there might be the last copy in Mankahar for all I know."

They packed everything they decided to take into a makeshift bag they made from the boat's sail, then struck a northwestern course through an area Brune called the Wetlands of Gunn. Their progress was slow, given Orjo's injury. By the end of the first day, the muskrat was running a fever so hot that Theo feared the worst. But the old omatje proved as tough as his reputation, and in changing his bandages and bathing his wound, Theo read from the scars on his patient's body that the muskrat had survived worse.

By the third day, Orjo had recovered enough to insist on walking, even if it was only in short spurts. Brune regarded the panting muskrat skeptically and motioned at the makeshift strap of ripped sail they had brought to carry him. "You can always get back in the sling."

Orjo grunted. "As the healer Zo said in his book, 'Lack of use leads to lack of limb.' I won't recover if I'm just a bundled babe on your back all the time."

Theo remembered reading that advice and had to admire Orjo's grit. The muskrat walked until he was clearly faint from pain, then submitted to lying in the sling and being positioned on Brune's back.

"You can tell us where we're going," Theo said as he helped tuck the sail cloth under his patient. "I promised to heal you and I will. We won't abandon you."

"I haven't lived this long by being naive, lad." Orjo said. "Let's keep to our agreement. We're headed in the right direction, and when you heal me, I'll tell you exactly where the Library is. And not a breath before." He twitched his whiskers.

"Does the Library hold the cure to pacification?" Theo asked. All these months seeking Orjo and the Library of Elshon had sharpened his curiosity about its secrets and powers.

"Is that what you're after?"

"Of course."

"Why?"

The question threw Theo. Wasn't it obvious? "Ending pacification and changing creatures back will save Mankahar. It's the greatest weapon we could have against the Urzoks."

Orjo winced as a bounce against Brune's back jolted his wound. "If you say so."

"What do you think is the most powerful weapon in the Library then?"

"Don't know, don't care."

"There's really nothing in the Library you think worthwhile or valuable?"

The muskrat patted his jacket pocket, where he had lovingly stored the book of songs. "Maybe I'd be partial to finding another work of Calgornan's if I could."

"I'd like to borrow it sometime, if you're willing."

"I'd have to be infinitely fonder of you than I am now, rabbit." He clapped his paws together and rubbed them. "Anyway, I'm hungry. Let's find some water lilies and snails."

* * *

"Do you trust him?"

The muskrat was safely out of earshot, reading his book next to Indigo under the shade of a green ash while Theo and Brune foraged for lilies. Even so, Brune kept his voice low.

"The griffin said Orjo knew where the Library was," Theo answered. "She wouldn't lie."

Brune's paw plunged into the water, pulling out a wriggling pike. "No, my question was, do you trust him?" The bear murmured a prayer to Aktu before biting into the fish.

Theo pulled a few leaves off a cattail, stuffing them in his jacket pockets. "I don't know."

"Good." Brune finished off the fish in two bites. "Because I think odds are he'll turn on us."

"Not while he needs us," Theo said. "He can barely walk."

"True, but it's only a matter of time," the bear replied. He wiped his muzzle with one burly paw and stood. "And he won't even tell us where we're going."

"He's worried we'll leave him while he's defenseless."

Brune shook his shaggy head. "You trust too much, Theo. This isn't Willago. This is Mankahar. And Mankahar is in dark times."

Theo glanced toward the tree. The muskrat looked up from his book, and Theo hastily turned back to his cattails.

"I know you think he's like you, because he's an omatje. But he's not. He's a killer."

"We've killed."

"That's different," Brune growled. "He's not your friend, Theo, no matter how much you want him to be. You two are like blueberries and nightshade. You may be similar on the surface, but he's deadly."

* * *

THE MUSKRAT TURNED from watching the bear and Theo.

"How long does it take to pick some lousy roots?"

"Pick your own if you'd like."

The muskrat watched the rabbit in silence as she repaired the quiver strap where it had frayed open. She ignored his gaze.

"You say little, but your hatred's louder than rain on a metal roof." Orjo scratched at the bandage on his side. "Are you the one who's going to kill me once we find the Library? Because you dislike me the most?"

She paused in her work. "You tricked me into saying we were going to kill you."

"They may not have been the words you wanted to say, but the truth tonic doesn't lie. So why do you wish to kill me? For fame?"

"I have personal reasons."

The muskrat frowned. "Then I take it we've met. Before you came to my island."

She looked at him then. "You don't remember."

"The only time I was in Alvareth was…" Understanding crept in. "Ah. The queen died while I was there, didn't she?"

"Queen Delamar and my sister, Azel. Killed with your dagger."

A tense silence fell.

"Well, this is awkward."

"So you remember now?" Indigo stood, unable to sit any longer.

The muskrat nodded, wistful. "I miss that dagger."

She digested this. "That's what you have to say? You miss your dagger?"

"It was a priceless dagger. I debated about getting it back." At her look, he held out his paws. "What?"

* * *

THEO AND BRUNE were halfway to the tree when they saw Indigo pull an arrow from her quiver, then slam Orjo to the ground with her full weight.

"Rot it," Brune growled, but Theo was already sprinting.

He arrived just as Indigo straddled Orjo, arrow point to his neck and a knee digging into Orjo's injured side. Brune was close behind him.

"Indigo! Listen to me!"

"Stay out of this, Theo."

"Revenge only works if you find the culprit." The muskrat's calm through his obvious pain surprised Theo, and he could tell Indigo was momentarily thrown.

Indigo pressed the arrow further until Theo was sure there would be blood. "You expect me to believe you didn't kill my family?"

"My dagger went missing before they died."

"You're lying!"

"No, I swear it's the truth."

Indigo looked as if she would drive the arrow through his throat, but she paused. "Let's find out."

She strode over to their supply bag and upturned the contents.

"Indigo, what are you—" Theo protested.

She picked out the green vial and held it out to the muskrat. "Drink it."

Orjo rubbed his throat. "Truth tonic is hard to come by. Think before you waste it on—"

"Drink it all, or I will put this arrow through your arm, and you'll never wield a knife again for the rest of your immortal life."

The two stared at each other before Orjo sighed. He sipped it.

"All of it!" Indigo insisted.

"Lass, I don't think—"

"Now." Indigo raised the arrow point.

Orjo shrugged. "Very well." He downed the vial's contents in one go and tossed the vial aside.

"Go ahead. Ask me anything."

Indigo drew a breath, and when she spoke, her voice trembled. "Did you kill my mother and sister?"

Orjo looked her in the eyes. "No. I did not."

Indigo blinked, but otherwise showed no emotion. Theo wondered whether she had even understood the muskrat's words.

"I told you. My dagger, the one you saw with the Forbidden Language on it, disappeared before they died." Orjo's tone was friendly and carefree, that of someone with nothing to hide. And perhaps, Theo thought, no way to hide it. "Your mother and sister were killed, but it was not by my paw."

"If not you, who?" Indigo looked as if her world had cracked open.

Orjo began laughing.

Indigo looked as if she would drive the arrow through his throat.

Orjo's laughter faded, and he looked at her, his eyes almost pitying. "You traveled very far for an answer that lies at home, Princess. You need to know your subjects' hearts above all. But you can't know that, because you don't even know your own."

"I'm one arrow point away from my heart's greatest desire."

"If that's true then you're not nearly ready to run a queendom, lass."

Theo wished he could have clapped a paw over the muskrat's mouth, but it was too late.

"Easy, rat," Brune warned.

"Take that back." Her voice had dropped dangerously low, and even Orjo seemed to realize that he had opened a very raw wound.

"You're the one who made me drink the tonic. I have no control over my words. And if you want to rule, you'll need to be strong enough to stomach some truth."

"That's it." Brune stepped forward and grabbed the arrow from Indigo. "You're here to lead us to the Library, so let's get walking."

"Then you'll have to carry me." The muskrat seemed to struggle to keep his eyes open.

"Rot it," Brune muttered. "The tonic."

"Don't worry, lass," Orjo slurred. "If you still want to kill me after we find the Library, I'll give you a fair fight. But if we do, don't be upset if you end up dead."

With a smirk, Orjo's chin dropped to his chest, and he was still jeering as he fell into sleep.

CHAPTER 19

The charred side of Nyatha was starting to heal, like some scabbed wound. When the fire had finally abated, over a third of Nyatha lay in blackened ruins. Even the stone structures were stained with soot, and from the manor, one could see the blackened husks of the pacification cradles. They were destroyed beyond repair, and there was talk that rebuilding would take the whole summer. Pozzi had managed to save the remaining prisoners from pacification. For now.

The damage had been extensive enough that even the house servants were delegated yard cleanup duty, spending days scrubbing the ash and smoke from the dairy, helping rebuild fences, and grumbling about the extra work. Stable hands, carpenters, bricklayers, and stone masons around the farm labored from dawn to well after sundown, chopping new wood, sorting tiles, and removing burnt debris.

Pozzi had managed to sneak back into the household and into Hassah's bed during the chaos, but he made sure to keep a low profile after the fire. Walnut had pestered him for the full story, but Pozzi had remained tight-lipped, which put Walnut in a sour mood for the week. Pozzi didn't need Walnut playing out the night's deed, as he usually did whenever he heard a new story. Keeva asked only one question, and Pozzi knew he hadn't brought the answer she wanted. He hadn't found any of their fellow villagers. He could only hope that they had escaped in the crowd, without his knowing.

He wondered where those rabbits had escaped to—and often found himself staring out in the direction of Redwood Forest, visible as a dark smudge in the distance from the balcony where Hassah played.

A few times at night, they could hear the howl of a wolf from the north. Were the escapees safe? Was Argasar trying to tell him to join them? Pozzi began listening each night and noticed answering howls from further away. If it was Argasar, he was no longer a lone wolf.

In the days after the fire, Master Ghazan's mood turned blacker than even the burnt structures, and he cut his farmhands' rations of meat. Imperial Day celebrations had to be canceled, and all business was postponed. In the days after the planned festival, Ghazan lived in the Nyatha trading halls, where crowds of disgruntled buyers and merchants wrangled with him from sun-up to well past moonrise, clamoring for compensation. With the master's stress, the whole of Nyatha seemed to spiral into a foul temper, with the house chamberlain snapping at the cooks and head maids, and they in turn taking it out on the house girls and errand boys. It wasn't long before even the sheltered Hassah felt the sting of her parents' moods.

Things came to a head roughly a week after the fire. Pozzi and Keeva heard the girl's wails first, then the approach of her running feet. Face streaked with tears and snot, she burst in and slammed the door shut before diving for her bed. There, she buried herself in her pillows, her dark hair prying free from its braids.

Walnut hopped over and pulled himself up on the bed. Pozzi watched from the windowsill, while Keeva peered out from under the bed where she liked to hide away occasionally and shut out the world.

"What's wrong, Hassah?" Walnut asked.

"Go away!" came the muffled reply. Walnut crept closer and tentatively slid under her arm. At first, Hassah resisted, but soon, she pulled him close, weeping into his fur.

There was a pounding on the door.

"Hassah! Your mother wants you." Farriah's voice was clipped.

"I'm not coming! Go away!"

"You'll get another smack if you don't."

Hassah screamed her response.

"Fine, but don't blame me if the mistress punishes you again." The nurse's footsteps retreated, and Hassah burst into a fresh round of sobs.

Keeva approached the bed and touched Hassah's foot. The girl sat up, rubbing at her wet nose, and Pozzi could see the fading red on Hassah's cheek where her mother's fleshy hand had landed.

"Mama doesn't love me anymore."

"That's not true," Keeva said. "She's just...busy."

"She's always busy with Sarkus," Hassah complained, brows bunched and voice thick with mucus and tears. "She never sits me on her lap or sings me songs anymore."

She was spoiled, self-centered, and the child of his enemy. But even so, Pozzi felt sorry for her. And a little guilty. If they hadn't helped the crows attack Sarkus, Sarkus wouldn't be disfigured, and the distressed Tansha might not be so quick to anger with her daughter.

Pozzi cleared his throat. "How 'bout we sing you a song, Hassah?"

"I don't want one!"

"You don't have to sing it. We'll sing," Walnut suggested. "Singing makes you feel better."

"No it doesn't!" Hassah said, teeth gritted.

Keeva shrugged. "I was going to sing the story of how the monkey lost his backside, but never mind."

A hairline crack appeared in Hassah's anger. "You can't lose your backside."

Pozzi nodded, serious. "Oh yes y' can. How does it go, Keeva?"

Keeva made a show of trying to remember. "Something about him sneezing so hard, that it fell off."

At this, Hassah gave in to a smile. "This isn't a real story."

"Happened to someone I know meself. Honest," Pozzi said, raising one paw. "And they wrote a song about it. It goes like this:

> *There once was a monkey*
> *Who had a big nose*
> *It stretched past his face*
> *And reached to his toes*
> *He'd pick it with his fingers*
> *And tie it in bows*
> *Until everyone said,*
> *That's a disgustingly long nose!*

> *Then a bug came along*
> *Who wanted a warm bed*
> *He crawled up one nostril*
> *And up monkey's head*
> *There he decided he'd like to stay*
> *So he cleaned out the cobwebs*
> *And set up some hay*
> *When along came a tickle*
> *And monkey said ha-choo!*

At this line, Walnut jumped up and sat heavily on Hassah, who squealed in surprise.

"And that's when his backside landed on you!" Walnut finished, laughing.

Hassah wiped tears from her eyes, but this time, they were of laughter. "Again!"

They repeated the song, taking turns being the monkey's backside, until they were all a tangle of limbs and fur on the bed.

Panting and spent, Walnut hugged the girl by the neck. "See? I told you a song makes things better."

Hassah sat up. "Thank you."

"That's what friends do," Walnut said. At this, Hassah looked downcast again.

"What's wrong?"

"Are we friends?" The girl looked vulnerable, unsure.

The question took Keeva and Pozzi by surprise, but Walnut answered without hesitation.

"Of course we are. Why wouldn't we be?"

"Sarkus says you're just animals. And animals aren't friends."

Sarkus was a warped boy with a warped soul. But Pozzi couldn't say he was all wrong. He could tell Keeva was unsure how to respond, while Walnut looked stung.

"We like you, Hassah." Pozzi searched for words. "But friends... Friends are equals."

"What's ee-kals?"

"Equals are when you're the same."

"But no one's the same," Hassah argued. "Everyone is different."

"Well, equal is when one of you doesn't own the other. You have to be free to be real friends."

"What does free mean?"

Pozzi and Keeva glanced at each other. "It means...you can make choices for yourself," Keeva said. "Do what you want to do."

Hassah smiled. "You make choices. Not like me. Nurse Farriah barely lets me do anything I want."

"We can't leave," Keeva said, quiet.

The girl frowned. "But you don't want to leave. Do you?"

"I don't want to leave," Walnut piped up.

"Walnut—" Pozzi began, but Keeva put a warning paw on his arm.

Hassah hugged Walnut to her, then looked at Pozzi and Keeva accusingly. "You want to leave?"

Keeva nodded.

The girl's voice turned wounded. "Why?"

"Because we were forced to come here. We want to go home." Pozzi's words spilled out, all of a sudden uncontrollable after months of putting on smiles for the sake of this child, for the sake of their own safety.

"You can't," Hassah said. "If you left, how would we play together?"

Pozzi decided to take a chance. "Hassah, sometimes the best friends are those who let each other go. If you helped us leave, we would—"

"No! You can't leave. You're my friends, and you're staying here."

"Listen, Hassah—"

"No! No leaving!"

She clutched Walnut to her and ran from the room. A tense silence fell.

"If she tells Ghazan…" Keeva started.

"I know." Pozzi doubted Hassah would tell her father, but that didn't mean she wouldn't curb their freedoms.

"We have to leave soon." Keeva looked out the open window, through which they could hear the unceasing ring of hammers, the steady chafe of saws, and the crack of stones being broken and stacked. Ghazan kept Nyatha working day and night to restore Nyatha's defenses and perimeter. "Once Nyatha is rebuilt, we won't be able to get out."

She was right of course. By the time Ghazan was finished repairing Nyatha, the place would likely be an impenetrable fortress. Leaving at night was out of the question, as they were securely locked in their cage without a key, and Hassah would be wary of letting them out of her sight. But how would they leave in the day? After the fire, Ghazan had hired extra mercenaries and guards and placed them around the perimeter, making sure no one entered or left Nyatha without being seen.

From the open window, Pozzi heard the neigh of a horse and the creak of wagon wheels. He looked out and caught sight of a familiar horse-drawn wagon entering the delivery yard near the kitchens, Kayden the driver slouched in the driver's seat.

"I think I've got an idea," Pozzi said.

CHAPTER 20

"I heard your Imperial Day Feast had a little complication."

Ghazan eyed Ornox wearily, clearly eager to get on with his other business. They were in one of the merchant trading halls, a large, airy room lined with long benches down the walls and a speaker's chair at one end.

Ornox had taken this chair while waiting, a gesture of arrogance that clearly irked Ghazan. "I'm also sorry to hear of your son's accident," Ornox added. "I hope he is recovering."

"I told you I can't help you, Ornox. Especially as I've lost over half of my livestock and have to rebuild Nyatha." The merchant rubbed his forehead. He had puffy gray bags under his eyes, and his nose was peppered in red, leftovers of his drinking and exhaustion. He clearly did not want to discuss his business or his son.

"I'm not here for help," Ornox said. "I'm here to make a business proposal."

"I told you, I have no funds."

"A good merchant doesn't deal solely in funds. You have other resources."

124

The master of Nyatha frowned, suspicious. "Even if I do, you don't have the coin to afford it."

Ornox smiled. "I have something better."

* * *

THE WIND RUFFLED the grass as they rode out of Nyatha's main gate, Ghazan on his stout quarter horse and Ornox on his war charger. Yod followed on his own steed, leading another mare with a saddlebag slung across its withers.

Ornox had learned to keep the clay orbs on a riderless horse after what happened to one of his men. He couldn't remember the man's name, which meant he wouldn't be missed, but the fool had lit his pipe while carrying a bag of the cargo and obliterated himself. Ornox had ordered their pipes and dried spike-plant supplies to be dumped, and from then on, the men were forced to take turns carrying the twenty odd balls of powder.

Ghazan led him around the side of Nyatha's outer walls. "What are we looking for, exactly?"

"Something we can destroy," Ornox replied, eyes scanning.

The merchant gave a dry laugh. "I have some traders I'd like to send to Blackhide."

"That would be messy." Ornox pointed toward a large, twisted ash tree on a hillock, its crown of branches so wide and expansive that it almost seemed to dominate the sky. "There."

Ghazan glanced at him, curious. "You'll need a big saw and fifty more men if you're wanting to bring that down."

Ornox simply smiled and kicked his horse into a canter. Yod followed, and after a moment, Ghazan urged his horse to keep up. When they were a few paces from the tree, Yod dismounted and carefully pulled out a clay ball from the mare's saddlebag. He handed it up to his master.

"What's that?" Ghazan asked, unimpressed.

"Our future." Ornox looked down at the ball, then motioned

to Yod. The servant took out flints and tinder, then dug a small hole in the earth and began a fire.

"I don't mean to be rude, but how long is this going to take because I—"

Ornox silenced him with a look. He might have lost his title, but he had lost none of his command over ordinary men. The warlord held the ball down for Yod to light the wick with a piece of kindling, and then he threw the ball toward the tree.

It bounced off a branch, hit another branch, and then fell like a stone onto the ground. It sat there, fuse alight, nestled in the crook of the tree's roots.

"Ornox, I don't see—"

The roar of ten dragons shook the ground, and the tree seemed to burst from the inside. The sharp crack of wood sent birds squawking in panic, and Ornox could feel his ears ringing. He had never felt more alive.

The tree was split in two, as if some god had taken an axe right down the middle. One half creaked as it broke free of the other, crashing to the ground in a flurry of leaves, broken wood, and splintered bark. The horses pulled at their bits, ears flat. If not for Yod's quick hand, Ghazan's horse would have run away with its master astride.

"What in Blackhide's name...!" Ghazan was shouting, clearly unable to hear himself after the roar of the explosion.

Ornox wiped the dust from his face. "No army can stand against these little griffin eggs."

Ghazan looked at him, stunned. "How many of these do you have?"

"The question, Ghazan, is how many can you make?"

"I don't understand."

"If you find an alchemist, Ghazan, you can be the richest merchant in Mankahar. How much does your livestock make you, even when you haven't lost half of it to negligence? Two hundred squares of gold a season? Three hundred? The emperor would pay you two thousand for every pound of this stuff, and consider it a bargain."

He could see the merchant's mind churning, calculating, putting this logic together. "What do you want for it?"

"Two dozen hardened men, fighters. And information."

"Theo Griffinrider?"

Ornox nodded. "You trade in information. I want to be first to know where he is, who saw him, and where."

"Very well. First to know."

"And of course a reasonable cut of your earnings."

"Ten percent?"

"A quarter."

"A quarter?" Ghazan looked indignant. "I'll be taking on all the risk. It's clearly volatile—"

"I can take this elsewhere."

"You're out of favor. There's not a merchant who'd risk the emperor's wrath and deal with you. I'll share a fifth."

"Nothing risked, nothing gained. A quarter."

The merchant made a sour face, but Ornox knew he had won. "You drive a hard bargain, but very well. You are welcome to have your pick of my best men. I will let you know as soon as I have word of the rabbit, Lord Ornox."

The warlord noted Ghazan's use of his title again. It felt good, like a familiar horse. Things were looking up for him; he could sense it. He would get his revenge and afterward, his throne.

CHAPTER 21

The tavern wasn't a tavern as much as a gathering of planks nailed together against the elements. Light spilled like cheap ale from its windows, and the travelers could hear the faint hum of conversation and the whine of an off-tune fiddle. The food and lodging on offer would be simple, at best, though that was not entirely the establishment's fault.

The growing war in Mankahar had meant leaner times for even the richer lands to the west and south, never mind this dingy outpost wedged between the sparsely populated marshlands and the farming communities of the plains.

"What are we doing here?" Theo asked, surveying the outside of the building.

"What do you usually do at a tavern?" Orjo retorted. He had recovered enough strength that he only needed Brune to carry him for half the day now. "Get a bath, have decent food, sleep in a bed."

"I admit, it's a clever way to get us killed." Indigo said drily.

"This place is likely overrun with bounty hunters."

Brune's words made Theo nervous. The handsome reward on his head had made them avoid towns and cities unless absolutely necessary.

"Listen, sleeping on the hard ground has been a real adventure. Reminds me of old times. But it does nothing for an old frame like mine, especially while trying to keep my ribcage from falling open." Orjo rubbed his paws. "Not to mention I'd kill for a cooked meal."

Brune scowled. "It's too dangerous. We're not going in there."

"Well, I'm not traveling another step unless we do. You want the Library, you give me a night in a proper bed and a proper meal."

He set out, not bothering to wait for an answer.

Indigo grimaced and undid her cloth belt. She wrapped it around her head like a band, keeping her ears down to hide the tattoos. She then shouldered Orjo's bow and quiver and followed the muskrat.

"Come on," she said. "The more we hesitate the more suspicious we look."

Theo looked at Brune. "You think it's safe?"

"Sure. Like suckling a baby lion."

Inside, the tavern was surprisingly cozy and well kept. A large hearth dominated the middle of the room, with chipped trestle tables and mismatched chairs arranged along the walls. A few ragged patrons sat in groups with their tankards and shared plates of bread and roasted garlic, while a fat fox with wine-colored fur and a broad-brimmed hat worked a fiddle in the corner.

Orjo had already commandeered a table by a window, and Indigo took a stool opposite him. Theo didn't excite much interest, but the sight of Brune gave everyone pause.

A small-eyed badger wearing an apron appeared almost magically from behind the bar, hurrying over while wiping her paws.

"We don't want any fighting," she warned.

Brune held out his paws. "Not here for a fight, friend. Just for a meal and a night's rest."

The badger nodded. "Go on then."

Theo and Brune joined Orjo and Indigo at their table, while the other patrons snuck curious glances in their direction.

At Brune's accusing look, Orjo shrugged. "We were never going to be able to travel to the Library without attracting notice. This way, we draw out the hunters and plant some false rumors."

"Rumors?" Theo asked.

The server sauntered over, a young badger whose eyes and gait clearly marked him as the son of the innkeeper they had just met.

"What'll you have, friends?" he asked, gracious but also openly curious.

"Four tankards of honey ale, two loaves of your best bread, a dish of soup—hearty, mind you, none of the watery stuff—a block of walnut cheese, and some salted herring. Oh, and a large leek pie."

"You expecting guests?" Brune growled. "You'll spend everything we have."

"It's my coin, remember."

Indigo surveyed the other patrons, noting their nervous stares and poorly veiled glances. "Everyone will know about us before sundown."

"Hopefully, not that long," Orjo said. "Now, if you stop talking and start listening, you might learn something."

The innkeeper's son came back with the pie and bread in one paw and a tray with four tankards on the other. "Here ya are. Been traveling long, I take it?"

"Indeed, lad," Orjo said, hefting a tankard. "And won't be many taverns up where we're going."

"Up?" Their server placed the last plate of bread on their table and counted the coins Brune left there. "Heading north then?"

Orjo shook his head. "I meant up as in up river. Oh look, my tankard's dry."

Brune glared at Orjo, but the badger headed off, happy for this business. Orjo immediately dug into the food.

"See? They now think we're heading north. Simple. Now eat. You're at a tavern for Aktu's sake."

Theo glanced at Brune and Indigo, then took a slice of leek pie. Indigo broke off a chunk of bread, and Brune sipped his ale. The musician began a lively tune above the hum of conversation.

Theo caught random words and snippets from a group of traders in the corner.

"…further south every day…"

"…worried so much coin is flowing…heard from a smithy…they must think it's serious."

"So what? One city is hardly Mankahar."

Indigo leaned in to their table, as if to take another piece of bread. Her voice was low, but excited. "Sounds like New Hegg has been liberated."

"Are you sure it was Hegg?" Brune said softly.

Indigo nodded. "That badger at that table said it twice."

Orjo popped a herring in his mouth and chewed. "Aye. They're all talkin' about it. The Order now controls New Hegg, it seems."

The bear closed his eyes, and when he opened them, there were tears. Orjo looked amused.

"Hegg is Brune's home," Theo explained.

"Was," Brune said, a hitch in his voice. "The empire burned Hegg and built the new city beside it."

"Congratulations. The Urzoks must be getting slack if they can't defend a second-rate city like New Hegg." Orjo licked the salt from his whiskers, then motioned at the unfinished pie on Brune's plate. "You just going to waste that?"

The bear motioned for Orjo to go ahead, evidently still trying to listen for more news of Hegg. The muskrat shoveled the last of Brune's pie into his mouth and licked his paws.

"I'm going to order another one of those. Anyone want anything else?"

They all shook their heads. Theo wondered how such a small creature could pack away so much food. They watched him walk toward the innkeeper, who was shelving cleaned tankards by the kitchen.

Theo saw Indigo watching the muskrat with narrowed eyes.

"You think he'll make a run?"

"It's likely."

"Stop worrying. He can't walk for long without resting. How far could he get?"

She sipped her ale. "He might be recovered more than we think."

The possibility hadn't occurred to Theo. He watched the muskrat and the innkeeper exchange words, then coins.

"How long does it take to order a pie?"

Theo watched more coins change paws. "He'll have spent everything he has by the end of this meal." Was it just him, or did the muskrat seem a bit furtive?

Indigo stood. "I'm going to see what he's doing."

Just then, the innkeeper nodded and turned away, and Orjo walked back and eased himself down onto his stool, wincing.

"You were gone a long time," Indigo said. "I hope you didn't order the whole larder."

"I was simply booking our rooms," the muskrat retorted. "Now, I could have been stingy and made you three sleep outside, as it's my coin, but I didn't. I'll even share my room with one of you. Any takers?"

* * *

THOUGH ORJO WAS right that having even a basic bed was a welcome change, Theo couldn't sleep. There was the threat that someone might alert the Urzoks about them, and the dubious leek pie that Theo regretted eating. But neither of these kept him awake as much as the occupant beside him in the bed.

She slept with her back to him, and he found himself watching the rise and fall of her silhouette despite the exhaustion that felt like a permanent part of his bones. Though Orjo had protested at their sleeping arrangements, Theo and his friends had little choice. The only rooms available were this small, glorified closet and a larger sitting room on the other side of the tavern that could accommodate Brune's size. Theo and Indigo had to bunk together, for Brune wouldn't hear of either of them being alone with Orjo.

Theo had offered to sleep on the floor, but Indigo had told him to not be ridiculous.

She turned over, and Theo quickly squeezed his eyes shut. He didn't want her knowing he'd been staring.

"Can't sleep?"

He opened his eyes and found her green ones fixed on him. "How'd you know?"

"You snore when you're asleep."

"That's not true!"

"It's very soft, don't worry." She paused, thinking. "I can't sleep either."

"Don't let Orjo get to you."

"It makes no sense. He has to be lying."

Theo thought on this. "He had the truth tonic."

"Maybe it doesn't work on him."

"Have you ever thought about who else could have done it?" At her intake of breath, he added, "I'm not saying it wasn't him."

"Then what are you saying?"

He paused, trying to find the right words. "Sometimes, we're so convinced of something that we forget to look at it from another angle."

There was a long pause, and she lay back, staring up at the ceiling. "It's been a truth for so long. He killed them, so I would kill him."

"I guess truths change. And we have to change with them."

"You're right. He's right. If the truth is he didn't kill them, I have to stomach that."

"Is it so bad that he's not as terrible as you think?"

She turned to look at him again. "He has a hold on you."

"I just want to find the Library."

"It's more than that. You're so happy to have found a fellow omatje that you can't see him for what he is."

"And what's that?"

"A killer. Just because he didn't kill my family doesn't make him trustworthy."

"True. But you've never had to be alone," he said. "Disliked. Hated, even."

He sensed her frowning in the dark. "You're not hated. Or disliked."

"But you wouldn't want to learn the Forbidden Language, would you?"

"I have no reason to."

"I was hoping—" He stopped.

"What?"

"Never mind. Good night."

She propped herself up. "No, say it. What were you hoping?"

"It's foolish."

"Tell me."

How could he explain that there would forever be a chasm between him and others? Between him and her? In that sense, Orjo, killer or not, would always understand him in a way that she never could.

"I was hoping that I'd be the rea—"

Her paw clamped over his mouth. "Shh! Did you hear that?"

Once he'd overcome his surprise, he tried to listen, but could only focus on the fact that she was practically on top of him.

"Don't move," she whispered, and he sensed, rather than saw, her paw reaching for the weapon she'd kept beneath her pillow.

The door crashed in, and a rush of dark-clothed figures filled the room. Three immediately fell on Theo, pinning him to the bed. Indigo leapt for her arrows, but a burly attacker—the fox with the fiddle, Theo realized—kicked the quiver under the bed and tried to push her to the floor. The princess took her attacker's arm and pulled him forward, using his momentum to smash him into the wall. He crumpled with a grunt before his companion, a badger who smelled of onions and wine, drew a knife and threw himself on Indigo.

Theo fought back as best he could, but he was outnumbered. A bag came over his head. He screamed for Brune but was cut short when something hard and big boned smashed into his cheek. He fell, mouth full of wet saltiness. Then all was still.

CHAPTER 22

Throbbing. Something was wrong with his jaw. And he was on a boat. A snorting boat going over hard, bumpy waves.

Theo forced his eyes open and was rewarded with a close view of a rough, woven sack. He was still hooded. Which explained why he couldn't seem to get enough air. He coughed at the overpowering smell of garlic and onion and tried to pull the bag over his head. His paws, he discovered, were tied with rope, but he managed to wriggle and squirm his way out of the head covering.

Threads of sunlight pierced small cracks in the roof, and Theo took in his surroundings. A fully enclosed cart—not a boat—only a few paces across, with myriad hooks in the ceiling and along the sides. From these hooks there hung ropes of dried garlic and onion bulbs, their papery skins brushing against one another and carpeting the wagon floor with crackly flakes. He heard another snort—a horse's—followed by a voice murmuring from outside the front of the cart. The driver, Theo guessed.

The cart lurched, and something kicked him in the back, making him cry out.

"Shh!"

He turned to see a writhing hemp sack on the floor behind him, its end tied with rope. A few holes, big enough to fit a digit through but not a paw, had been cut into the bag to allow airflow.

"Stay still." Even whispering pained his jaw, though being able to speak at all gave him hope it was just a fracture and not a break. With his bound paws, he untied the top of the sack and pulled the cloth down, freeing Indigo's head and ears. Her look at seeing his face made him realize he must look terrible.

She pulled her paws, which were bound like his, out from the sack and began undoing Theo's bonds, looking around her for any hints of how they could get out. Once she had his paws free, he undid hers, and they silently worked the ropes off their legs.

If the cart drivers heard them through all this, they didn't let on.

Indigo checked the back of the cart, but the door was securely locked from the outside. She moved to the front and peered out through a chink in the wood, trying to sight the driver. Theo held one paw against the swaying cart wall and felt his jaw. Swollen, painful, but likely just fractured.

Indigo held up two digits to signal two captors. At least they were evenly matched.

She began exploring the walls, looking for any way out. For all its stink and plainness, however, the cart had been sturdily built. The floor and walls were solid for a simple vegetable-seller's wagon, and for the first time, Theo noticed the coils of rope hung on the hooks. Stinking onions and garlic could easily overpower the smell of blood and discourage anyone curious about exploring a closed wagon. As if following his logic, Indigo mouthed, "Bounty hunters."

Theo wrestled a knot of fear. After the encounter with the bats, he had become too aware of how many enemies he had. Wherever they were being taken, he didn't think he'd like the destination.

They hit a rock, which sent the wagon lurching. The ropes of onions and garlic swung, and something clattered above them. Indigo looked up and pointed.

Following her gaze, Theo saw a small square grate in the ceiling, just big enough for a rabbit to squeeze through. Indigo looked around and, choosing the sturdiest-looking rope of onions, gave it a hardy tug. It held. She motioned for Theo to give her a boost. He held his paws together and she stepped up, then pulled herself onto the rope. She stretched up until she could reach the grate and pushed at it. Though it had been wishful thinking to hope it might open, Theo felt a stab of disappointment when it held.

There came the sound of excited voices, then the cracking of a whip. Without warning, the cart leapt forward. Indigo's pawhold slipped from the grate, and she fell, crashing into Theo and sending them both flying against the back door. The cart was speeding now, and Theo could hear the gallop of the horses' hooves.

Just then, something giant landed on the cart's roof, blocking all light. The cart slowed, but whatever had landed made the horses panic, for they ran faster. The prisoners heard someone fall off the cart with a grunt; then came a scream.

Theo and Indigo pounded on the back door, trying to force it open. Whatever new threat was above them was obviously much worse than whoever had abducted them. The cart hit another rut, throwing them and the giant on top of the cart to one side.

There was a curse from above and then a crash as whoever it was fell off the cart. Freed from the attacker's weight, the horses shot forward, the cart jolting and bouncing the two prisoners as the fear-blind horses fought to escape.

Before they could find their feet, one of the cart's wheels left the ground. Indigo gave a shout of warning as they careened first against one wall of their prison, then slammed back again as the wheel came down with a bone-bruising thud. They landed in a tangled heap of garlic and rope against the back door, the cart resuming its breakneck pace.

"You all right?" Indigo called.

Theo managed a nod before the wood next to Theo's ear exploded with a deafening crack. The tip of a giant axe blade protruded from the cart door, its sharp edge gleaming just whiskers away from Theo's skull. He and Indigo scrambled to get away, clawing at the lurching walls for any purchase. Indigo yanked a string of onions from a hook, and tossed one to Theo.

"What's this for?"

"It's all we have!" she shouted. "Throw them when the door opens!"

The wheel cracked and bounced against a rock, and the cart door flew open. A giant hairy paw gripped the side. Theo glimpsed the shaggy head too late, and the onion caught the bear square in the eye.

"By Aktu!" Brune's back paw slipped from the cart, sending the bear's body over the back and onto the ground speeding past below.

"Brune!" Theo was so happy to see the bear that he barely noticed the pain in his jaw from shouting.

The horses kept on, dragging Brune who was holding on to the embedded axe with both paws. The bear managed to get his feet under him and pull himself back onto the cart's stepping board.

"To me!"

The rabbits crawled toward the bear, the cart still jolting and bouncing wildly. They took his outstretched arm.

"Hang on!" Brune gripped them to him, then with a mighty yank, he jerked his axe head free of the cart door, and they were crashing and rolling onto the ground, the cart careening away.

Bruised and scraped, but safe and on solid ground, the rabbits stood. Brune shook the dust from his coat and gripped his axe in one meaty paw. "Everyone all right?"

Theo nodded. "Sorry about your eye."

Brune rubbed at it. "First time I've been attacked with onions. Come on. Orjo's back there somewhere."

They half walked, half ran along the wheel tracks. They were in a vast scrubland, and Theo didn't recognize any landmarks. The sun was well over the horizon. They came across Brune's fallen helmet, which the bear picked up and fitted back to his head. Before long, they had caught up to Orjo, who stood with his belt in his paw over the bodies of an Urzok and a fox. The fox from the tavern, Theo realized.

Orjo beamed. "There he is, Theo Griffinrider!"

Theo winced. He was beginning to really dislike his nickname.

"You killed them?" Brune growled.

"What? You wanted to make friends?"

"We won't know if there are others." Indigo scanned the area.

"We'll know when they try to kill us." The muskrat rifled through the fox's pockets, examining a small pocket knife before discarding it. "Where is it, you little—Aha! Here it is." He pulled out the well-worn book from the fox's inner pocket and turned the pages lovingly before tucking it away in his robe. "Let's go. And you were right. No more taverns—that was a bad idea."

* * *

At Orjo's insistence, they found the horses and cart at the riverbank, still skittish but spent and willing for Brune to take the reins.

"What'd I tell you?" Orjo remarked, inspecting the wagon. "They wouldn't cross the river." He wrinkled his nose at the smell of garlic and onion. "And now we get to travel quickly, if not in style."

They searched the wagon and found water skins beneath the driver's seat, along with rope, flints, bedding, a kettle, and some dried biscuits in a cloth.

They filled the water skins from the river, then boarded the wagon. Theo took the reins and drove the horses upriver until they were crossing the Plains of Fire. The name had stuck because the grasses here looked like spindly flames year round, Brune told them, turning from amber yellow in spring to gold to an ember red and then an ashen white in winter.

Theo glanced back at Orjo, who was lying on the folded pile of hemp sacks in the wagon reading his book, rolling with the rhythm of the horses.

"You must really love this omatje."

Orjo didn't look up. "Calgornan was more than an omatje. He was a bard. Music and words that make you laugh or cry, that's true magic."

"What was it like? Back when the Forbidden Language wasn't banned?"

Orjo made a dismissive grunt. "It's past. That time's never coming back."

"But what if it could?" Theo pressed.

The muskrat read in silence for a moment, making Theo think he hadn't heard. But then Orjo shut the book.

"You want me to tell you it was a golden age, Griffinrider? It wasn't. Those who knew the Forbidden Language, and most did, had knowledge. What some might call wisdom. So what? It wasn't worth a beetle's belch in the end." An exhaustion crept into his voice. "Greed, war, death, power—these things all existed then as well. Nothing changes except who's oppressed and who isn't. The Forbidden Language won't cure that."

"If it will defeat the Urzoks, then it's good enough for me," Brune remarked.

"Besides," Theo added, "it might not have been a golden age, but it was better than it is now, wasn't it?"

Orjo considered this, then snorted. "You're like a disease, Theo. Stay around you too long and your naivete becomes infectious."

CHAPTER 23

"Gentle fingers, Mistress Hassah, gentle," the nurse admonished.

A deformed mess lay in front of Hassah on the work table, all that was left of what was supposed to be a bowl. The girl pouted.

"I'll never be able to do this!"

"Let's make plates instead!" Walnut was already pounding his ball of clay into a flat pancake. Keeva and Pozzi were each working a potter's wheel, Keeva for Farriah and Pozzi for Hassah.

Hassah giggled and began pounding her warped bowl into a flat cake as well.

"Enough!" Farriah said, standing up and moving to Hassah's side. "If you don't want to learn how to make proper pottery, we'll practice your needlework instead."

Hassah, Pozzi knew, hated sewing. Obediently, she began shaping the clay the way Farriah had shown her.

The door to the workshop swung open. Everyone faltered and tried to cover their unease.

"Morning, Farriah," Tansha said, her hand on Sarkus's shoulder. Though the boy's face was less livid and the wounds had nearly all healed over, it was clear no one would be able to look upon him without wincing. The reactions of everyone in the room did not go unnoticed, though Tansha ignored them.

"Morning, m'lady," Farriah said, straightening.

"Sarkus would like to join you today. Isn't that so, Sarkus?"

Pozzi wasn't sure if the scowl on Sarkus's face was permanent or really did deepen, but either way, it was clear that Sarkus wanted to do no such thing.

Farriah gave her most encouraging smile. "Why of course, Sarkus, come join your sister. We're making bowls."

At a push from his mother, the boy walked over and settled himself onto a stool opposite his sister. She shoved her clay toward him.

"Here, you can have mine."

The boy made no move. Tansha seemed to sigh inwardly before saying, "Give it a try, son. See if you can stay out of trouble for the morning. If you still want to, I'll ask your father to take you hunting later."

At this, Sarkus perked up and picked up the clay in one hand. He looked about at the rabbits as if just noticing them.

"You've got good strong hands for pottery, Master Sarkus," Farriah said encouragingly. "Just knead it a bit and then we'll try the wheel, shall we?"

Sarkus began pressing the clay between his hands.

"That's the way," Farriah said and began helping Hassah scoop more clay out of a pot on the table.

Keeva shivered, and Pozzi tried to control his own unease. Sarkus's presence made the air go cold.

"Look, Sarkus made a bunny!"

They all looked over at where Sarkus had flattened the clay into a rough semblance of a head and two long ears.

"Not bad for a first try, Master Sarkus." Farriah sprinkled water on Hassah's clay to dampen it.

Sarkus said nothing, but instead watched Pozzi as he dug a

thumb deep into the clay's face, making an eye. Pozzi felt his neck fur stand up.

"Perhaps it could be used as a spoon rest," the nurse said, encouraging. "I'll put it in the kiln for you."

She took the clay rabbit head and arranged it on a wooden ladle. Sarkus stared at Pozzi, eyes murderous under the deformed brow.

Pozzi could see Keeva watching him. He knew what she was thinking. They had to escape Nyatha, for even if Hassah never told her father of their desire to leave, Sarkus would find a way to hurt them. It was simply a question of when. They had to make sure they weren't here to find out how.

* * *

"The last two days of the week."

"You sure?"

Pozzi peered around the fish barrel by the kitchens, toward the outer delivery yard. There, Kayden, the wagon driver, was loading up pelts with the burly man's assistance.

Pozzi, Keeva, and Walnut were playing hide and seek with Hassah, and when Pozzi had spotted the wagon, he motioned for Keeva to hide with him so he could tell her his idea.

"That's what's happened the last two weeks, and I've overheard them talking." Pozzi watched the wagon door shut, then turned to Keeva, who looked slightly ill at the sight of the blood-flecked furs. "It's our best chance."

"What about our clothes?"

"We'll hide them in this fish barrel, then dash for it," Pozzi said. "There won't be much time, as we'll have to climb in just as the wagon's 'bout to move. But that's the only time when they won't see us."

Keeva was clearly hesitant.

"You think this is our best chance?"

"I think it's our only chance, Keeva."

Just then, Hassah's face popped over the barrel, grinning. Since their argument, no one had mentioned leaving again, and Hassah seemed to have forgotten about it in the way only children can.

"Found you! Now you have to find me!"

As the girl ran away to hide, Keeva and Pozzi glanced back at each other. The wagon creaked into motion as Kayden cracked a whip over his horse's back. Keeva and Pozzi watched the wagon disappear through one of the delivery-yard gates.

"Next week then?" Pozzi asked.

Keeva glanced back in the direction of the wagon, then seemed to harden herself. She nodded. "Next week."

CHAPTER 24

The warlord called a halt before telling Yod to assemble five of his men to accompany him.

He looked behind him at the garrison Ghazan had equipped him with. The thirty he had picked from Nyatha were not of the greatest caliber. But what he lacked in quality, he hoped to make up for with his ten griffin eggs.

Yod rounded up the five remaining original men from Vyad. After their return to Nyatha and their hearing Ghazan call Ornox by his title again, all the men rode straighter, took the time to shine their armor. No one wore their hair loose anymore, but braided it in tight plaits. They knew that fortune's light was starting to shine once more on their master.

"Have the troops wait here." Ornox motioned for the men to follow, then spurred his stallion into a canter. They left Yod and the rest of the battalion, riding toward the ramshackle tavern that sat on the outskirts of nowhere.

Time to see how reliable Ghazan's information was. If the rabbit and his companions had been here, Ornox was determined to know every last detail.

The warlord walked in first. The ambience shifted, the half dozen badger and fox patrons clearly uneasy at human presence.

His soldiers' arrival only thickened the unease, especially when the troops spread out and took seats at various tables to bar the exits. Everyone seemed fascinated by the dregs of their tankards and didn't dare look any of the newcomers in the eye.

Ornox walked past the bowed heads and silent tables, straight for the bar where the innkeeper stood gripping a tankard like it was a shield.

"What can I get you?" she managed to whisper.

He pulled out a stool and sat at the bar. "I'm not after food or drink."

The innkeeper had clearly been dreading exactly that. She surveyed his men. "Then what do you want?"

"I'm after information. About some travelers that stayed here a few days ago."

"The muskrat? Traveling with a bear and rabbits?"

"You're a clever badger."

"I already told the other one everything I knew."

Ornox leaned forward and folded his hands on the bar counter, frowning. "What other one?"

"The thin Urzok—man, I mean," she corrected her use of the slur. "I'm sorry, I don't normally—"

"What did he want?"

"He was asking all about the muskrat. Which way he headed. I told him what my boy told me—"

"What did this man look like?"

She swallowed, nervous. "Tall, thin. Scarred face."

"What kind of scar?"

"Pockmarks. And a large straight one, from here to here." The badger drew a claw from one eye across the cheek below.

Caldrik. The Child's man had been here.

"Tell me what you told him," Ornox said. "Every word."

CHAPTER 25

Theo was in a grand, ornate chamber, surrounded by shelves. Shelves of books.

He'd been here before. Or at least, he'd dreamed of this before.

The shelves rose on all sides to the domed ceiling, brimming with multi-colored books of every hue and size. He looked up at the archway above and read: The Library of Elshon.

He suddenly remembered what happened next in the dream. He turned around, and there they were—the books were leaping down from the shelves as if pushed by invisible paws. As they landed, they transformed into rabbits running toward him. As they drew closer, they seemed to slow, and Theo could see them clearly.

They were all him.

Or at least, they all looked exactly like him. Thousands upon thousands of Theos, leaping from the shelves and stampeding toward him and past him. It was a whole army, running away and disappearing into a yawning dark cavern on the other side of the Library.

"Wait—I'm looking for the cure—where is the cure for pacification?"

The rabbits ignored him, some knocking into him in their hurry.

He grabbed one by the arm. The eyes looking back at him were his and not his.

"Tell me, where's the weapon? The one that stops pacification?"

His dream-self twisted from his grip and bolted off.

Theo tried to chase after these identicals of himself, but found that no matter how hard he ran, he barely moved. It was like he was in a bubble of tar, and every step only slowed him further. He looked up and saw that all the versions of him were disappearing into the hungry dark cave on the other side, from which a dreadful, high-pitched noise slowly grew, like a scream.

He became aware that he was moving, being swept along by the tide of Theos, closer and closer to that yawning abyss with the heart-stopping wail.

"No, no no no..."

He tried to dig in his heels, to stop his forward momentum. He turned to flee the other way, but found himself facing a giant, leathery tortoise. Its shell was thick and ridged, its eyes as ancient as the moon.

You can't slay a nightmare, Theo, without going into the dark.

Helplessness mounted in him until he cried out and woke to a canopy of stars blinking down.

He moved his legs. No tar. Only a dream.

He stretched his limbs, stiff. He looked at the shadow of the cart, the horses tethered nearby. The smell of onions and garlic seemed embedded in the cart's every plank, so much so that after riding in it all day, no one wanted to sleep in it at night. Instead, they all opted to sleep out in the open air. Brune was stretched out some distance away in the long grass, chest rising and falling rhythmically, while Orjo lay on his side, asleep with his head on his book.

"Bad dreams?" Indigo lay on her back, looking at the stars. The coals in the cooking pit were still aglow, but barely.

Theo sat up. "Just…strange." He looked up toward all the winking lights above. "What are you doing?"

"Learning that it'll storm tomorrow." She turned and looked at him. "You never finished what you were going to say." At his confused look, she continued, "At the tavern. You were telling me why you wished I would learn the Forbidden Language."

His heart thudded. But he was too tired to summon the words, too tangled in the remnants of his dream to tackle the barrage of emotions he had when it came to her. "It's not important. Get some rest."

"You're sure?"

He nodded. "It's almost time for my shift anyway." He also didn't want to revisit his recurring dream. Indigo pulled a pack under her head and closed her eyes. Theo watched her for a little while, then looked up at the stars. He had a sudden memory of Father Oaks when Theo was little. They had sat outside their warren, and Father Oaks had pointed out the brightest stars in the inky heavens. He remembered how his grandfather told him the stars were pieces of the sun, broken off and scattered around so that the creatures below wouldn't be lonely in the dark.

Theo would give all the stars above to have his grandfather with him instead. But there was no one to bargain with. He looked for something to distract him, and his eyes landed on the Calgornan book beneath Orjo's head.

The muskrat seemed fast asleep, as were Brune and Indigo. Theo hesitated, debating. After a moment, he reached out and touched a corner of the book.

No reaction.

Theo slipped his paw beneath the spine and began gently pulling. He almost had it free when the muskrat's bony paw clamped around his own.

"Don't."

"I'm sorry," Theo said. "I was just curious."

Orjo let go of Theo's paw, then pushed himself up, eyes hard. "Did you steal *The Miraculous Cures of Zo* too?"

Theo grew defensive. "No. It was given to me."

"Well keep your paws off this."

Theo watched the muskrat carefully tuck the book into his inner robe. The movement made Orjo grimace.

"Pain?"

"Just a little burning."

"Let me have a look." Theo stoked the coals in the cooking pit, trying to coax more light from them.

"Are Zo's other cures real? Like changing hearts, or other parts of the body? Or bringing the dead back to life?"

Orjo looked at the coals for a moment. "Many said Zo could return the dead to life, though I never witnessed it. But yes, the other cures were all common then." The muskrat looked back at Theo. "Miraculous now."

Theo pulled the bandage off, examining the wound. "The Library must be full of other books by Zo and Calgornan."

Orjo grunted, and Theo wasn't sure whether it was a sound of agreement. "What makes you think any of those books is going to do any good for Mankahar?"

"*The Miraculous Cures of Zo* saved Indigo from pacification. What's to say another book can't save Mankahar?"

The fire was bright now. Theo motioned for Orjo to move closer to the light. The muskrat obeyed, and Theo pressed around the wound, making Orjo hiss. The pink flesh had puckered around the scar, and wiry fur was already growing back. "The wound looks clean, Orjo."

"You sure? No signs of infection? Bleeding on the inside? I knew a stoat once. He thought he was healed after a knife wound but then just died on his feet, without warning."

"You'd know if you had bleeding inside." Theo looked up. "You have any headaches? Numbness? Tingling?"

"None."

Theo smiled. "Then I can't see anything wrong."

"That's a relief." Orjo pulled his shirt down and sighed, then regarded Theo quietly. "I suppose I should say thank you."

Theo looked at Orjo, surprised. He saw a genuine gratitude there, and something else that seemed a mixture of admiration and regret.

"But I'm not good at thank-yous," the muskrat said gruffly. "So I'll just wish you luck."

The muskrat's paw flew forward. Theo felt a sharp pain in the section where his neck joined his shoulder, and then all the pieces of sun in the sky sank into the night, leaving nothing but darkness.

CHAPTER 26

*H*e wasn't sure what woke him—the sound of metal and a furtive hushing, or the ache in his bruised neck. A gray, moody dawn was breaking on the horizon, and by its tepid light, Theo could see the silhouette of the horses, packs slung across their withers.

A short, stout figure was mounting the larger horse, and even in the faint dawn Theo recognized Orjo's wild fur.

"Hey!"

Orjo's head snapped in his direction. Theo's shout had woken Indigo and Brune, who were scrambling to their feet.

There was the loud crack of reins, and then the horses were off at a full gallop.

Brune roared and set off after them, as did Indigo, though Theo knew there was no way she could outrun horses.

The bear was gaining, his legs eating up the distance with impressive speed. Orjo glanced over his shoulder, trying to keep his balance on his horse's bare back. He slapped the horse's neck with his paw, urging it into a fresh burst of speed. Brune held on for a few breaths, but soon, the gap between him and the horses widened, until he had to finally give up, panting.

After a few moments, Indigo and Theo caught up to him,

watching Orjo and the horses disappear against the brightening horizon.

"Rot that lying rat's mangy hide!" Brune swore and slapped the ground with a paw.

"How did he catch us all asleep?" Indigo asked.

"He didn't." Something more than anger stung Theo's eyes and heart. "He hit me in the neck." He half hoped Orjo would come back, to say he'd been just teaching Theo a lesson, but deep down, he knew Orjo was gone. And it was his own fault.

Brune looked at Theo. "I'm sorry. I know he was our hope to finding the Library."

Something on the ground ahead caught Theo's eye. He walked forward, then bent and held up a cloth-wrapped package.

"What's that?" Brune squinted as Theo opened the package.

Theo showed them the muskrat's well-worn book. He could just make out the faded words *Songs of Calgornan* in blue on the front.

A rumble sounded from above, and Brune sniffed the air. "It'll be raining fish and feathers in a while. If we need to think about next moves, we may as well do it dry as wet."

They returned to the cart just as the first heavy raindrops appeared, like ink spots against the ground. They squeezed into the cart against the downpour. There was only silence between them for several moments before Indigo's voice broke in.

"This is my fault." Indigo shook her head. "We should have used the truth tonic to make him tell us where the Library was. Instead, I wasted it."

"I was the one who let him get away," Theo countered. "I trusted him too much."

Brune made a disapproving noise. "As my father always said, blame and regrets catch no salmon. The question isn't what we did or didn't do, it's what we *will* do."

"I'm not sure we have much choice." Theo felt drained, beaten.

Brune and Indigo looked at each other. Indigo turned back to Theo. "Did Orjo give any clues as to where it was?"

Theo shook his head. "None. And we'll never find it on our own."

"We could follow Orjo. Try to take him."

Theo sighed at Indigo's suggestion. "We'd have little chance. As I told him myself, he's almost fully healed, and with horses, he's making double what we can do in a day."

"What say you, Brune?" Indigo turned to the bear.

The giant ran a paw down his face. "Theo's right. It's not impossible. But we'd need five pounds luck and ten pounds miracle, as my father would say."

A defeated silence fell. The rabbit looked out at the rain pounding the earth outside, the heavy drops like thunder on the roof of the cart. Any tracks Orjo left would be washed away. Orjo had probably never intended to take them to the Library, and led them on only as long as he needed Theo's healing skills to survive. *This has all been a waste.*

Theo turned back to Indigo and Brune, resigned. "Without Orjo, we don't have a hope of finding the Library. So it's time to rejoin the Order, if they'll have us."

He couldn't read their faces. Disappointment? Relief?

"Of course they'll have us," Brune said after a moment. "Lord Noshi will always welcome you both."

"But are you sure, Theo?" Indigo added, quiet.

Theo nodded. "It was worth giving Orjo a try. But we've reached the end."

They each considered these words, glum.

"We might as well sort out what we can carry. Perhaps it'll let up by then." Indigo peered out at the sky, then surveyed the ground where they had slept, the packs they had used as pillows now sodden in the rain. "That'll also give our packs a chance to dry." She jumped out of the cart and began gathering their wet things.

"Don't blame yourself." Brune's gruff voice cut in through

Theo's thoughts. The bear caught sight of him glancing at Indigo. "She doesn't blame you either."

"How do you know?" Theo asked. "She only came so she could find Orjo and have revenge."

Brune grunted. "Then she'd be off hunting him down, not helping you find the Library."

"She was right. You both were. I should never have trusted Orjo."

"Maybe. But that doesn't mean you should stop trusting yourself."

"Yes it does. I was wrong about him, and now, we'll never find the Library. We wouldn't be in this mess if it wasn't for me."

"As my father always said, wisdom isn't gained by being wise. It's gained by being foolish, and learning."

* * *

THE RAIN CONTINUED, relentless. As the princess and the bear began sorting through the cart's contents for transportable food and tools, Theo opened the book. He knew he would take it with him, even if it reminded him of Orjo. A book was too precious to leave behind.

For a long time, he simply stared at the pages until, despite himself, his anger and defeatism gave way to curiosity.

Something about the paper and the words was different. Almost all the books he had seen had been written with a quill, and indeed these pages were covered with copious amounts of notes in the margins, but the main text of this book looked different. Every glyph of every word was spaced evenly, with no spots to show where the nib had newly been dipped in ink, and no discrepancies between how the same glyphs were written.

"You look like you're far away."

He realized he had been staring at the book for several moments. He looked up at Indigo. "I've never seen a book like this. The writing is all the same, as if someone had the ability to catch words in exactly the same way every time."

He went back to the book and began releasing the words, letting himself sink into the rhythm of the songs. He studied the many notes in the book, captured words that appeared in blue, black, and sometimes green ink. Were these words captured by Orjo? Or some other omatje long ago?

The more he read, the more engrossed he became. The songs were unlike any he had ever heard. They were by turns bawdy, sad, bitter, ecstatic, and lovelorn, but above all, they held a defiant humor such that he could almost hear the bard laughing behind each sentence. All the songs he knew or had heard used genteel language, but Calgornan seemed to delight in using highborn as well as everyday words, no matter how callous.

"What's wrong? You look embarrassed."

Theo glanced at Indigo. "It's nothing, just that this omatje has a crude style. Maybe that's why he's so famous."

Brune checked a pitcher for cracks, then placed it outside to collect rainwater. "Crude how?"

Theo drew a breath and read. "'I'll sing my songs in the morning, be I clothed or naked or poor, and my guitar'll keep me warm at night, though I sleep on the wine-soaked floor.'"

Indigo flicked an ear. "I can see why Orjo liked this bard." Noticing Theo's change in expression, she looked from him to the book. "What?"

He continued, excited,

> *You can kill the bird, but how do you kill its song?*
> *Though I'll be seeing Aktu*
> *Before the shadows grow long*
> *My music will walk away, carefree when I'm gone.*
>
> *You can bury a body, but how do you bury its soul?*
> *Though Elshon's ruins lie*
> *Beneath gleaming new Jaipri town*

Its power will seep through, like water through a stone.

"Jaipri?" Brune asked. "You mean the city of giant serpents?"

Theo looked up. "Unless there's another. And if Elshon's ruins lie beneath it, then the Library is under Jaipri."

"By Aktu." Brune leaned in toward the book, as if he too could make the words speak to him. The bear frowned, thinking. "Isn't Jaipri where you found that book, *The Miraculous Cures of Zo?*"

"I didn't find it. Lyusa gave it to me." He remembered when he and Brune had last been in Jaipri. The serpent commander Lyusa had led him to the abandoned underground palace and given him a fully supplied medicine pouch, along with the book.

"You think Lyusa was trying to tell you something?" Indigo asked. "That the Library is in Jaipri?"

Theo thought on this. Could the old serpent have been trying to guide him? "I don't know."

Indigo looked at Brune, then at Theo, questioning. "So do we go to Jaipri?"

"I know it's not much to go on." Hope flickered in him. "But it's all we have. The Library just might be there."

Indigo looked at Brune. "How far is it?"

The bear rubbed his muzzle thoughtfully. "At least a quarter moon. And that's if we cross Urzok territory to get there."

"So a long dangerous journey through enemy lands for a whisker-thin chance of finding the Library?"

"Exactly, Princess." The bear pulled his helmet to him and grinned as he fitted it to his head.

Indigo smiled at Theo. "So, more of the same then."

"No," he answered, excited. "Now, we know where we're going."

CHAPTER 27

$\mathcal{I}$t took them the better part of three days to retrace their passage back south, over the undulating grasslands toward the base of the Purple Mountains, toward Jaipri Forest.

At the end of the fourth day, Indigo noticed a patch of scorched earth in the ground.

"Urzoks camped here recently." She rubbed at the soot with her boot, uncovering remnants of a meal: some bird bones, a fruit rind, and a stick with a charred end used for cooking. "Hunters, most likely."

Brune nodded. "There'll be more and more of them the closer we get to Doria. That whole area has been Urzok held for scores of years."

Indigo flicked one tattooed ear. "We can't just walk through. Two rabbits and a bear won't go unreported."

"We'll travel by night," Brune said. "Stay off the roads."

"And during the day?" Theo asked.

"Easy," Brune grunted. "Try to be invisible."

* * *

THE SKIES STAYED clear and dry as they traveled west, and spring fully relented into summer. Foraging meals became easier as they neared the densely treed valleys surrounding Doria, though they also saw more evidence of Urzok hunters and travelers. Here, mulberries, mushrooms, and wild leeks grew in abundance, along with cat's ear and the occasional hazelnuts.

A day's walk out from the furthest borders of Doria, they decided to stay close to the fringes of the thick forest that Brune guessed from the towering, bearded fig trees was the Southern Jungle. Here, they could disappear between the trees if Urzoks approached. They had already had to do so twice in the last day, and when they spotted a caravan of Urzoks traveling by horseback, Indigo called a midday halt.

"We'd best not travel by day anymore. From now on, we should only travel after nightfall."

Theo couldn't fault her logic, but he knew he wouldn't be able to sleep. Brune and Indigo, used to hard, discreet travel, could turn their thoughts off at will, but not so Theo.

They chose a sheltered hollow beneath a giant spreading fig, and Theo offered to keep watch. He sat back against a tree and listened to their breathing as it slowed and evened. He couldn't quite explain why he didn't feel comfortable freeing words from the book in front of his friends. They had accepted his taboo knowledge and followed him to the ends of Mankahar, even. But it still felt strange to read in front of them, as if he was doing something secret and private, because he knew neither of them had completely overcome their mistrust of the skill.

Once he could hear the soft exhales coming from Brune and only the regular sounds of the jungle remained, he took out Calgornan's songs again and began to read. He read a song about love, another one about an unjust king, and then he flipped a page and came across one called "If I Were a Star."

> *If I were a star*
> *I'd sail on light*

> *Through the sands of time*
> *Through the darkest night*
>
> *If I were a star*
> *I'd find you in the deep*
> *You'd know I was with you*
> *An immortal eye that knows no sleep*

The mention of immortality reminded him of Orjo. Where was the muskrat now? Theo's anger and sense of betrayal had worn away to leave a pervading sadness.

"So that's why you wanted first watch."

He turned to see Indigo regarding him. Her tone was light, but Theo still felt a hint of rebuke. He closed the book.

"I didn't mean for you to stop."

"No, it's my turn to rest anyway." He lay down and closed his eyes, his mind still far away with the stars.

"Theo?"

"Yes?"

"Do you enjoy knowing the Forbidden Language?"

"More than anything," he said without thinking.

"Why?"

"I can't explain it." He turned to her. "But I could teach you."

"No." She said it so quickly it felt like a cut. Swift, clean, reactive.

"Of course. I'd forgotten how much you hate omatjes." *Omatjes like me.* Even if Orjo hadn't killed her family, he knew she had despised the Forbidden Language for too long to simply stop now. How could he put into words why he felt her rejection of the Forbidden Language was also a rejection of him? It made no sense. But feelings seldom did, he was learning.

"Theo, I don't hate omatjes. If you let me—"

"You don't have to apologize. You owe me nothing." He turned back around and closed his eyes, and was thankful that she didn't press.

* * *

BRUNE WOKE him up as the shadows were stretching across the jungle floor and the light was softening. They gathered their few things, Theo careful to keep the book protected in its cloth and tucked safely in his vest, and also careful to avoid eye contact with Indigo.

They kept to the jungle fringes, listening to the night creatures stir and take over from the day, now hearing crickets and fruit bats, long-tailed mice, and pygmy owls. By the time the moon had risen a quarter of the way through the sky, all the creatures of the night seemed to be going about their business, some surprised at the sight and smell of the foreign bear and rabbits.

"How many nights will it take us to pass Doria?" he asked.

"At this rate?" The bear didn't slow but kept pressing through the brush. A startled lizard darted away. "Five if we're lucky and we don't get rain."

"Two if you fly."

The strange voice came from above, making Theo look up into the trees. He tripped and fell face first onto the ground.

"You all right, Theo?" Indigo came back to help him, but he refused her outstretched paw. She quickly withdrew it.

He rubbed his leg and looked behind him.

"Must have been an exposed root," he said.

"It's a trap, friends!"

They all looked up at the voice that came from above within the trees. The canopy was a mass of shadow and whispering leaves, but they could just make out the silhouette of a net, with someone winged inside. Brune drew his axe, and Indigo put a paw on the hilt of her sword.

"There're traps everywhere in these parts," came the voice again.

"Who are you?" Brune growled.

"Just someone in need," the voice replied. "Please, get me out,

162

tonight's my sister's wedding you see, and my mother will pluck me alive if I'm late."

Theo examined the spot where he had tripped, and found a taut rope. Indigo joined him. "Looks Urzok made."

The creature above them cawed in agreement. "The Urzoks hunt our feathers. Please get me down? All you have to do is cut that rope."

Theo went to do just that, but Brune stayed him. "We'll let you down, but nothing sudden. Understood?"

"You have the axe, bear."

Brune grunted, satisfied with this, and with a swift heave of his weapon, he severed the rope. The netting crashed through the branches to the ground just before them, a small mass of feathers and beak and rope.

Theo had the impression that there was more than one beast in the trap, for the moving shape before them was so active it couldn't possibly be one being. But as the thing tore at the ropes and struggled out, the misshapen mass slowly formed and stood, into a bird. She was slightly larger than Theo, and seemed like an uncontainable ball of energy.

The bird examined her wings and then took a few steps, testing for injuries. In the shadows of night, Theo couldn't make out much color, except for a few impossibly bright golden feathers sprouting from the bird's head. The bird caught them staring.

"As mother says, beauty is a curse," the bird commented. "Our head feathers are worth a fortune in Urzok markets, so these forests are full of traps." She flexed her feathers up and down for good measure, as if to make sure they were intact. "I can't thank you enough. And a Proudfeather always repays a favor. Come."

Brune sheathed his axe. "There's no need. Aktu be with you."

He began walking, and Indigo and Theo were about to follow, when the bird called out.

"Wait! You're Theo. The Griffinrider."

Indigo let her paw rest on her sword hilt again. "You a bounty hunter?"

The bird made a reproachful sound. "Hardly! My name is Nyra, daughter of the matriarch Proudfeather. You helped me, and a Proudfeather always returns a favor. Always."

"Thank you, but we don't need anything in return," Theo said.

"So you wouldn't be interested in crossing Doria in two days instead of five?"

They all looked at the bird then.

"You need to cross Doria, don't you?" Nyra looked at the three of them.

"Yes," Brune said, cautious. "But how—"

"As I said, it's two days if you fly. And I can help you fly."

CHAPTER 28

The bird Nyra led them deep into the forest's heart, gliding easily from branch to branch above them. By moonrise, they had reached a seemingly unremarkable clearing in the trees, but Nyra seemed to recognize that they had crossed some invisible border.

She stretched her wings and gave a long, low call, and soon, five great birds dropped from the trees around Theo and his companions. Theo realized with a start that Nyra must be a youngster—all the other birds were at least three times her height, towering as high as Brune's waist. Their distinctive golden crown feathers arced long and shimmering in the moonlight, a shocking fountain of color in their otherwise modest brown-and-white-flecked body feathers.

One of the birds, wearing a woven necklace of bright stones, strode forward a step, head feathers jutting up in a way that gave her height and an aura of authority. "Where have you been, Nyra? Of all days for you to disappear, you choose today?"

"It wasn't my fault, Mother—"

"It never is," the grand bird complained.

"I was in a trap, but these three cut me free."

At this, the tall Proudfeather's anger turned to concern. "A trap? An Urzok trap? Why were you so far away?" She fluffed her head feathers, as if her thoughts were so much dust she could shake off. "Never mind, there's no time now to get into your constant wandering off." She turned and looked Theo and his companions up and down, sighing. "I am Hygra, matriarch of the Proudfeathers. I thank you for rescuing my very impetuous and unruly daughter."

"Also your favorite, remember."

The mother gave her daughter what was meant as a stern glare, but it was obvious the youngster spoke the truth. "We of course must thank you properly, but I'm afraid we'll have to discuss that later."

"They need to cross Doria quickly," Nyra cut in.

Hygra frowned at this.

"And how do you think we can help with that?"

"I simply need ten of our family to help me take them."

The matriarch's feathers stiffened further. "I can't ask that of our kin!"

"Mother, who do you think they are? A bear and two rabbits? This is Theo Griffinrider, the famed sword Indigo, and a messenger from the Order itself."

At this, all the Proudfeathers seemed to regard them with new interest.

"Besides, I've already agreed to repay them with safe passage."

From above, several horns sounded, drawing an impatient sigh from Nyra's mother. "If you've agreed, then why are you even asking me?" She cocked her head, eyes stern. "We'll provide ten of our own to take them. But not until tomorrow, after the wedding, is that understood?"

"Of course, Mother." Nyra, it seemed, was all meekness now that she had gotten her way. She turned to the two rabbits and the bear. "You'll join us for my sister's wedding, won't you?"

"We'd be intruding," Brune said. "Time is against us, and we can't delay."

"Then you must stay," Nyra insisted. "Wait for me to take you tomorrow night. I'll have you at Jaipri in two days, maybe less. On your own, it'll take you five nights, assuming you don't get trapped by the Urzoks like I did."

Brune, Theo, and Indigo looked at each other.

"Well," Brune conceded, "who doesn't like a wedding?"

* * *

NYRA INSISTED they didn't need to stand on ceremony, but Indigo refused to attend with the grime and dust of travel on them.

Nyra led them to a nearby rock stream where they could wash the layers of dirt and mud from their clothes. They took turns dousing themselves in the cheerful water, and they each tried to comb their fur as best they could. Theo avoided looking at Indigo, still raw from their conversation the night before. For her part, Indigo gave him his space, and their silence didn't go unnoticed.

Brune finished putting his harness on, and smoothed the unruly fur on his head as he tucked his helmet beneath one arm. "Something's gone sour between you two, but for all our sakes, sort it out."

The bear left them in the moonlit stream in awkward silence.

Theo tried to think of something to say, when the sound of wooden instruments filled the air. Nyra materialized from the trees, landing on a rock before Theo and Indigo.

"The sky dancing will begin soon. You won't want to miss it."

Theo couldn't imagine birds dancing. "Where?"

"You'll see."

The rabbits followed Nyra back to the clearing where they had first met Hygra, and where Brune now stood, his helmet on.

"You'll have a better view from above," Nyra said. "Climb on."

"Both of us?" Theo asked. Indigo shot him a look that he couldn't interpret.

Nyra looked indignant. "I'm small, but I'm strong."

"What about Brune?" Theo asked.

"I'm not that strong."

The bear shook his head, grinning. "Don't worry about me. I'm a bear. I could climb trees before I learned how to eat honey."

Indigo was already on Nyra's back and looking to Theo.

He climbed up behind her, his long ears flushing as she reached back for his arms and wrapped them around her waist. Nyra swiveled her head.

"Just remember one thing, Theo."

"Don't look down?"

Nyra winked. "Hold on tight."

The bird launched herself into the air, taking the rabbits with her as she wobbled and then found her balance. Indigo's grip on his arm tightened, and somehow, he didn't mind the ground pulling unsteadily away from them and the tree branches rushing past. Theo clung, eyes closed.

"You can look now," Nyra said, panting.

He did and, for a moment, forgot everything but what was before him. They had cleared the treetops, and here, the jungle canopy spread before them in an unending sea of silver-kissed green in the full moonlight.

Nyra came down on the end of a gnarled branch that jutted up over the other trees. Theo and Indigo slid off the bird's back, not without some regret on Theo's part, and stood on the branch. Their perch was so wide that it would have taken Theo ten paces to cross it, which eased his fear of being so high up.

"I have to join the others in the dance," Nyra apologized. "And then I'll be back to take you to the feast."

She spread her wings and pushed off, gliding on the air until she had disappeared into the trees below.

Theo took a seat beside Indigo, and for a while, they simply stared at the space around them. It felt free, powerful somehow, to be above the world. A slow, rhythmic drumbeat began to sound, sending flocks of birds up and away into the air. The drumbeats continued, steady, until the rapping of wood on wood joined in, a staccato punctuating the drums.

"Look!" Indigo pointed.

They watched as a line of Proudfeathers shot up from the canopy, in perfect formation. They rose and then formed a ring until, from the rabbits' view, they had created a halo around the high moon. They flew like this at a languid pace, first one direction, and then on a signal from the drum, abruptly turned and flew in circles the other way. Theo thought he recognized Nyra's small form but couldn't be sure from this distance.

The wooden instrument picked up its tempo until a crescendo echoed through the jungle. Two giant Proudfeathers, tails streaming garlands of flowers, flew up into the middle of the circle and began a series of spins and dives.

"It's beautiful," Indigo murmured. She looked thoughtful. "Do you think they love each other?"

"Why wouldn't they?" Theo looked at her, surprised.

"It might be arranged." At his confusion, she added, "They might have been chosen for each other by their parents. Especially if her mother's the matriarch."

Was she trying to tell him something? He couldn't be sure. "So would you not have a choice? As crown princess?"

"I have a choice," she said, a hint of defensiveness in her voice. "But the queendom would have to approve."

"And who would the queendom approve?"

She watched the two birds do a sharp dive then split apart and fly in widening circles up toward the pale clouds. "They have to be born in the queendom, be from one of the powerful families, and..."

"And?"

"Be over a certain height."

He found himself laughing. He didn't fit a single criteria. Not one.

"What's so funny?"

"Nothing." As soon as the laughter came, it went, leaving behind an ache. He was such a fool. "It's just… silly."

"I'm sorry my queendom's customs are silly to you," she said, cold.

"No, that's not what I meant. I was—"

"How about you? You just get to choose anyone you like?" she countered. "Who would you marry, if you were back in Willago?"

"Me?" Was she trying to shame him?

"Yes, since you clearly have the freedom to choose anyone for yourself, who would you have chosen? There must have been someone special. Who?"

He watched the birds dancing in the air and was brought back to another wedding, so long ago, it felt he had dreamed it. His brother Harlan's wedding, where Theo had watched his brother marry Keeva.

"Aha!" She caught the look on his face. "So there was someone."

"I thought I loved her. She was never interested in me."

"Why not?"

"Why do you think?" he shot back. "Would you want to be with an omatje?"

There was a heavy silence, and Theo wanted to be anywhere but here.

She drew a breath, and when she spoke, the anger had left her voice. "I'm sorry. It's none of my affair."

He felt his own anger follow hers, evaporating in the night. "I don't think your traditions are silly."

She smiled. "Actually, they are a little."

"Maybe you'll change the rules when you return."

Indigo flicked one tattooed ear. "Maybe."

He knew how unlikely that would be. Indigo followed her queendom's rules. No matter what.

A cracking and rustling in the branches nearby made them turn. Brune's paws appeared on the platform, followed by his helmeted head. He hauled himself up, then sat down next to the rabbits.

They watched the bride and groom do a spin, and then the other birds joined them in a joyous loop around the rising moon. The birds came together in a final flourish, the wedding dance ending.

"What a sight." Brune took in the view, the birds concluding their dance, then turned to the rabbits. "So… seems like you two are friends again?"

Theo and Indigo looked at each other. The princess nodded.

"Yes. Still friends."

Brune looked at Theo, and the rabbit knew his mentor wasn't fooled by Theo's cheerful tone.

ife can be divided into two parts.

Ornox remembered sitting in on a trial lesson between his young daughter and her future tutor, Caldrik.

"Life is all about action, and waiting. The wise person knows when to act and when to wait." It was then that Ornox had decided Caldrik was the right teacher for his daughter. In her hunting lessons, Agacheta had always shown herself a great tracker, excellent at finding her mark, but she lacked patience. And Ornox knew that the best hunters were patient.

Ornox and his men had been waiting since late afternoon. The reeds that hugged the banks of Lake Lostgone provided ample cover for his small force, but nothing for their patience. To an experienced eye, their telltale shiftings in the reeds were as obvious as lanterns in the night. Ornox would have traded them all for his daughter. She would have waited days for their quarry if need be.

Lake Lostgone was the biggest lake in Mankahar. It was a vast, watery maze, and hence its name. One could disappear amongst the hundreds of islands and reeds here and never know which way led back to the main shore. It made sense that the muskrat would pay the innkeeper to organize a boat to take him into these parts, for he could disappear for another hundred years here. What puzzled Ornox was why the bear, or Theo, would agree to follow.

He glanced up at the amber half-moon. The boat would appear soon, if it was on time. If the innkeeper had been truthful. And Ornox was confident she had been truthful. A knife to her son's throat had guaranteed her honesty.

The wind shifted, and he heard it. The soft trodding of hooves. There it was again. He waited, patient.

The hoofbeats started once more, and soon, he could make out a horse with a cloaked figure on its back. The figure was too short to be human, even a child. Ornox tried to look for signs of a tail protruding but could see none. Perhaps it was one of the rabbits. Theo even. The possibility made his skin prickle.

Where were the bear and the other rabbit? He saw no sign of them. Were they waiting, hidden somewhere? That would make sense. If so, best to wait until they showed themselves.

The soft splash of water drew his attention out toward the lake. A small skiff, no longer than the length of a tall man, was poling toward the shore, a cloaked gibbon standing in the bow.

The horse neighed as the boat bumped gently to the pier. From his place in the reeds, Ornox watched the rider pull on the reins until the horse knelt. The figure dismounted, then pushed off his hood, revealing a wild mane of hair and stubby ears. The muskrat.

The creature pulled a pack off the horse's back and began walking toward the skiff. Ornox frowned. Where were the others? It was just beginning to dawn on him that the muskrat might be alone when he heard the shouting.

The ferrier and two men with swords—hidden under the furs—had leapt out of the skiff and were running toward the muskrat. The muskrat, evidently having sensed a trap, had already dropped his pack and was sprinting for the horse. He got to the animal and was trying to pull himself up when the men caught up to him and dragged him off. The horse, startled, clambered to its feet and kicked, sending the gibbon flying off the pier and into the water. The men circled the muskrat, swords drawn, as the horse galloped away and into the night.

Both men lunged for the quarry, blades out. But the muskrat was ready. He pulled a dagger seemingly out of nowhere and dove straight for one man's ankles. The muskrat sliced through the boot, disabling the first attacker. The second grabbed the muskrat's cloak, only to find himself clutching empty fabric. His momentary confusion allowed the muskrat to dart between the man's legs, sweep his dagger backward, and sever the tendons behind the man's knees. The assailant went down on the pier, bellowing curses.

It was time to act.

Ornox gave the signal and charged. His men burst out from the reeds and clambered up the wooden jetty. The two men from the boat barely had time to register their attackers before they were cut down where they lay, their swords clattering.

The warlord pulled himself up on the pier, dripping wet. He surveyed the muskrat, who eyed him warily.

Ornox bent down and picked up one of the swords. The hilt was fine, the blade well crafted. An expensive weapon, with an insignia Ornox recognized. The Child's.

"You have powerful enemies, Orjo." Ornox tossed the blade into the water. "It is Orjo, isn't it?"

"What do you want?"

"I expected to find Theo. Is he here?"

"You seem to have eyes. You see a rabbit around here?"

Ornox regarded the muskrat, debating. "Tell me where he is."

"What if I don't know?"

"Then Lake Lostgone will be grave to one more soul tonight." Ornox bent down until he was eye level with the muskrat. "So, do you or do you not know where he is?"

The old creature looked longingly out at Lake Lostgone, then sighed.

"We seem to be at what's called an impasse. Which usually can only be broken one of two ways—"

Ornox's boot to the muskrat's injured midsection sent the creature sprawling onto the pier, the pain seemingly so great that he could barely catch his breath.

"I don't believe in impasses," Ornox said calmly. "Only in who gets their way. Do you or do you not know where Theo is?"

The muskrat wheezed for several breaths, then managed to hold up a paw when Ornox lifted his boot again. "I can take you to where I last saw him."

Ornox lowered his foot. "That's a good start."

CHAPTER 30

The night after the wedding, the clearing in the Proudfeather forest was again a basin of silver, the tree branches muttering in the summer night.

Theo, Indigo, and Brune looked doubtfully at the oddly shaped bundle that Nyra and her ten family members had laid before them.

"What is it, exactly?"

Nyra took one end, and a large Proudfeather she had introduced as her sister, Irah, took another. They lifted and unfolded the package until a great mesh net lay out on the clearing floor. Brune reached out to feel it.

"Fig bark and triple-woven hemp," Nyra said, the feathers on her head standing up in pride. "Strongest stuff in Mankahar."

"How is this going to get us across Doria?" Theo asked.

The Proudfeather's eyes twinkled. "Prepare to fly, Theo Griffinrider."

"Are you sure it can hold?" Brune pulled on the netting, testing it. Theo could understand the bear's worry. Bears didn't make light passengers.

"Don't worry, bear," Irah assured him. "We keep this for

when we have to hunt and trap large game. This can withstand the sharpest tooth or claw."

"I think what he's saying is," Indigo cut in politely, "can you really carry a bear all that way?"

"I can't. But ten of us can."

The other Proudfeathers all nodded in agreement with Nyra.

"Outside of the griffin, I think you'll find we're the strongest beasts in the sky," Nyra boasted.

Irah craned her neck, beak open. "We'd best be going, there's rain coming."

Tamping down his misgivings, Theo stepped onto the net. Rabbits weren't meant to fly. But they weren't meant to find long lost libraries either. The net was closely woven, at least, so that Theo didn't have to worry a leg or arm would fall through.

"That's the way. You two coming?" Nyra looked at Indigo and Brune.

The bear tightened his axe holster. "Not letting Theo go without me."

The two climbed aboard, and the ten Proudfeathers took their positions around the net. Theo saw that the edges had been strengthened with twisted hemp, the better to grip and withstand strain.

"Ready?" Irah asked. At a nod from Theo, she cried out a signal and the Proudfeathers launched, their wings stretching so far that they blocked out the moonlight. The net pressed against Theo as they lifted off, and the wind rushed by, pulling on his stomach like an invisible sash. Then just as suddenly they stopped rising, and his stomach settled.

They had cleared the treetops and were skimming just above the forest spires. Here, the sea of stars flowed in a frozen river above them, closer and brighter than Theo ever thought possible. Ahead, he could see for leagues. The smudge of what must be the Purple Mountains, the glimmer of the sea to their east, and straight before them, what appeared to be a carpet of tree tops that rolled away into the distance, endless and thick.

"You all right?"

Theo looked up and over to see Nyra holding the side closest to him. Her wings pumped the night air like mad, keeping up with the others who flew with an effortless rhythm.

"Yes." And he meant it. The rush of air against him smelled of earth and faded woodsmoke, and something about being this high above Mankahar, above these tree spires, gave him a sense of freedom. Of hope.

Theo turned at the sound of Brune's booming chuckle. "By Aktu! Last time I flew, I was fleeing bloodthirsty Urzoks. I hadn't a chance to enjoy my wings."

Indigo smiled, the view before them seemingly enough to dispel any discomfort for her as well.

"How long to Jaipri at this rate?" Theo asked.

"Two days," Nyra answered. "If we're slow."

Two days. Theo tried to temper his excitement. Two days until they reached the Library, and the secrets within.

"You should sleep," Nyra advised.

How could he? Here above the forest, suspended between treetop and sky, he had entered a magical netherworld, a world where time seemed to slow and even stand still. There was too much to see, too much to take in. He noticed a glow far in the distance, in the direction they were heading. It was too late for sunset and too far away to be a lone fire.

"Something's ablaze," he said.

Brune smiled, his teeth a crescent of white like the moon. "It's Doria. In cities, lights are kept burning in every window, so many that you can barely see the stars."

"Will we fly over it?" Indigo asked.

"Yes," Irah answered. "Don't worry, though. We'll fly higher up to avoid being seen."

The next leagues passed below them in smooth patches of shadow and light, and they slowly climbed higher as they neared Doria.

"How about there?" Indigo pointed. "Is that a city too?"

They all looked. A bright light burned in the distance, just under a cloud, flickering.

"That's no city," Irah said, concern creeping into her voice. "That's lightning."

Theo noticed the wind had picked up, having first assumed it was just the Proudfeathers flying faster. "Should we be worried?"

"Not yet, Griffinrider," Nyra said. She gave another signal to her team, and they heaved. The net went with them as they climbed higher into the sky.

Theo's hair stood up, and the sky went bright, as if someone had struck a flint.

"It's closer." Indigo pointed. Moonlight silhouetted a mass of clouds that blotted out the stars, flashes of light crackling closer and closer.

"We can outfly it!"

Theo vaguely realized that Nyra was arguing with one of the other birds.

"It's faster than it looks, Nyra!" Someone on Brune's side shouted back.

Thunder drowned out the rest of the words. The smell of metal hung sharp in the air, and Theo could feel the net shuddering beneath him from the wind. How had the storm moved so fast? It was pushing from behind, driving them toward the lights of Doria.

Another flash and another thunderclap, sooner this time.

"We have to land!" Brune roared above the noise.

"To ground!" One of the Proudfeathers began the descent, and the others followed. They dropped fast, and Theo's stomach lurched.

"We're over Doria, we can't land here!" Nyra protested. They were so close to the city roofs now that Theo could make out individual windows with their candlelight, the lines and cracks of roof tiles. One chimney came so close he felt the fleeting warmth from its smoke.

A claw of light flashed, blinding Theo, and something hissed close to his arm. The net gave way, and Theo instinctively grabbed with both front paws as his back paws swung into open air. The stars had all disappeared, swallowed by a rippling dark cloud above.

"Pull up!" Someone screeched, but the wind snatched the words. Then the broken net he was holding was on fire, disintegrating with every breath. Indigo was reaching for him, eyes panicked, but then the net in her paw ripped clean away and she fell against him, sending them tumbling to the roofs below.

Voices.

The voices prodded Theo into consciousness, and he became aware that he was bruised, in pain, and itchy. His first instinct was to sit up, get his bearings, but something about the voices warned him to keep still.

He opened his eyes instead, and found himself under a suffocating pile of something rough—hay, his nose told him. It smelled of wet straw, horses, and dung, and something else unusual yet familiar—

"Will you quit your *I told you so?*"

Theo froze, realizing he wasn't alone.

"Well, I did," an exasperated female voice said. "That roof has rotted to nothing, and now it's caved in from a little storm."

The male mumbled something, but Theo couldn't hear over the neighs of a horse, and then there was the clomp of boots, the creak of a ladder.

"Stop griping and get the carpenter," the female said. "Don't need sodden hay on top of it all."

There was another indistinct reply, then the scrape of a large gate being latched shut. Theo strained to hear if anyone else was still nearby. But the only sounds were the stamping of hooves, the creak of wagon wheels from somewhere outside, and the distant pealing of a bell.

He began digging his way out of the straw when he felt someone else trying to dig in.

"Theo?"

He could have laughed with relief at hearing Brune's voice. He sat up, sending straw and hay tumbling off him, and saw the bear and Indigo, straw sticking out from their fur at odd angles.

"Where are we?"

Brune glanced around. "In a blacksmith's stable."

"In the middle of Doria," Indigo added, plucking a piece of straw from her ear.

"So those were Urzoks."

Brune nodded. "We only just found you when they arrived."

"We couldn't risk your making a noise, so we covered you up where you fell, and hid instead."

Theo looked up toward the morning sunlight streaming through three holes in the roof. He had to agree with the woman; the roof was badly rotten, which had been lucky for Theo and his companions. Where they might have cracked a bone or two in their fall, they had instead crashed through the weakened roof and into what looked like a mezzanine used for storing hay. Below the mezzanine was a space for horses, with one of the walls low enough so that the animals could lean their necks out into the adjacent courtyard.

"Are you hurt?" Brune asked. "Can you walk?"

"I don't know."

He stood. Everything seemed to work fine, though he hadn't fallen through unscathed. He could feel the sting of several scrapes along his arms, and his vest was torn in several places.

Panicked, he patted his vest and was relieved to pull out Calgornan's book, still intact.

"You seem happier to see that book than to see us," Indigo said drily.

Theo looked at her. Was she mocking him?

"Never mind," Brune interrupted. "We have to get out of here before those Urzoks come back."

"Then let's go," Theo said, testing his legs.

Indigo shook her head. "Look outside."

Theo moved to the lowest of the holes in the roof, on the opposite side from the courtyard. The hole was too high, so Brune gave him a paw up.

"Welcome to Doria, Theo."

Outside was a sight unlike anything Theo had ever seen. He hadn't seen many cities, but the ones he had seen were full of different creatures, large, small, clawed, furred. This city, from what he could see, had mostly one type of inhabitant. Urzok. The road outside was full of them, all walking, riding horses, pushing carts. He had never seen so many Urzoks in one place, other than the battle at Ralgayan.

"We can't go anywhere without being noticed," Indigo said.

"And we can't hide here." Brune lowered his paw to put Theo back on the ground.

"We could sneak out at night."

Brune shook his head at Theo's suggestion. "There are bound to be imperial guards patrolling the streets, even at night. Bounty hunters will be looking at every bear and rabbit."

The sound of a pipe's music drew Theo's attention back to the hole. He could hear clapping and shouting.

"What's that?"

Brune peered out, frowning. "Some sort of show."

Theo pushed a bale of hay under the hole and clambered up. Over the rim, he could just see the wide public street below, with its tamped down earth. A ring of spectators ringed an Urzok—a man, who wore a festive red hat with brightly dyed feathers. He held a ribboned hoop, through which three small, spotted dogs took turns jumping. Bright scarves had been tied around their necks—one rich yellow like a yolk, another holly red, and the third robin's-egg blue.

"Pacified pets," Brune snorted.

Theo watched the dogs perform another round, jumping through the hoop before sitting obediently in a line as the man bowed to applause.

"Thank you all, people of Doria!" The man's voice was melodious and carried easily, a voice used to reaching the furthest ears. "Our show must travel on, but Reenan's Spectacular will be back in Doria before summer's end, especially if it's made known we will be welcome." He made a subtle gesture toward his hat, which he swept off his head and held out in one smooth movement. The crowd came forward to toss coins in.

"Poor dogs." Indigo had joined Theo on the hay bale.

"That's how we're going to get out of Doria."

Indigo frowned at him. "What do you mean?"

"Sometimes, the best way to hide is in plain sight," Theo said.

"It may work," Brune admitted. "Except that everyone and their fleas would recognize Indigo's tattoos. Not to mention the famous griffinrider."

The bear was right. Bounty hunters had been given a description of Theo's gray face with the black eye patches, the black paws.

"You said this is a blacksmith's?"

"The forge area is across the courtyard," Brune explained. "His hammering was what brought me to."

Theo scampered down the ladder to the horse pen below. There were three of them, one gray and two white, and they tamped and huffed at his intrusion.

Indigo peered over the edge of the hay mezzanine. "What are you doing?"

"Finding our disguise. Brune, find anything with bright colors, or decorative. Indigo, keep an eye out, and let us know if the Urzoks come back."

Indigo nodded, while the bear lowered himself down the ladder. The horses whinnied in panic, and Theo and Brune shot nervous glances toward the courtyard, but no one came.

Brune opened the gate to the courtyard, taking care to keep

the horses from getting out. He and Theo walked across to the open forge area of the blacksmith. Here, a yawning half-moon furnace held a huddled heap of coals, their glow winking like sleepy eyes amongst the soot. Metal tools lined the walls, and baskets of nails, keys, axles, cutlery, and other odds and ends crowded the shelves. A well-scarred anvil and a large barrel of water dominated the center of the space.

Theo went straight for the furnace, while Brune began searching the walls.

"Bright colors," the bear grumbled. "This place has about as much color as the inside of Blackhide's backside."

"There must be something!" Theo scooped the cooler soot from the furnace into his paws, testing the color and fastness. It would have to do. He rushed back across the courtyard and called up softly to Indigo until her head appeared at the mezzanine.

At the sight of his sooty face, she asked, "You think this'll work?"

"It just has to last us out of Doria."

She came down the ladder toward the gate.

"I'll get Brune to open—"

But before he could finish, the princess had jumped up and grabbed the ledge of the wall, effortlessly pulling herself up and over into the courtyard.

Of course. He had forgotten how she made things like this look so easy.

He followed her to the forge, where Brune was still rummaging. She took a pawful of the soot and began rubbing it into her ears until her blue tattoos were completely covered.

"This was all I could find." Brune held out two threadbare kerchiefs, striped blue-and-white, and a set of reins with bells stitched on.

"It's a start. But what about your axe?" Theo nodded toward Brune's harness. "And helmet? That won't help us stay unnoticed."

The bear grinned and pulled out a rolled-up red-and-green horse blanket from under his arm. He threw it over himself like a cloak, covering the axe.

At their skeptical looks, Brune growled. "I'm not leaving it."

"We have to get out of Doria, Brune."

"And entertainers don't carry axes or wear helmets," Indigo added.

"Where would we hide it?"

Theo looked at the forge and its dozing bed of coals.

"No. No, no, no."

"If you hide it, it'll be found," Theo insisted.

"He's right," Indigo said. "We can't risk it." At Brune's hesitation, she took a breath and said, "I'll go first."

She undid the sword at her belt, hefted the blade, and threw it onto the coals. The sheath began to smoke and blacken, and the coals stirred to life.

She turned to Brune, expectant.

Brune looked like a dozen arguments were brewing inside. At the rabbits' silent faces, however, the bear nodded, pained. He took a poker leaning by the forge and reluctantly stoked the sleeping coals until they were awake and roaring with hunger. Brune took off his helmet and rubbed it fondly.

"Farewell, old friend." He tossed it into the flames, watching it settle into the coals. He then unstrapped his harness and cradled the axe for a moment.

"How are we going to defend ourselves?" he asked, his paw resting on the axe head.

"With our wits, hopefully," Theo replied.

The bear sighed. "Nothing wrong with our wits, but I'll miss this axe." He looked at it one last time, then pushed it in. The fire embraced it, metal and all, crackling around the weapon.

Brune turned to Theo. "Your turn."

"What?"

"The book."

Theo looked at Indigo.

"He's right. Entertainers don't wear helmets or carry axes. And if anyone finds that thing on us, we'll be sent to Kalyun-eh."

"But it has the key to finding Elshon!"

The bear shook his head. "You've had days with those songs. If they had any more to offer on the Library's whereabouts you would have found it by now. If I can give up my axe and helmet, you can give up Orjo's book."

Theo took the book out, feeling it one last time in his paws. "It's one of a kind. The last in Mankahar."

"So was my axe."

At Brune's grieving look toward the furnace, Theo held out *The Songs of Calgornan*. The bear took it, and fed it to the flames. Theo felt as if he, and not the book, was on fire. Somewhere, he imagined Orjo screaming.

"Chin up, rabbit. If we find the Library, you might find another of those."

* * *

THE STREETS SMELLED OF ALE, dust, oils, and dung. Theo's nose reeled under the scents and sounds of so many Urzoks, but he tried to follow Indigo's lead, walking confidently, as if he did this all the time.

Brune lumbered behind them, his tasseled horse cloak only just reaching his tail. Passersby scuttled out of the way and pointed at the great hulking beast, momentarily surprised but then overcome by fascination. Theo tried to ignore the discomfort of the bandana around his neck, which in his nervousness, he had tied too tight.

The princess shook the bells occasionally, adding to the charade that they were performers. They wove through small streets, always trying to keep a general northern course. Theo wasn't sure how Indigo knew where to go, as the buildings around them closed in so high and tight that he couldn't make out the sun's position.

They turned down a narrow alley and into a maze of lanes before finding themselves at a dead end.

"We should take the bigger roads," Brune suggested.

"And hurry," Indigo said, looking up at the sky. "The gates will likely close at sunset, big city or no."

They turned to retrace their steps, but froze. Blocking the lane were two city guards, dressed in leather armor with officious red-and-black cloaks. Curved swords hung at their belts, and one of them wore gloves despite the heat.

"What's your business in Doria, you three?" The gloved one's voice was gravelly, as if he was too fond of smoking pipes.

Indigo was the first to react. "We're performers," she said smoothly and gave a courteous bow.

"Who's your sponsor?"

"Sponsor?" Indigo kept her voice neutral, but the gloved guard's eyes narrowed.

"Every animal in Doria, pacified or no, needs to have a human sponsor. It's the law."

Theo tried to control his nerves. In the rush of leaving, they hadn't discussed details, or what they would say if they were stopped.

"Of course it is," Indigo answered. "And we would never consider breaking law."

"Then where is your sponsor?" The one without gloves rested a hand on his sword hilt.

"He's mending some of our supplies," Indigo said smoothly. "We're waiting for him."

"What's his name?"

Theo glanced at Indigo. "His name?"

"Are you parrots or are you rabbits?" The gloved guard moved closer. "I asked you for his name."

"Reenan."

The guards turned. Behind them stood the performer Theo had seen below the window, his dogs at his heels.

The gloved guard eyed him dubiously. "These animals are yours?"

"Yes, sir, I'm their sponsor. Reenan's my name."

"And you have a permit to perform in Doria?"

"Of course!" The man smiled, mouth full of charm, and produced a wooden token from an inner pocket. He held it out to the gloved soldier, who examined it before handing it back.

The guards glanced at Theo, Indigo, and Brune. "Good day, then. Remember to keep your animals in sight at all times while in Doria."

"I will. And thank you for the advice," Reenan said. He watched the guards leave, then turned back to Theo and his friends.

"Thank you," Indigo said. "Reenan, is it?"

Reenan beamed. "Reenan the Spectacular! And these three are Hops, Pepper, and Dash." The three dogs wagged their tails at their names. "So, does the bear dance?"

"I'm sorry?" Theo hadn't even considered what kind of performers they were.

"Can the bear dance?"

Brune bristled. "Look, I'm not one of your pacified dogs."

"Because a dancing bear could get out of Doria. As part of a sponsor's troupe. And as you can see, you three need a sponsor."

Indigo's eyes darkened. "Is that why you're helping us?"

Reenan held up his palms, his voice low. "I just thought you could use a friend. I can get you out of Doria. But you'll need to play a part for it to work."

Brune looked at the rabbits, then nodded. "I'm the best dancing bear you'll find in these parts."

Reenan nodded and tipped his hat. "Then welcome to the Spectacular!"

CHAPTER 32

When the patter sounds started in the early morning, Pozzi cursed. Please pass, he prayed. But instead, the summer drizzle intensified, hitting the gables and the cobblestones outside in cheerful, fat droplets.

"Should we wait until next time, Uncle Pozzi?" Walnut suggested quietly as they finished their breakfast of date porridge and watermelon, but Keeva shook her head. They had already waited an extra week, as the last two collection days had failed. The first time because Hassah had misbehaved and been confined to her room the whole morning, and the second time because the kitchen maids had commandeered the courtyard to sand all the cast-iron cookery. Hassah had been forbidden to bring her pets there to play.

Pozzi looked at Keeva and knew they had to try. Rain or no, they would have to go today.

He picked up a watermelon rind and hefted it, thinking.

"Pass me that knife."

Keeva did as he asked and watched as he made some quick cuts to the rind, then pushed a fork into the hollowed bottom so that it stood up.

"Mistress Hassah!"

The girl didn't look up from braiding a ribbon into her doll's stiff hair. Pozzi moved closer.

"Mistress Hassah, wouldn't it be more fun to play outside?"

The girl frowned, still absorbed with her braiding. "It's raining."

"Exactly!" Pozzi said, smiling. "Wouldn't it be fun to play in puddles?"

Hassah blew a wayward lock out of her eyes. "Nurse will whack me if I get my dress muddy."

"Then don't wear a dress. Have you ever raced watermelon boats?"

The girl looked up, curious. "What are watermelon boats?"

* * *

OUTSIDE IN THE COURTYARD, the rain settled to a steady drumming and created wide pools of water. With the breakfast knife, Pozzi had created boats for all of them out of the melon rinds. Each boat had a small fork as a mast, with a triangle of cloth tied to it for a sail. Hassah, dressed in an oilcloth cloak and hood, was racing them with Walnut, squealing with every splash.

As the morning wore on and the cart didn't appear, Keeva grew fidgety. "Maybe there's no delivery. Because of the rain."

Hassah had gone to race her boat in the gutter, where the water flowed at a merry clip. Keeva glanced toward the outer courtyard, obviously worried Walnut was right and they should wait.

"They'll deliver," Pozzi said, but he was as unsure as Keeva was. Kayden always picked up the pelts in the morning. The horse wagon was punctual, without fail. But he hadn't seen them in the rain.

"Walnut! Come here!" Hassah squealed, and Walnut gave them a last look before racing off to join the girl.

Pozzi couldn't give up, not unless he had to. Any moment now, the nurse would become suspicious as to why Hassah was so quiet in her room, and come looking for her. Any moment now, Hassah would tire of this game and insist on escaping the wet. Any moment now, their chance at freedom would be gone.

There was a hacking cough and the sound of something being spat in the outer courtyard. Pozzi never thought such a filthy habit could sound so welcome.

"Wetter n' a fishmonger's floor, eh Kayden?" remarked the burly man.

"That's the truth," Kayden grunted. "Roads were bogged, made us late."

Pozzi looked over at Hassah and Walnut returning with their boats. He turned so his back was to them and broke his and Keeva's boats to pieces. As the little girl arrived, Pozzi looked apologetic.

"I'm sorry, Mistress Hassah. I tripped and stepped on them."

Hassah pouted. "Then how will you race?"

"Why don't you find some more rinds?" Keeva suggested.

The girl looked at the boat in her hand, reluctant to abandon her fun. "You get them."

"The kitchen maids won't listen to us," Pozzi said. "Only you."

Hassah sighed the sigh of the young who have to do everything and began trotting for the kitchens.

As soon as she had passed the doorway, Pozzi and Keeva bolted for the outer courtyard. Pozzi turned to see Walnut looking at the spot where Hassah had disappeared.

"Walnut!" Pozzi called, his heart catching. *Don't let him change his mind now!*

With one last glance toward the kitchens, Walnut raced toward Pozzi and Keeva, who were already stripping off their clothes and hurriedly tossing them into the fish barrel. Keeva helped Walnut with his and then followed Pozzi as he sprinted across the courtyard and into the archway that led to the outer keep.

"That the lot?"

"Aye, that's it for today. See you tomorrow."

The driver grunted as he closed the wagon door with a bang.

Pozzi looked back at Keeva and Walnut, nodding for them to get ready. He peered around the corner at the wagon and could see Kayden's boots splashing in the mud on the other side of the wagon as he made his way back to the driver's seat.

"Now! Go!"

Pozzi turned back to pull Keeva and Walnut with him, but instead found himself face to face with a pair of boots. A pair of very familiar boots.

"Go where, rabbit?"

He felt the fist connect with his head, a shower of heat and pain spreading across his cheek.

"Run!" he managed to shout at Keeva and Walnut, who were some distance away—Walnut was lying on the ground, motionless, and Keeva was trying to rouse him. Pozzi tried to stand and go to them, but Sarkus pulled Pozzi up by the neck, and the rabbit's vision blurred.

The boy turned Pozzi to face him and smiled, which with his maimed features now looked more akin to a snarl. "Pretty rabbit. Let's make you not so pretty."

CHAPTER 33

The potter's workshop was silent but for the pounding of rain outside.

Sarkus lit a lamp on a workbench with one of the wall torches, his other hand still keeping a firm grip on Pozzi's neck fur. By now, the flesh there was numb with pain, not helped by Pozzi's constant thrashing.

Sarkus surveyed the tools hanging neatly on nails on the wall. At Pozzi's continued squirming, the boy brought his arm under the rabbit's legs, taking some of the pressure off his neck but holding his prisoner's head still to look at the various tools.

"A scraper. That's a good start." Sarkus pulled a carving tool off the wall, testing its curved blade against the wooden bench. "Perhaps we'll carve you a new mouth, rabbit."

Pozzi fought a sudden nausea. He eyed the open door to the workshop. If he could just somehow twist his head enough to bite that hand, he might be able to get the boy to drop him, and make a run for it.

As if reading his mind, Sarkus grinned. "What sharp teeth you have." He walked to the kiln, searching. "Here we are." He pulled out the kiln gloves and, keeping Pozzi pinned under one arm, pulled the gloves on.

"Hassah will tell your father!" Pozzi protested.

Sarkus's face darkened. "You think he cares what I do with a rabbit? He lets me do anything I want, as long as he doesn't have to see my face." Pozzi could hear the bitterness in the youth's voice. The boy's eyes lit up. "This! I have no idea what this is." Sarkus examined a tool that had a screw on one end and a chisel-like triangle on the other. "I've never taken out eyes before." The boy put them down on the workbench, his hand pressing Pozzi's neck into the wood so that the prisoner found it hard to breathe. "You asked the crows to come for my eyes, didn't you? They tried, you know. Like this."

Pozzi winced as Sarkus placed the edge of the chisel next to the rabbit's right eye. He struggled with all his might, clawing at the glove with his paws, but his captor's hand and forearms were completely protected.

The boy's lips attempted a smile at Pozzi's expression. "Ready for your new face?"

Pozzi closed his eyes and tried to think of something else, anything else. Home. Keeva. Walnut. Keeva—

"Sarkus!"

Though the pressure on his neck didn't lessen, the blade at his eye was gone. He opened his eyes and saw Tansha standing in the doorway, strands of her braided hair wild around her stern face. It seemed she had rushed here. Huddled against her skirts were Hassah, Keeva, and Walnut.

For a few tense heartbeats, they all simply stood there, looking at each other.

"What do you think you're doing, Sarkus?"

"They were trying to escape."

The mistress of Nyatha's voice remained hard. "That may be, but it's no cause for torturing the thing. Let the rabbit go."

Sarkus hesitated, then stepped back, surly.

"Now back to your lessons, son. I want no more of this fighting over silly pets."

"But—"

"I'm your mother, and you will obey me!" Tansha snapped. "Now to your lessons."

Sarkus gave a last glare at Pozzi, then slunk out of the room, his anger trailing behind him like a shadow.

Hassah ran up to Pozzi and hugged him to her. "Thank you, Mama."

Tansha sighed and herded them out of the workshop. They entered Hassah's room, where Hassah held the cage door open and pushed them inside. Tansha locked the cage and pocketed the key.

"It won't happen again," Hassah promised. "Please don't tell Papa."

"Your father makes the rules, and he was clear. You had to be responsible for your pets. Or what would happen?"

Hassah grew teary. "Please, Mama. No."

Pozzi's heart skipped a beat.

Tansha bent down to eye level with Hassah. "Rules are rules, my daughter. And these animals are making you and Sarkus fight. They're more trouble than they're worth."

"But they're my friends."

"They're your pets," her mother corrected. "And they'll still be your pets, I promise."

"It won't be the same!" Hassah wailed.

The truth hit Pozzi. Tansha was going to have them pacified. He almost wished he was back in the workshop, back facing whatever Sarkus had in store for him. One look at Keeva's face let him know she knew Tansha's intentions as well.

"What won't be the same?" Walnut asked.

Tansha glanced at him before turning back to her daughter. "We'll have them pacified tomorrow, and everything will be all right." Tansha stroked Hassah's hair. "You'll see. Now go and play. I'm going to have a word with your nurse."

"No!" Keeva shouted, paws gripping the cage. "Hassah, don't leave us!"

Tansha guided her daughter toward the door. "Shush, rabbit. Come Hassah."

Still teary, the girl obediently let her mother lead her out of the room. As the mistress of Nyatha closed the door behind her and her daughter, Pozzi felt as if he was being sealed in a tomb.

I asked you for that fire, Brune roared, the flames shooting from...

CHAPTER 34

The western gate of Doria rose like the arched back of a stone cat, its faded yellow flags swimming lazily in the summer breeze.

"Let me do any talking." Reenan looked pointedly at Indigo and Theo, who rode on Brune's back. "It'll go easier if they assume you're pacified."

None of them needed reminding. Their one chance out of this teeming Urzok city was Reenan, along with the three dogs who trotted obediently next to him.

The closer they drew to the gate, the more crowded the streets became. As many streams converge and then flood into the sea, so the road grew packed with traders, pilgrims, workers, and smiths leaving and entering Doria with their wares, their profits, their tools. Theo's senses were overwhelmed with the smells of bodies pressed together, of mud and discarded fruit peels churned under hundreds of feet and hooves. Beggars and thieves wove among the crowd, making full use of the noise and the crush.

That's one advantage we have, Theo thought. The crowd kept a good distance between themselves and the traveling show group, for no one wanted to bump up against Brune. Those next to them stared and whispered, but no one jostled them, and no one tried to get close to rob them.

They slowed as they approached the gate. Indigo peered over heads and frowned.

"Don't worry," Reenan said under his breath. "This is standard. They stop anyone they think they can squeeze a coin from. The dogs perform a few tricks, charm them a bit, and we leave the city."

Theo looked at the dogs, unsure. They were wearing bright-green scarves with bells around their necks that made a pleasant tinkling sound as they trotted along. It was true they looked innocent, some might even say charming.

As they came within sight of the gate guards, Theo saw an officious-looking Urzok in robes and a cropped beard sitting on an elevated chair, with a view of the crowds passing through. Occasionally, he would point at someone, and a guard would motion them forward. A series of questions would be asked, a bag or cart examined, and then the traveler would either be waved on or have something confiscated.

Theo knew it was pointless to not look, for the official was bound to see them. They stood out like hens at a fox party, as Brune would say. It was time to test his argument about hiding in plain sight.

Theo looked up to see the official pointing a long tapered finger at them and whispering to a guard. The guard nodded and motioned at them to move to the side and away from the crowd.

"Here we go," Reenan whispered. "Just stay quiet, do as I say, and we'll glide through this like money through a fool's hand."

The travelers around them seemed to melt away, grateful to have avoided attention. Reenan led his group to the side, just under the official's raised chair.

"My good sir, such a pleasure to meet you!" Reenan's voice, Theo found, could turn as sweet and thick as syrup when needed. "Perhaps you've heard of us, Reenan's Spectacular?"

"I have not." If Reenan's voice was melodious and smooth, the official's was blunt and seemed to take great pleasure in putting others down as a hammer does a nail. "What's your business?"

"We're performers, good sir," Reenan replied, unruffled.

"Any of these unpacified?"

"No." Reenan's smile never wavered. "Unpacified animals are harder to manage. Some go for them, but not me."

The official frowned down at them, his cropped beard trimmed as sharply as a knife's edge. "I've seen dancing dogs. What do the bear and rabbits do?"

By now, some travelers had stopped to gawk, and even the guards seemed to have forgotten their duties. Reenan had a natural magnetism that turned everyone into a spectator. Theo could feel Brune's shoulder muscles tensing beneath him, and though Indigo's breathing was even, he knew she felt as nervous as he did. If they betrayed too much emotion, the guards might suspect they weren't pacified.

Reenan kept his blinding smile throughout the official's frown. "Well, perhaps you've heard of a dancing bear, or a—"

"Show me."

"Show you what?"

"The bear. Make it dance."

A murmur went through the crowd around them, and the guards took greater interest. Reenan's smile never wavered, but Theo felt a rush of fear.

"Good sir, he's a little out of practice. I'm afraid that—"

"If you want to leave this city, you will show me a dancing bear."

Reenan paused, then nodded. "A good entertainer always obliges." He turned to Brune.

Theo could feel Brune's hesitation, in the way he eyed the official and the crowd.

Reenan gestured. "Let's not be shy, bear. Show them your spectacular!"

Brune sat, so that Theo and Indigo could slide off his back.

The bear stood to his full height, and the crowd instinctively stepped back, an expectant murmur running through them. Everyone had given up the pretense of passing the gate and simply stood to watch the show.

Brune kept a stony expression, but Theo could tell he was tense, unsure. The bear hopped from one hind paw to the other a few times.

Reenan's smile looked frozen, and a few titters arose from the audience. At this, Brune pulled himself to his full height.

He shuffled his back paws and raised his fore paws. A few spectators began clapping. Emboldened, he hopped in a circle, his steps surprisingly light for such a large beast. Cheers arose, and at a signal from Reenan, Brune spun first one way and then another, while the dogs barked excitedly around him. Reenan looked relieved, and Theo could see him tempted to try to solicit some coin there and then.

Brune whirled to a stop, panting. The crowd applauded and then, as if remembering why they were there in the first place, pushed forward to get past the guards before they could be pulled aside and searched or made to pay a tithe.

"And there you have it!" Reenan said with a flourish.

The official nodded. "Pay two bits and be on your way."

Reenan's eyes narrowed, but he kept his best smile. He dug out two bits from his pocket and handed it to the guard, who passed it up to the official.

The official examined the coins, then waved them through. Theo felt light with relief and could see that Indigo and Brune felt the same way.

As the stone archway of Doria's western gate passed over them, Reenan patted Brune on the shoulder. "By Blackhide, friend, you really are the best dancing bear in these parts."

CHAPTER 35

The road out of Doria proper was crowded for a league or so, before it branched into three, thinning out the foot traffic.

Reenan and his troupe took the middle road, which led toward the western city of Bhenkar. By the time the sun had climbed to its zenith, they were virtually the only souls on the road.

"Thank you for what you did," Theo said.

"You're welcome."

"You took a great risk for us," Indigo added. "Why?"

Reenan shrugged. "Been a performer all my life. I spend more time with animals than with my own kind. These three here"—he indicated the dogs trotting happily next to them—"are my family. And I don't agree with much of the empire's views on animals." He paused, as if thinking, then continued, "I don't know where you're headed, but you're welcome to join us. We could use a dancing bear and some company. Pay's good, and there's always shelter."

"That's very generous," Theo said. "But we need to get to Jaipri."

"Forest of the serpents?" Reenan raised one eyebrow. "Why?

Doesn't seem like a safe place for you, even if the empire doesn't bother with that wild jungle." At their clear reluctance to give an explanation, he waved a hand dismissively. "Sorry, not my affair. It's true. Well, in that case, you'll want to start heading north in a few leagues."

They stopped under a tree at noon to avoid the heat of the sun, which the rabbits appreciated not so much for the rest as for the fact that they had noticed the soot on their fur was turning into a slick glue in the heat. They were about to wipe off what they could and start back on the road when the sound of galloping hooves made them turn. A large cloud of dust was moving up the road from the direction of Doria.

"Someone's in a right hurry."

The first riders appeared, and sunlight glinted off them. Armor. Theo's chest tightened. There were thousands of reasons the empire's soldiers would be on this road. It didn't mean they were after Theo.

The soldiers slowed with a whinnying of horses and a clash of metal bridles and stirrups, and Theo's optimism waned.

There were fifteen in all, led by a short, stocky man with a red cape and imposing helmet, beneath which a long, black braid protruded and coiled around the man's neck. Their arrival brought Dash, Hops, and Pepper to their feet, baying.

"Greetings!" Reenan said, putting a hand down to quiet the dogs. "Can we help you, friends?"

"This bear yours?" The man in charge pointed a sword at Brune, who bristled but stayed silent.

"He is. Is there a problem?"

"What about these rabbits? They belong to you too?"

Indigo flicked her ears, and Theo forced himself to stay calm.

"They are." Despite his even tone, Reenan was evidently nervous. Unlike the soldiers in the city, these were imperial men, not mere city guards. The dogs seemed to sense Reenan's unease and growled.

"Where'd you find them?"

"Can I ask why—"

"I said where'd you find them?"

Theo looked at Reenan, nervous, and noticed that Brune's hackles were raised.

"I really don't remember. Some market somewhere."

"You'll need to come with me," the lead soldier said gruffly, then motioned at another soldier mounted on a gray mare. Theo noticed several chained collars hanging from the mare's saddle. "Chain them."

"No."

The commander turned, trying to find the voice.

"It would be best for all if you let us go," Brune said.

The commander frowned. "So they are unpacified. I suggest you don't resist."

Two of the soldiers dismounted, pulling their chains with them.

"Perhaps there's a misunderstanding," Reenan insisted. "I'm simply a performer on my way to Bhenkar, I—"

"Well, now you're a performer on your way to Doria's garrison."

Reenan's face blanched, and the dogs snarled. Brune shot Indigo and Theo a look that said to be ready.

Brune let the soldiers get close enough to try and throw the chain over his neck, before rearing onto his back legs and hooking the chains hard toward him. The two soldiers lost their footing and pitched forward toward the bear, scrabbling for their swords. But Brune was faster, his paws lashing out like bladed mallets that cut through armor and flesh, felling his attackers.

"Seize them!" The lead soldier had leapt back onto his horse, urging the others forward.

The remaining Urzoks drew their swords. Five rushed Brune, who had pulled out his dead opponents' swords, while another three came after Theo and Indigo. Reenan turned to run, with the dogs following, but the remaining four soldiers closed around him with their horses, the dogs baying ferociously. As the soldiers dismounted to subdue Reenan, the dogs leapt at the attackers, locking jaws on ankles and wrists.

Indigo rolled forward, dodging a soldier's blade, and wrapped one of the fallen Urzok's chains around her paw, yanking the collar out from underneath the body. Her attacker turned to take another swipe, but she brought the metal collar swinging around, catching him hard under the eye. Indigo took advantage of his distraction to kick the sword from his hand.

"Theo!"

Theo reached for the weapon she directed at him, but too late. A second soldier, muscular and with a missing forefinger, stepped on the hilt before Theo could grasp it, and drew his own sword. Four Fingers' companion joined him, weapon drawn.

Theo leapt back as Four Fingers' blade came dangerously close to his shoulder. Hands grasped his arm, and instinctively he sank his teeth into the flesh.

The man swore but didn't let go, instead using his other hand to grasp Theo by the ears in an attempt to pull him off. Theo kicked with all his might and felt his boots connect, but his captor barely flinched.

Then without warning, the man cried out and let go, and Theo fell to the ground. His attacker crashed face down next to him, his back seeping red. Behind the fallen soldier, a panting and blood-spattered Brune stood, a sword in each paw.

"Down, Theo!"

The bear raised the swords high above his head. Theo dove for cover and felt a sting in his ear before looking up and seeing Brune's bulk above him, the blades whistling down with a deadly speed. Theo heard something crack before Brune pulled his swords free, and a soldier's body slumped to the ground next to the other one. Theo recognized Four Fingers.

Brune reached down and pulled Theo up. The rabbit spotted Indigo fighting off the last remaining soldier, with a short sword she'd taken off someone. The sole survivor from Doria seemed to sense that the tides of battle had changed. His commander had already fled. There were two horses left that hadn't bolted, and if he stayed, he would be dealing with the giant bear with the swords.

Theo watched the man weigh his options before taking off for the nearest horse and leaping onto it. The man pulled the reins up and slammed his heels against the beast, galloping back to Doria.

"Everyone all right?" Brune asked. One cheek was cut open, and his flank was dark with blood, though from the way he was walking, Theo guessed it hadn't gone deep.

Theo went to Indigo, putting a paw on her shoulder. "Minor cuts," she assured him. "I'm not sure about him though."

Theo looked where she indicated, and saw Reenan sitting, cradling Dash's head in his lap. He was stroking the dog's muzzle with one hand, and his shoulders trembled.

Theo felt sick. He walked toward Reenan and stood next to him, silent. Hops and Pepper had been slain, and only Dash was still conscious, whimpering as he tried to lick Reenan's hand. The dog's breathing slowed, his tongue drooping to one side. Reenan stroked his companion's ears even after he lay still.

"I'm so sorry." Theo hated how empty, how hollow, his words sounded.

Reenan didn't look up.

"We have to go," Indigo added.

"They were my family. You don't leave family on the road."

"You have to go," the princess said. "Soon Doria will send more troops, and you can't be here when they arrive."

"But they died for me."

"If you truly care about them, you'll make sure to live," Brune said. "And that means running."

Theo rubbed at a patch of his face until the gray fur beneath showed. "I'm Theo. This is Indigo, and the bear is Brune."

Reenan stared, connecting the names, the pieces. The last moments seemed to have added years to his face and an invisible weight to his shoulders. "The Griffinrider? I helped the Griffin-rider escape Doria?"

Guilt flooded Theo. Reenan had risked much, but he hadn't known how much.

"Let us help you bury Hops, Pepper, and Dash so that they're safe."

"We don't have time, Theo," Brune growled.

"They died for us as well."

Reenan looked at him, expressionless. Brune and Theo got to work with what little they had, while Indigo searched the remaining horse and soldiers for what weapons they could take with them. Reenan gently retied his dogs' scarves around their necks before letting Brune lay them in the rough grave they'd prepared.

"Did you want to say something?" Theo asked the man. They didn't have the luxury of time, but Theo had to ask. Reenan said nothing, the shock still heavy on him. Theo looked at Brune, expectant.

The bear looked hesitant, but Theo nodded encouragement. Brune coughed, lowered his head, and murmured:

> *In Aktu's balance*
> *Nothing is created*
> *Nothing is destroyed*
> *Through death shall be born life*
> *And through life shall be born the balance*
>
> *Leave in joy and return to the earth*
> *May you re-enter Aktu in peace.*

Brune and Theo picked up pawfuls of earth and began covering the bodies. Reenan joined in after a moment, and soon, they had the trio buried.

The neighing of the horse drew their attention to Indigo. She had a short sword at her waist and held the reins to the remaining horse, a bay stallion.

"If we ride, we can make Jaipri by nightfall tomorrow."

Theo looked to Reenan. "Come with us."

Reenan looked dubious. "I'm in enough trouble as it is. The forest of serpents is no place for me."

"The empire might execute you for helping us," Indigo said. "Or worse, torture you to find out where we are."

Reenan looked uncertain. "I'm not sure being caught with you is safer."

"I've a better idea," Brune said. "Go to Lord Noshi."

"The traitor?" Reenan asked, incredulous.

"That's what the empire calls him, but to us, he's leader of the Order." Indigo brought the horse closer. "You can find him at Mt. Mahkah."

Brune shook his head. "New Hegg is closer; it's only two days' hard ride from here. Tell the Order that Brune of Hegg sent you. They'll keep you safe as a cub in winter."

"This would mean giving up my life."

The rabbits and bear looked at each other. "I think the life you knew is already gone," Brune said softly.

"This is not an easy choice. And you'll have to choose quickly," Indigo added. "Those soldiers will be back. With lots of friends."

Reenan looked from them to Doria, then to the fresh grave. Something about the sight of the fresh earth over his dogs seemed to tip him.

"New Hegg it is."

CHAPTER 36

Ornox's band started on the straight road that cut through the Stone Forest toward the Plains of Fire. The Stone Forest received its name from the countless oblong stones, some taller than three men standing on each other's shoulders, which stood all around, visible between the trees. Some said these were the teeth of a giant, left behind by old gods, and others said they were quarried and built by ancient men, markers for some ritual only they knew.

Ornox cared nothing for the history of the Stone Forest, just that it had to be crossed to get to the spot where the muskrat claimed he had left Theo. Getting here had been smoother than the first part of their journey from Lake Lostgone, given there was a derelict but usable road that cut straight across the forest. Only the very poor took this route, and even so, they did so infrequently, for the stones and the trees provided perfect cover for thieves, wild animals, and—for the superstitious—ghosts.

But Ornox didn't fear thieves or wild animals, much less ghosts. He looked over at the muskrat riding tied to Yod's horse, paws bound behind him.

"You seem a capable warlord. Is it really necessary to have a muskrat tied?"

Ornox ignored him.

"I give you my word that I won't run. How's that?" Orjo lifted his paws behind him.

Ornox debated clubbing the animal into silence, when his servant Yod interrupted.

"My lord."

Ornox turned his gaze ahead and saw two figures on horses in the distance down the road, one tall and the other noticeably shorter. Though travelers on this road were rare, it wouldn't be unheard of. What was strange, though, was the fact that they weren't moving.

As Ornox and his retinue approached, he recognized the smaller figure.

"Have the men be on guard."

Yod nodded and turned in his saddle to give a signal.

Ornox didn't change his horse's pace until they stopped within a stone's throw of the two figures.

"Lord Ornox," the smaller rider trilled, shifting on his gray gelding.

"Brel. Emperor's business?" He could smell the musk from the Child even at this distance and recognized the tall man on the accompanying tan gelding. Caldrik, who had once been his daughter's tutor. And there was a third party, Ornox realized now. An old rabbit with one jagged ear, locked in a wooden cage that was strapped behind Caldrik's saddle. The warlord felt the painful stab of a memory of his daughter—standing in a tent with this very same disfigured rabbit, just before she went to battle. To her death.

"The emperor's business is what I tell him it is. Now, I believe you have something of mine," Brel said. "I don't mind your killing of my men, but I would like to have my goods back."

"You mean that?" Ornox pointed at Orjo sitting on Yod's horse. "He appears to be mine at the moment. And I have use of him."

Brel smiled, indulgent. "I'm feeling generous. Give me Orjo, and I will reinstate you. All your lands, your title, your wealth." He pulled out a key and seal from his pocket, and Ornox recognized them. "I have the emperor's ear. You can turn around right now and go home to Vyad."

Ornox put his hands on his pommel. "You should have made that offer when I was in Kalyun-eh."

Brel's smile grew brittle, and he pocketed the seal and key. "Don't let pride keep you poor and powerless, Ornox. Besides, why do you even want him?"

"That's my business, not yours."

"Very well. But think about what I'm offering. Give me Orjo, and your life goes back to what it was before."

"My life will never go back to what it was before." The anger in Ornox's voice crackled. "Now get out of my way."

Brel sighed, as if tired. "I do believe we're not done negotiating."

Caldrik whistled. The singing of armor sounded all around, and Ornox saw armed men in battle gear stepping out from behind the giant stones. There were easily six dozen men, all with bows and arrows trained on Ornox's party, closing off any avenue of escape. His own soldiers drew their swords, their horses stamping as riders tightened their grips on their reins.

"Looks like he's got you by the dangles," Orjo said drily, looking about at all the bowmen with their arrows trained on the warlord's small force. Ornox didn't reply.

"Now," the Child said, impatient. "Give me the muskrat."

Ornox looked back at Yod, who tapped his thigh with one finger.

Ornox turned back to the Child and Caldrik. "You'll have to come and get him."

At a signal from Yod, Ornox's men all leapt off their horses, pulling their mounts to form a protective barricade around them.

Ornox unsheathed his sword and spurred his stallion forward, charging into Brel and Caldrik. The two reeled away, and Ornox heard the hum of arrows flying, the neighing shrieks as those arrows hit the shield of horseflesh defending his soldiers. Ornox continued his charge straight for the Child. A ring of Brel's soldiers was trying to form around their master and Caldrik, but Ornox barreled through them, slashing left and right as he went.

Brel's remaining men scattered and tried to regroup, but Ornox charged through again, oblivious to his own safety. He used his charger's pure mass to knock into his opponents' horses, catching them off guard and sending their parries wildly off course. Ornox hacked down another two before he heard the crack of the first explosion.

Stone, sand, and wood rained down on the battling sides, and Ornox's ears rang with the aftermath of the griffin's egg. As expected, the explosion tore through the enemy and stunned them long enough to allow his men to stand above their shield of horses and send off a volley of arrows. Several enemy soldiers fell, and Ornox took the opportunity to dispatch another one of the Child's men. There were only three fighters now left defending Brel and Caldrik, and seeing Ornox spur his horse toward them, Brel took flight.

Caldrik tried to follow, but an arrow from one of Ornox's soldiers found his horse's neck, and it crashed to the ground, the cage with the old rabbit still on it. Caldrik shrieked a curse, his left leg pinned under his dead mount. The remaining men looked torn about whether to help but decided to join forces against the formidable threat of Ornox.

The warlord held his sword ready as the three encircled him. Just as they were about to rush him, the earth shook under another explosion, sending one of the Child's men toppling off his horse while the two others instinctively ducked for cover. Ornox swept in like a hawk, stabbing one soldier through before turning around to deal with the other. This one proved faster to recover and parried Ornox's blow with his right hand before sinking a short dirk into Ornox's thigh with the left. The warlord grunted as he slammed the butt of his sword hilt into the soldier's helmet, delivering enough force to make the man slip halfway off his saddle. As the soldier tried to pull himself back up, Ornox brought his blade sideways and down, cutting through the man's leg before the panicked horse took off, dragging its rider with it.

Ornox looked at his thigh and the blade lodged there. Time for that later. He scanned the area and, through the debris and bodies, saw Brel up ahead on the road, spurring his horse as if Blackhide was after him.

Ornox slapped his horse with the flat of his sword and gave chase. He knew his beast had the speed, and soon, the charger's sturdy legs were grinding up the distance between him and his quarry.

Ornox bent low, sword out, knees gripping his steed as he gained on the Child. Brel kept glancing behind, fear etched on his face. As Ornox closed in, Brel jerked his horse and took off between the stones, trying to lose his pursuer. But Brel was no skilled rider, and the sudden change of direction confused the horse, who lost its footing and stumbled. Brel toppled over its neck and went crashing into the ground, his riderless horse galloping off out of reach.

Brel pushed himself to his feet while Ornox circled him on his charger.

"We can work something out," the Child said, holding out scraped palms.

"I told you, I gave you that chance in Kalyun-eh."

"Yes, you're right," Brel agreed, "but I can give you anything you want. I can make you emperor. I can give you the Library. You will be the most powerful man in Mankahar."

"I don't need you anymore, or the Library," Ornox replied. He pulled the knife from his thigh, then dismounted, ignoring the pain.

Hope flitted across Brel's face. "Please. Name it. I can do it."

Ornox limped to stand in front of Brel.

The Child pulled the seal and key from his pocket and held it out. "Take these!"

Ornox looked at the seal and key—his seal and key—but made no move.

"I can give you more than this, Ornox, you know that. With me alive at court, you can have whatever you want."

The warlord leaned down, as if to whisper in the advisor's ear. "What I really want…"

He thrust the knife deep, feeling it hit breastbone.

"…is to see you bleed."

The Child blinked, as if the idea that anyone could forego wealth and titles for emotional satisfaction was just too perplexing to grasp. Ornox waited until the life left the Child's body, then let him fall.

The warlord bent over his enemy and picked up his key and seal. He felt their familiar weight and designs, then tucked them under his shirt before limping back to his horse and mounting with his good leg.

He rode back to the site of the ambush. The bodies of men and horses lay everywhere he looked. Most of the horses were his. Most of the men were not.

He was pleased to see that one of the survivors was Yod. His servant was bloodied, his face sooty from the griffin's egg, but he immediately made his way over.

"How many did we lose?"

"Eleven men, my lord, but over half our horses are dead or injured."

"What of the griffin's eggs?"

"Three left, my lord."

Ornox swore to himself. A heavy price to waste on the Child. "Where's Caldrik?"

Yod led him to where his daughter's former tutor was still lying beneath his dead horse. He seemed to have calmed down and put on a civil face at Ornox's approach.

"Caldrik."

"Lord Ornox."

The warlord leaned against his horse's pommel and idly pressed a kerchief Yod handed him to his wounded leg. "You trained my daughter in war tactics, in strategy. What would you advise her to do if she were in my situation?"

"It depends, my lord." Caldrik swallowed. "Do you need soldiers? These are the best. They—and I—have many uses."

"I need to travel fast, not feed excess mouths." Ornox tapped one knee. "Surely, the clever Caldrik, the one who taught my daughter that mercy is weakness, would counsel me to kill every last man."

"If it was advantageous, my lord." Caldrik suddenly looked hopeful. "Though you could take just half of them."

"And how would I determine which half to take?"

"Pit them to the death. Take only the survivors, or in other words, the best."

"Now that's the clever Caldrik I remember." Ornox turned. "Yod, split the prisoners into two even rows. And find some men to help our dear Caldrik."

Caldrik's relief was palpable as Yod motioned at two of Ornox's nearest soldiers. One of them unstrapped the cage with the disfigured rabbit, then they both began heaving the dead horse off Caldrik. Yod and several other soldiers rounded up the sullen prisoners and began grouping them into two lines.

"Take the rabbit and put him with the muskrat," Ornox commanded one soldier, while the other one helped Caldrik to his feet. The man's leg was not broken, but it was bleeding and clearly causing pain.

"Thank you, my lord. It is an honor to return to your service."

Ornox's smile was cold. "But you haven't."

"My lord?"

"You have to earn your place, just like everyone else." At his nod, the soldier roughly pushed Caldrik toward the other prisoners, standing him next to a particularly ferocious-looking giant with a broken nose.

Ornox led his horse to the head of the two lines, while his soldiers formed a ring around the line of prisoners, preventing escape. The warlord addressed the Child's soldiers. "You will each battle the man opposite you. The one who lives will join me and be paid well. Does everyone understand?"

There were expressions of confusion, then understanding and a ripple of fear. Caldrik looked ashen.

"Begin."

There was a split moment's hesitation, and Ornox thought he'd have to intervene. But then one man launched himself at his adversary, and like flame to tinder, everyone's instincts to survive took over. It was messy and ugly, as none of the men had proper weapons. Ornox watched them battle each other in the dirt, with bare hands or daggers or even rocks and parts of their own armor.

Broken Nose was the first to earn his place. Grinning at his good luck, he dispatched Caldrik with a simple kick to the wounded leg and a twisting of his opponent's neck. Ornox nodded his approval and motioned for Broken Nose to stand and join his men.

Soon the last victim fell, and Ornox was looking at the bloodied, dusty survivors.

He nodded. "Good work. Yod, give them water and weapons. We leave within the hour."

CHAPTER 37

*P*ozzi, Keeva, and Walnut spent the rest of the day fruitlessly trying to escape their cage, followed by a restless, defeated night slumped against the slats. Except for a tight-lipped Farriah coming to give them some food and water, they were left alone in the room, locked in their prison.

As light crept up the windowsill, Pozzi wondered whether this would be the last sunrise he would ever see as a living, thinking creature. Keeva had fallen asleep with her head against his shoulder, while Walnut lay with his head against her chest.

"Do you think it'll hurt?"

He looked over. She was staring out the window, at the bleeding dawn.

"Hassah will fight for us. She'll convince Ghazan to change his mind."

Keeva didn't challenge him, though he could tell she didn't believe him. He didn't believe himself, but he wasn't ready to give up hope just yet.

"Pozzi?"

"Hm?"

"Why did you never show your feelings for me? Or ask me to marry you?"

217

Once he'd gotten over his surprise, he snuck a look at her. She was watching him, calm, but sincere. Had she always known how he felt? He struggled to untie his tongue. "You were in love with Harlan."

"What I was was a fool." Her paw found its way into his.

Tears that he hadn't known were there spilled out onto his face, wetting the fur.

The door opened, and Pozzi squeezed Keeva to him, as if he could protect her from what was coming.

Hassah appeared, tousled and red-eyed. She pulled the key from around her neck and unlocked the cage door.

"Quick, wake up Walnut."

Walnut sat up, rubbing his face. "What's going on? Where are we going?"

"Shhh," Hassah whispered, looking at the door. "We have to hurry."

They followed her out into the corridor and toward the stairs. They could hear the faint sounds of the first servants waking, as well as the beginnings of another light summer rain on the roof.

They moved stealthily down the stairs, avoiding the kitchens where the maids were getting kindling ready for the morning bread. Hassah led them out to the main courtyard where they usually played. The rain had strengthened, drumming steadily against the cobblestones.

Hassah motioned for them to stay hidden in the portico as a maid raced outside toward the cistern. When she had finished scooping out a fish for the day's lunch and returned, sodden, to the manor, Pozzi peered out.

"Where are you takin' us, Hassah?" he asked.

Hassah cupped her ear. "Shhh. Do you hear that?"

They all listened. The sound of the rain's patter on stones and tile was most obvious, along with the occasional shouts and bangs of pans from the kitchen, but then Pozzi heard something else. The creak of a wagon wheel, a hacking cough. The neigh of a horse.

Hassah motioned for them to follow, and they raced through the rain, the puddles soaking their feet and the girl's slippers. She led them to the archway that opened onto the outer courtyard, where the pelt cart stood.

They watched from the courtyard archway as Kayden and the cart driver loaded the skins into the wagon. There was no color scheme today. A bloody tumble of browns, tans, blacks, and grays.

"I don't want you to be like the others," Hassah whispered.

Keeva threw her arms around the girl's thigh, hugging her. Walnut joined in, followed by Pozzi.

"Thank you," he said. "We won't forget this."

The girl nodded and rubbed at a nose that had turned runny.

"Follow my lead," Pozzi said to Keeva and Walnut. "And whatever you do, once we're in there, don't let go of each other."

He peered around the archway and saw that the furs were almost all loaded. He waited for Kayden to latch the wagon gate shut, then as soon as the cart driver started pushing the empty cart back toward the southern gate, Pozzi sprinted for the wagon.

He reached the wheel, its spokes twice the length of his body, and looked up. It was a long climb, and he'd have to make it quick. Keeva joined him, then Walnut.

"You're first," he said to the young rabbit and pushed Walnut up onto the first spoke.

The horse whinnied and stepped back. The wheel jolted, and Walnut's paws slid off the wood. He scrabbled, regained a pawhold, then pulled himself over the lip of the wagon bed and out of sight.

Walnut's brown head popped back up over the rim. He looked like he might be ill.

"Eyes on me, Walnut!" Pozzi hissed. "That's it! Don't breathe in, just keep your eyes on me!" Even from down here, in the rain, the smell of blood and fur made him glad they hadn't eaten since last night.

Pozzi cupped his paws together and helped Keeva up. He heard the groan of the wagon seat as the driver settled into it and knew they were running out of time.

Kayden unwound the reins from a hook at the front of the wagon. Keeva scrambled up from the spokes to the wheel rim, where Walnut reached out a paw to grasp hers. The young rabbit struggled to pull her heavier frame, but she managed a pawhold and pushed herself over.

Pozzi began to climb after her. They had to hurry, before the wagon started, before—

His back paw shot out from under him.

The rain had made the wheel slick, and before he could grab a spoke to steady himself he was on his back, the breath slammed from him, a shower of fire raining before his eyes.

When the fire dissipated, he looked up into Hassah's face. She reached out and hauled him up.

"What's going on back there?" They heard Kayden's annoyed voice from the wagon seat, then the groaning of wood as he dismounted.

Hassah gave Pozzi one final squeeze, then stepped up on the wheel's spoke. She took a moment to balance herself and then threw with both hands.

Pozzi hit the side of the wagon with a bruising blow, but the momentum was enough to topple him onto the pile within. He saw Keeva and Walnut an arm's length away, crouched against the wagon side, arms over their noses.

"Mistress Hassah?" Kayden barked from within his rain hood. "What're you doing here then? Where's your hat and coat?"

"I lost my ball."

"Well it's not here, Mistress," Kayden said, in a kindlier tone. "Now, your nurse should tell you not to play near wagons, understand? Especially in the rain. I nearly ran you over, I did."

"Yes, sir."

The wagon seat creaked as Kayden settled himself back in, and then a sharp crack sliced the air and the wagon jerked into motion. Pozzi clambered across the skins to Walnut and Keeva, who squeezed his paw as if she would never let go. Pozzi cautiously peered over the side of the wagon.

Hassah stood in the rain, hair wet and clinging, watching the wagon roll out the Nyatha manor gates. Pozzi's last view of the prison that had been their home was of this lone girl receding away from them.

No, not just a girl, he corrected himself.

A friend.

CHAPTER 38

$\mathcal{D}$espite being tightly strapped just behind the saddle, the cage still bounced and slid against the mare's hindquarters. Inside, Orjo and Father Oaks tried not to jostle each other in the tight space, each holding on to their side of the cage with clenched paws.

Ornox's retinue had left the Stone Forest and was keeping up a punishing pace south. Ornox only agreed to slow when the sweat flew off the horses like snow.

Father Oaks could feel the bruising in his bones. It was hard to believe things could have possibly gotten worse since the Child died. But worse it was. Instead of serving someone who genuinely seemed content to leave Theo alone, Oaks was now in a cage with a conniving muskrat. A muskrat who had not only divulged where Theo was, but was serving a warlord whose only goal seemed to be finding Theo and killing him.

As the horses slowed to a canter, and then to a panting walk, Oaks observed his companion, noting the closed eyes, the tangled mane. The shirt on his side rode up enough to reveal a healing scar.

"How did my grandson come to be with ye anyway?"

The muskrat didn't open his eyes. "He wanted to find the

Library of Elshon."

"And did ye?"

"No."

"So ye don't know where it is?"

"I do. But it's best if he doesn't find the Library. I did him a favor."

"Says who?"

"Says common sense."

"And so ye just abandoned him to fend fer himself." The old rabbit didn't hide his disgust.

The muskrat sighed and sat up, eyeing Father Oaks as if he were a fly that wouldn't go away. "I left him at the grasslands with a bear and a warrior. They'll protect him more than I could."

"So ye abandoned three folks, not just one."

"I'm not responsible for him."

"Is that how ye repay his saving yer life?"

Orjo considered the old rabbit. "What makes you think he saved my life?"

"I taught him to sew wounds, though he never did master it. I'd recognize that uneven pattern anywhere." The rabbit squinted. "Deep wound, by the looks of it."

The muskrat grunted in answer.

Father Oaks glanced at the soldiers, then lowered his voice. "Help me get out. We have t' find Theo and warn him."

"I agree to getting out. As to warning Theo, my answer's no. He's your grandson, not mine. And I wouldn't give my life up for my own grandson anyway."

"I see why ye've got lots of enemies and no friends."

"I don't need friends. I need you to stop talking."

"Ye're an island, is that what ye think?"

Orjo didn't bother answering.

Father Oaks made a derogatory sound. "All islands are connected underwater, ye know. Ye're not an island, ye're a mole. Blind and livin' in the dark."

* * *

THE HORSES SEEMED to instinctively find a narrow trail that ran along the forest's edge. After galloping hard across plains that Father Oaks had thought would never end, Ornox had reluctantly agreed to a slower pace to allow the horses to recover. Here where the forest grew, great towering figs practically blocked out the sun, and a strange birdsong that Father Oaks couldn't recognize echoed between the trees.

He peered into the forest. One could disappear in there. If one had the strength and younger legs. The old rabbit sighed, knowing he had neither, even if he could escape his prison.

"You don't want to run for it, rabbit. The birds in there hunt animals four times your size."

Father Oaks looked up. The tall Urzok rider on whose horse they rode had plaited, raven-black hair, which was pinned into a round crown on his head. In fact, everything about him was round. His face, his nose, even the fingertips that gripped the reins.

"I'll take birds over you lot," Father Oaks muttered.

Roundy gave a malicious chuckle. "These aren't just any birds. Proudfeathers weigh about as much as this horse here, and can carry one off too. Them feathers are worth something to make your eyes water."

"Why's that?"

"They're long and pure gold," Orjo cut in.

"Aye." Roundy grinned. "I seen one once. Like holding a shaft of sunlight in your hand."

Father Oaks squinted. "Like that?"

The rider looked over at where he was pointing and gave a low whistle. "By Blackhide."

Sitting in a high, crooked fig branch a stone's throw away was a bird the size of a large rabbit, busily trying to dislodge something from a tree. A sprout of gold feathers winked above its head.

"That's not so big," Father Oaks harrumphed.

"It's a juvenile." Roundy slowed his horse imperceptibly, and his voice had dropped low. "Even so, just one o' those feathers would buy a house and a plot o' land."

"Why don't you kill it?" Orjo suggested.

Oaks looked over at the muskrat. "What?"

But the muskrat ignored him, directing his words to Roundy. "You want to be a mercenary all your life, lad?"

The soldier's voice held an edge of defensiveness. "Nothing wrong with being a mercenary."

"Sure. But it's never going to buy you land and a house. Nothing risked nothing gained."

"Ye're a bloodthirsty bastard," Oaks said, repulsed.

The muskrat shrugged. "No. Just practical."

Roundy glanced up at the riders ahead, clearly torn.

"It's a juvenile. Can't fly fast." Orjo's tone was that of one debating the benefits of a hot or cold breakfast.

"That's why ye shouldn't kill it!" Father Oaks snapped.

"It's just a bird, you old toad." The muskrat smirked, then turned back to Roundy. "It's but a moment's business to take it down, and then you'll be rich as a fat man's stew. Your choice, but in my experience, successful men are those who recognize luck when it shows itself."

The muskrat leaned back and closed his eyes, nonchalant. The man glanced at his companions pulling further ahead of him, then seemed to make a decision. He unslung his bow and reached toward the quiver hanging at his horse's withers.

Roundy gripped one of the arrows, and glanced back at the bird. It was still in the tree, trying to free something from a hollow.

In one smooth movement, Roundy had his arrow in his bow and let it fly.

The juvenile fell to the ground with a cry of pain, and Roundy whooped in triumph. A few of the Urzoks ahead of him turned at the sound, curious, as Roundy spurred his horse into the trees.

Another cry came from the injured bird, and all at once the forest seemed alive with bird calls. Angry, screeching bird calls. Clearly, the juvenile was not alone.

Roundy hadn't even reached the fig tree where his quarry had fallen before a dozen giant Proudfeathers, dwarfing the injured juvenile, descended on Roundy and his passengers, tearing at the horse and rider with talons as long as Father Oaks' arm. Roundy jerked his horse first one way and then another, yelling for help as he tried to free his sword and fight back.

One of the birds, a large male with a snowy white head, shouted, "Go! Help Nyra!"

Two of Roundy's attackers flew off in the juvenile's direction. Oaks and Orjo crashed into each other as Roundy's horse reared, trying to avoid the beaks of the white-headed Proudfeather and his companions.

Then the world was tipping, and Father Oaks found his face pushed painfully against the cage as Orjo fell on top of him.

"Get off o' me!"

Father Oaks tried to breathe from under Orjo's suffocating weight. The horse must have fallen to its side. He tried to make sense of Roundy's screams, the clanging of metal, the flapping of wings, and the thunder of horses' hooves approaching as Roundy's companions rushed to his defense. Oaks was able to extricate his head from under Orjo and saw weapons flash as Ornox's men began attacking the Proudfeathers. Oaks saw the white-headed one take a blow to the wing and fall, as the rest of the birds were forced to retreat, taking their injured juvenile with them.

Then the ground and trees ripped away from Father Oaks, as Roundy's horse found its feet. Its movement threw the rabbit back against the other side of the cage, along with Orjo, as the horse, now riderless, bolted into the forest with the two prisoners still strapped to it.

CHAPTER 39

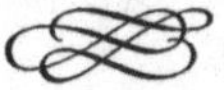

Ornox stepped on the dead bird's wing and pulled his sword from its broad back. It was a large male, a giant of a bird, its crushed and ripped crown feathers spread in a halo of gold and blood around its milk-white head. Its eye, angry even in death, stared sightlessly up at Ornox.

The warlord looked up as Yod pushed a man forward through the other soldiers. Ornox hadn't lost any men, fortunately, though the first half dozen to the fray had some new gouges in their faces and arms courtesy of the flock of Proudfeathers. All of the birds had fled once they had realized they were outnumbered—all except this large, white-headed male that Ornox had brought down himself.

The soldier kneeling before him was neither old nor young, but Ornox vaguely remembered choosing him out of Ghazan's garrison at Nyatha. He was on the plump side, which Ornox disapproved of, but he had scars that proved he had seen battle and could shoot a target three out of three from impressive distances.

Ornox bent over, picked up the three crushed feathers, and held them up against the light. Even bent and broken, they caught the sun's rays and shimmered, each wispy barb like a tendril of molten gold. "Do I not pay you enough, soldier?"

"I'm sorry, my lord. It was foolish. I was just— It was the muskrat. He said—"

"Such a light thing to carry such a heavy price." Ornox hefted the feathers, then let them waft to the ground as he reached for his sword.

"My lord, please, I—"

A flash of metal, and a dull thud cut his words short. The man's head rolled gently against the bird's wing, the blood mingling with the crown feathers. The body fell to the forest floor, loud as a crash in the silence that had fallen over the remaining men.

"If you want it so badly, you shall have it." Ornox bent down and tucked the feathers, quill first, into the dead man's belt. He stood, and looked over the other soldiers.

"Who else would like one of these feathers? Go on, there are three for the taking."

No one moved or spoke.

"Good." Ornox wiped his sword against the soldier's shirt. "Now, find me those two vermin."

* * *

THE MARE CRASHED through the forest like a wild thing, and Oaks was sure all his bones would break before she was done.

Something hard and heavy—one of the low-hanging tree branches, Oaks guessed—cracked against the cage with bruising force, and they were flying, cage and all, through the air.

"Hold on to something!"

He heard Orjo's warning, but before he could get his bearings, they came down hard against a rock. Oaks felt a sharp pain in his shoulder, then he was rolling head over backside down a rough hill. When they came to an abrupt, whiplashing stop, the old rabbit's head was reeling, and his body was nothing but pain.

But pain meant life. He wasn't dead. And neither was Orjo, judging by the movement on top of him. Oaks groaned as a great weight lifted off him, then coughed uncontrollably as his lungs and ribs creaked their way back into place.

"Move over. You're on the broken part."

Broken part? He felt like all his parts were broken. Paws pushed at him, making his bruised sides scream. "Stop it, ye bastard!"

The muskrat sat back on his haunches, impatient. "The cage has to have split somewhere, I need you to move so I can check under you."

Father Oaks closed his eyes. "What happened to bein' an island? Not needin' anyone to do anything?"

"If you won't move, I'll kill you and move you myself."

"That might be a blessing, actually."

"Is that your final choice?"

Father Oaks forced his limbs to obey and sat up. Pain shot through his skull, and for an instant, his eyes dimmed. Orjo pushed him roughly aside and began pulling at the cage slats.

Oaks looked around. They seemed to have fallen down a dried ravine of rocks, moss, and broken tree limbs. The fig trees towered above them on either side, and there was neither sight nor sound of the mare.

Oaks gingerly felt his limbs, his head. The gods had somehow spared him broken bones, if not some terrible cuts, bruises, and knocks. And a fair bellyful of anger.

"Was that yer way of escaping?"

"It worked, didn't it?"

Orjo gave up on breaking the cage slat. He cast about, searching. A nasty gash above the ear was matting his mane with blood, but otherwise, it seemed Oaks had taken all the knocks and left the muskrat nearly unscathed. Orjo reached through the bars and grasped a rock.

"We're still in a cage," the old rabbit griped.

"Not for long. If you'd help, we might get out even sooner."

Orjo took a swing against one of the weakened slats, but the close quarters meant he couldn't bring much of his arm into it. The cage bars were made of toughened yew, and the metal lock, though scratched, had survived better than either of the occupants.

Orjo tossed the rock away and searched for another. He stretched his arm out and rummaged until he found one with a sharp edge, then began smashing the edge against the bars.

A sharp crack of wood echoed through the ravine. Encouraged, Orjo began striking harder.

Crack.

Crack.

"Nearly there."

The sound was giving Oaks a headache, and he wished he could just stay in the cage and rest, if it meant peace.

Crack.

Crack.

A shadow blocked the sun, making Oaks look up.

"Oh gods." The words were barely out of his mouth before a gust of air nearly knocked Oaks over. A giant Proudfeather with a crown of golden feathers descended on them, its giant talons closing around the cage top.

Orjo was about to bring his rock against the talon when the Proudfeather screeched and hauled the cage, occupants and all, into the air. Both the muskrat and rabbit lost their footing, the rock tumbling out of Orjo's paw as they flew up and away.

Everything spun in a dizzying kaleidoscope of trees and sky as the cage swung with the bird's darts and turns. Then Father Oaks felt a jolt as the cage was dropped onto something solid. Something motionless, thankfully.

He was almost too tired and battered to do anything but lie there—when had he gotten so *old?*—but he forced himself to try to sit up. And look.

Orjo was already on his feet—that's what came with immortality, Oaks supposed. They were in the crook of a giant fig, crook being more like a large basin. Oaks sensed, before he saw, the dozen or so great giant birds perched in the branches around them, like hulking guardians of the sky. Some were tending their wounds, others were murmuring among themselves, their talk punctuated by the occasional soft sob.

"Sister, I brought you something to eat," said the bird who had hauled them here. She was large, Oaks saw, her head and fine gold crown feathers towering over many of the others.

Oaks looked at who the bird was speaking to and saw the juvenile Roundy had tried to kill, its neck feathers specked with blood. Another large Proudfeather, wearing a stone necklace, perched on the edge of the basin, anxiously fussing over the juvenile.

"It hurts too much, Irah," the small Proudfeather complained to her sister.

The one called Irah pinned Orjo to the tree with one giant claw. The muskrat fought, but Oaks could see it was like fighting a metal vice. "You must eat, Sister."

The one with the necklace bobbed her head. "Irah's right. You need strength to heal, Nyra."

"You don't want to eat us," Orjo said, calm.

"Talk won't fill a belly," a large male in the trees nearby argued. He hopped to a lower branch and addressed the wounded Proudfeather. "Eat, Nyra."

"Stop!" Orjo said, more urgently this time. He pointed at Father Oaks, who was still sitting winded on the platform. "He can heal her. Nyra, is it?"

The large Proudfeather with the necklace looked toward Oaks. "Is this true? You can save my daughter?"

"He's a healer. Look!" Orjo pulled his torn shirt open to display his wound. "This is his work." At the large male bird's unimpressed look, Orjo continued, "This is actually his grandson's work. The old one's much more skilled than Theo."

"Theo?" The juvenile raised her head. "Theo Griffinrider?"

"Do you know any other?" Orjo indicated the old rabbit. "This is his grandfather, Oaks."

The juvenile turned to Irah, earnest. "Let him go! He's Theo's family!"

The tall Proudfeather hesitated, then stepped back from Father Oaks. "If he's Theo's grandfather, who are you?"

At Irah's question all eyes bore down on Orjo, and the tall birds shifted forward to hear his answer. "Are you Theo's family too?"

"I'm a friend," Orjo said smoothly.

"Is that true?" This time, the young bird's question to Oaks drew all eyes to the rabbit.

Everyone waited. The old rabbit and the muskrat shared a look. Oaks could see the tension in Orjo's mouth.

"Theo saved his life," Oaks said quietly. "Which means they're friends. Isn't that so, Orjo?"

Orjo nodded.

The tall bird, Irah, turned to Oaks, eyes hopeful. "So we ask again. Can you heal my sister?"

"I'll have t' see. But I'll do my best."

CHAPTER 40

As they neared the fringes of Jaipri Forest, Brune made attempts at banter, knowing Indigo was skittish about entering the jungle home of Mankahar's giant serpents. But when his jests seemed only to make her more nervous, he gave up and simply hummed instead.

By the second day, they had progressed deep into the forest of towering yamba and fig trees, and Theo felt, rather than saw, eyes on them everywhere. Eventually, he caught glimpses of the serpents camouflaged in the boughs above them. Their browns and greens and scarlets mixed with the forest canopy, their scales occasionally whispering against the bark. He had a memory of the last time he and Brune had been in Jaipri Forest. The trees and foliage still looked pristine and untouched by the outside world, a haven from the war beyond its borders.

"May Aktu go with you," Brune called out when they reached a clearing ringed by moss-clad yews. "We come as friends of Queen Mercusa and her brother, Commander Lyusa."

A long serpent, its body as thick as Theo's torso, detached from the gnarled wingfruit tree just in front of them. His scales were shot through with gray, as if he had crawled through ashfall, and his eyes were black and brittle.

"Greetings," Brune dipped his head. "I am Brune of Hegg, Messenger from the Order, and this is—"

"We know who you are," the ashen serpent's voice held no welcome. "Jaipri is neutral, but we do not shelter omatjes."

A dozen serpents descended then, like a curtain of scales and hisses that spread in a ring around them.

Brune and Indigo instinctively took defensive stances, and Theo wondered if they had made a mistake coming back here. He had not been entirely welcome last time either. Each of the serpents was twice Brune's length or longer, and as thick as the bear's arm. They were designed to squeeze the breath out of prey four times their size. There was a good reason the Urzoks left Jaipri Forest untouched.

"We are not here to speak of war," Brune said evenly. "We are here to see the queen."

The ash-flecked serpent coiled his tail and regarded them for a moment, assessing. He motioned to the other serpents with a jerk of the head. They disappeared back into the trees, as if they had never been.

"Come then."

They followed Ash through the thick forest, on a path that only the serpent seemed to see.

"We're well liked," Indigo commented to Theo. "Good thing we didn't bring Orjo as well."

They heard the sound of rushing water and broke out of the trees onto a rocky cliff that cut straight down into a river. Its width was at least twenty times Ash's length, and the drop was longer. Two thick tree trunks lashed together served as a rough bridge across the chasm, with no rails or pawholds.

"Are you coming or not?"

Ash was already halfway across, and Theo realized he was standing frozen at the start of the bridge. Indigo and Brune were already a quarter of the way across, following the serpent, who coiled like a corkscrew around the trunk bridge.

Theo released a lungful of air he hadn't realized he'd been

holding in and forced himself to breathe. He took a step, trying not to look down at the waters far below.

"Keep going!"

He saw Indigo in front of him, encouraging. Suddenly, he didn't feel as high up, and the tree trunks, he noticed then, were thick, sturdy beneath his paws. They didn't even bounce under Brune's weight. Theo took a step, then another, until he was all the way across. Once safely on the other side, he couldn't resist looking down over the edge at the brisk river below. A shudder passed through him.

They walked in silence, making their way through dense jungle until they broke through a tangle of giant fronds.

Theo stared, the memories seeping back. Everything looked the way he remembered—the palace set into the hill, the miniature red-furred, monkey-like creatures known as Grodlyns scurrying at various tasks, the yawning stone gates that led into the labyrinth underground den of the giant serpents.

"Come," Ash commanded.

"Just remember, they hate me more than they want to eat you," Theo reassured Indigo.

"That's not comforting," she said.

They followed Brune and Ash through the carved-sandstone gate marking Jaipri's outer palace. Here, the large tunnels were wide enough to accommodate five serpents abreast and tall enough to allow for a complex network of walkways overhead, where the miniature Grodlyns scurried back and forth on various errands. The tunnels soon began a sharp descent into the earth. Several other serpents slid by, all of them staring at the rabbit with open curiosity—all wary, some hostile.

Ash increased his pace, and the din of Grodlyns and serpents moving along the passageways had grown so much in the underground space, that it was hard to be heard. Theo tried to ignore the stares, the whispered conversations as a crowd began to gather and follow.

Knots that had started when they first entered the forest now doubled and tightened within his stomach. He remembered the funeral for Brune's brother, the suspicion the head Grodlyn had shown toward him, and the wondrous, abandoned underground palace to which Commander Lyusa had taken him. He tried to focus on this. This was why he had come. For the underground palace.

They turned several corners, crossed numerous outer chambers where serpents and Grodlyns alike slowed or stopped to watch them pass. At one archway, their guide conferred with a serpent with a green jewel affixed to the flat part of his head. Theo remembered that jewels denoted rank, but couldn't remember which colors were for which level.

The green jeweled serpent nodded and jutted his head to the right before disappearing into a side archway crowded with onlookers.

"This way," their surly guide said, muscling his way through the crowd. Theo followed and realized that although he was pressed from every side by giant, scaly serpents, he was not nearly as discomfited by their carnivorous natures as by their naked fear and suspicion.

Ash pushed aside a feathered curtain and motioned for them to follow. They entered a generously sized chamber decorated in cushions and low tables around the perimeter.

"Wait here," the serpent said, then slid out. Indigo looked relieved at having some space from the giant snakes.

Brune gave them a reassuring smile. "Commander Lyusa and I are old friends. We won't come to harm while he's here."

The curtain parted, and a Grodlyn wearing a floor-length robe entered.

Theo tensed. Eluk, head of the Grodlyns and royal chamberlain to the queen of Jaipri, had the same narrowed eyes, the same wrinkled, black nose, and the same posture that made Theo think of a large rat with reddish fur. A large, ill-tempered rat.

"Welcome, Brune of Hegg. And you have brought back Teo of the Forgotten Lands," the Grodlyn said, in a tone that was more reprimand than welcome. Theo didn't bother correcting the pronunciation of his name. Something told him that the queen's chamberlain had deliberately mispronounced it.

"Hello, Eluk." Theo would have to try his best to be polite.

"We'd like to speak with the queen and Lyusa," Brune said.

Eluk bowed, stiff. "I'll relay your message."

"This isn't an invitation to a honey-tasting that we can just pass on," the bear said. "We need to see the queen. Now, if possible."

Eluk scowled but directed his gaze at Theo. "Jaipri does not welcome omatjes."

"I know your stance on omatjes," Theo said. "But Jaipri may have the key to defeating the Urzoks."

This seemed to only deepen Eluk's hostility. "If so, it puts Jaipri in danger. Our neutrality is what keeps us safe."

"It won't forever," Brune growled. "Come now, Chamberlain, you have a duty to let Lyusa and the queen know we're here."

"My only duty is to keep Jaipri safe," Eluk shot back, pushing his arms further into his wide sleeves.

The curtain parted again, and a serpent with skin the color of malachite slid through. The old commander had aged so much that Theo nearly didn't recognize him, if not for the stubborn spark in the eyes—faded but not extinguished.

"Commander Lyusa! You look younger every time I see you," Brune said fondly.

"Ha! Liar. It's a wonder I still have my teeth." The commander looked at them each in turn. "I thought I'd misheard when someone said you were here. And look, it really is you, young Theo." The serpent's tongue flicked in a genuinely pleased hiss. "Of the Forgotten Lands, but certainly not forgotten. And this must be Princess Indigo?"

"Theo is an omatje," Eluk hissed.

Lyusa looked at him, amused. "Yes, everyone with ears has heard. But he is still a guest." He turned to Theo. "Forgive our chamberlain. I want to hear all about the battle at Ralgayan and what brings you back to Jaipri."

The commander led them out and through meandering passages until they reached a wide dining hall. Here, a row of bore holes in the ceiling allowed sunlight in, illuminating a low wooden table in the middle, flanked by multi-colored cushions. At the sound of their approach, a Grodlyn with his mane tied in two tight braids appeared from the doorway. He nodded to Lyusa and Eluk before disappearing back through the doorway, shouting orders.

"Sit down, sit down," Lyusa said, motioning at the cushions with his tail. Indigo followed Brune's example and sat. Theo took the cushion next to her. The chamberlain kept a respectful distance, seating himself at the end of the table.

"The queen will be with us soon, but you must be hungry," Lyusa said.

Before long, a troupe of Grodlyns streamed in from the doorway, bearing generous platters of roasted yamba, an assortment of pickled mushrooms, sliced taro fried in nut oil and sugar, and tubes of elderberry wine, which they poured into everyone's goblets.

"Thank you for the welcome," Brune said. "I'm afraid we're here to ask for your help. Again."

"Jaipri is neutral," Eluk said. "We made that clear when you were last here."

Lyusa smiled. "Eluk is one of our greatest assets but notoriously prickly, and defensive of Jaipri. Some might say to a fault. If we can help, without breaking our rule of joining in war, then we will."

The dining curtain parted. A serpent with interlocking amber-and-wine-colored scales entered, a ring of feathers encircling her neck. But it was her bearing, the look of quiet command in her eyes, that gave her away as queen much more than any elaborate accessory.

"Ah! My sister, Mercusa," Lyusa said. "You know most of those here. Except for the princess of Alvareth, Indigo."

The queen nodded. "Welcome." Her voice was as smooth as Lyusa's was rough. The only indication that they were related was the dark banding around their tails. "I do indeed know most here. Everyone knows about the Griffinrider of Ralgayan, no?"

"Your Majesty, I never rode—"

"Don't tell the empire that," the queen said with a quiet laugh. "They fear the one who commanded the griffin! And it's about time the Urzoks were afraid of something." She turned to the bear. "It's good to see you again, Brune of Hegg. And I finally have the pleasure of meeting the famed warrior of Alvareth, Princess Indigo."

The rabbit bowed her head, touching it with one paw. "It is I who have the pleasure of meeting you, Queen Mercusa. Kuno had the greatest respect for you."

At Kuno's name the mood dampened.

"My brother would not want us to mope about him." Brune gruffly broke the silence, raising a goblet of elderberry wine. "A toast! To friends and to the queen's health."

Everyone raised their cups and toasted.

"Now," Lyusa said, motioning for a server to refill their plates, "How can Jaipri be of service?"

"We seek the Library of Elshon," Theo explained.

He felt the queen's and Lyusa's full attention shift to him. If they were surprised, they didn't show it.

"I'm sorry, Theo, but what does that have to do with Jaipri?" the queen asked.

Theo instinctively reached for his vest pocket before remembering the book was gone. "We found Orjo the Terrible, who had a copy of the *Songs of Calgornan*. One of the songs talks about Elshon being underneath Jaipri."

"You came all the way here because of some caught words?" Eluk said, incredulous.

"And because of the book Commander Lyusa gave me."

At this, the queen and Eluk looked surprised, and the old commander cleared his throat. "The old palace below has bits and pieces of artifacts from days long gone. The book was one such relic."

"I believe the Library is in the old palace, under us," Theo said.

"Your Majesty, we cannot allow this," Eluk protested. "Griffinrider or no, he is an omatje, and worse, he's wanted by the empire and every bounty hunter alive. I strongly advise we ask them to leave Jaipri. Now."

"The Library holds a great weapon," Theo countered.

"Possibly the secret to defeating the empire," Brune added. "We're not asking you to join a side, we're asking that you allow us to find the Library."

The queen shared a look with her brother and chamberlain.

"It is not going to war, Eluk. It does not break our rules."

The Grodlyn scowled. "Three days. No more."

Indigo frowned. "That's hardly much time."

"Those are the terms we must have, my queen," Eluk insisted. "How long will it take for word to spread that Theo is here? How long will we risk Jaipri so that this omatje can find the fabled Library? Which may or may not exist?"

Mercusa looked back at Theo, Brune, and Indigo. "We will give what help we can, but my chamberlain has a point. We will grant you three days to find the Library. And after that, I'm afraid you must leave."

CHAPTER 41

Ornox dismounted from his charger and picked up the broken piece of wood that lay wedged between two boulders by the ravine's edge. The mare's tracks clearly led here, and this wood was certainly from the cage. But where was the cage? If the rabbit and muskrat had gotten out, why were there no paw prints? He and the dozen men he had with him had combed the nearby area and found no telltale fur in the undergrowth, no clue to where the two prisoners could have gone.

A cold trail. As if they had disappeared, cage and all, into thin air.

He was about to order his men into the trees, to see whether they could see any signs of the fugitives in the surrounding forest, when Yod appeared on his horse from between the fig trees. Ornox had split his men into three groups to cover more ground, and Yod would only be here if he had news. Yod dismounted before the horse had stopped and hurried over.

"My Lord, we found the rabbit."

"About time. And the muskrat?"

Yod shook his head. "Not the old rabbit, my lord. The one called Theo."

Ornox's pulse quickened.

"Go on."

"Travelers from Doria said there was a garrison killed some days ago, just outside Doria. Killed by a bear and two rabbits with a man."

"They escaped?"

Yod nodded. "So they say. But the travelers don't know anything more."

"Gather the men. We're leaving for Doria."

"And the muskrat?"

Ornox glanced at the trees. "The birds and foxes can have them, now that we have a lead on Theo."

* * *

THOUGH THE IMPERIAL troops had been trying to tamp down the rumors in Doria, it had been quick work for Ornox to learn the story being repeated and embellished on every street corner. Every vendor and beer slinger in the city could talk of little else besides the garrison that had been decimated just half a day's journey outside the city's western gates.

Ornox had wasted little time finding the spot himself. Blood and a fresh grave near a spreading tree marked where the skirmish had taken place. He had carefully examined the ground, forcing himself to take his time and not give in to impatience. Hastiness now would lead to potentially costly mistakes. The area had been trampled and combed over multiple times already. Ornox recognized the distinct horseshoe shape that was issued to imperial guards. No doubt the empire's forces had returned here trying to track the beasts. Those hoof prints told a story of the troops circling the area, disturbing many of the prints, before galloping off in pursuit of tracks that went directly north.

Ornox frowned. Clearly, the imperial guards thought the rabbits and bear had gone north, with a horse. But a horse couldn't carry a fully grown bear.

He walked carefully around the perimeter of the area,

searching. When he didn't see anything obvious, he circled again.

He finally found what he was looking for in a patch of crushed grass and mud, and squatted down. He examined the large indent with the five toes and claws, its breadth almost double the width of his own hand. The bear. The bear was a servant of the Order, and the Order had chosen the rabbits. The bear was duty-bound to protect the rabbits, no matter what. Where the rabbits went, the bear would follow.

"Look for bear prints," he commanded. His men immediately obeyed, dismounting and bending over the dirt.

"Here, Lord Ornox!"

It was Broken Nose. Ornox walked over and examined the prints, smudged and incomplete, but definitely those of a bear. There were no rabbit prints, which meant they were riding the bear to make faster time.

Ornox mounted his horse. "We head west." Excitement flared in him, and he recognized the feeling as one he hadn't had in a long time. He was gaining on his prey.

CHAPTER 42

Oaks pulled the last stitch into place and broke the end of the thread. "There ye are. Done."

The patient looked relieved, as did the matriarch, Hygra, who touched her head against her daughter's. They were in what Father Oaks had learned was the Matriarch's Nest, a giant architectural feat that spread between four branches of one of the oldest figs in the forest. It was larger than Father Oaks' entire home and could comfortably fit two giant Proudfeathers.

"Ye don't want to fly today, or ye'll open it back up. But by tomorrow, ye'll want to be on yer feet, and day after that, ye can start making short flights."

"You have my gratitude," the older Proudfeather said. "We'll do what we can to help you find your grandson."

Oaks nodded. "Thank ye. And ye're sure they're not in Doria anymore?"

"Positive." Nyra moved her crown feathers up and down. "All anyone can talk about in these parts is how that garrison got killed on the road out of Doria by two rabbits and a bear."

"Ye said they're headed to… What was that name again?"

"Jaipri. About two days' flight."

Oaks calculated. That probably meant a five-day walk from Doria. If you were young. He'd be lucky to make it in ten.

"It's much to ask, Hygra, but—"

"Of course we'll take you there. I'll see to it personally."

"You will?"

"He says I'll be better tomorrow. Can I take him, Mother?"

"No."

"Please!" Nyra begged. "Irah can come with me."

Hygra's head feathers stood up. "The answer is no."

"You never let me go beyond the forest."

"With good reason!" Hygra said, stern. "We've lost a member of our family already, I'll not have you be the second. You have never obeyed me before, but you will obey me today. Is that clear?"

Something in the mother's tone seemed to let Nyra know that there was no negotiating or sweet talking her way to winning this argument. The youngster nodded, meek.

Hygra lay down and let Oaks climb gingerly onto her back. His old and battered body still protested at every little exertion. Once he had a secure grip, she launched off the branch, quickly clearing the canopy. She landed on a wide platform with a view of the trees, where Orjo sat looking out over the horizon.

Oaks slid down with a grunt and a wince. The bruises from the ride through the forest, he knew, would take days to leave him.

"I'll be back to pick you both up once I've made arrangements for Nyra's care," the matriarch bird said.

Orjo looked over. "Thank you, but I won't be going."

Oaks wasn't surprised, but Hygra cocked her head. "Where will you go then?"

Orjo pointed to the distance, over the treetops toward a bank of clouds that drifted across a rose-hued horizon. "It's not far to the Bay of Bhenkar. Lot of islands that are perfect for a muskrat like me."

Hygra looked toward where he was pointing. "That's not a short journey. I'll have my daughter Irah take you."

Orjo regarded her, seemingly debating this generosity, then nodded his acceptance.

"I'll let her know." Hygra flew off from the branch and disappeared into the canopy.

Oaks hobbled over to Orjo and debated about sitting. Getting up and down was a pain now that he was black and blue. In the end, he decided he was too tired to stand. He lowered himself next to Orjo.

"Funny," Father Oaks said. "I thought ye meant what ye said about bein' Theo's friend."

The muskrat looked at him. "You and your grandson are very alike."

"I hope so."

"That wasn't a compliment."

"I know that. But yer ideas about good and bad are like a weathervane. Ye always know which way the wind's blowin', but ye'll never find yer way home."

Orjo looked over at him, assessing. "Good luck, Oaks," he said finally. "I hope you find Theo."

The old rabbit nodded, grim. "Goodbye, Orjo. I'd say take care of yerself, but I know ye don't need me to tell ye that."

CHAPTER 43

The queen assigned Theo and his team two dozen Grodlyns with mops and water to clean the grime off the surfaces of the underground palace. The torches the Grodlyns had lit and mounted on the walls showed chambers and halls of dusty mosaic, much of the design so hidden by dust and cobwebs that one could barely see what the original artist's intent was.

Likewise, much of the floor had been overgrown with vines and fungi, spots of damp mold blooming in corners where moisture pooled from cracks in the ceiling. Grodlyns bearing long hacking blades, brooms, and gloves got to work alongside Indigo and Theo, and with Brune's brute strength helping clear the vines, they sent the resident beetles and spiders scurrying for new shelter. By late afternoon, they had cleared the floor, revealing a faded but intact central mosaic of interlocking serpents.

The Grodlyns worked quickly, if loudly, keeping up a lively chatter until their water buckets ran black with mold. Eluk watched all this with proud disapproval, but just as Mercusa promised them, never interfered. When the last of the cleaning and vine clearing was done, he ushered the Grodlyns out to give

Indigo, Brune, and Theo space to study the walls and pillars of the main chamber.

The bear and rabbits stood in silence for a while, taking in the vivid hues and pictures around them. One wall showed a street scene, with youngsters holding books, booksellers hawking wares, papermakers rolling out their sheets of pulp to be cut into swathes and bound. In the middle of it all was a grand, circular building with pillars and multiple floors. Theo had been so overwhelmed the first time Lyusa had brought him here, he hadn't even noticed this painting beneath the dirt that time had layered on it. But now, he was sure it was a painting of the Library of Elshon.

He reached out to touch the wall. It felt cool, secretive.

"What are we looking for, exactly?" Brune peered skeptically at the cleaned walls.

"Anything that looks like a secret door, a hollow space." Theo tapped on one wall. Solid.

He stood back to take in the painting of the Library, admiring how grand and large it must have been. He noted its great domed ceiling, its pillars of veined white marble. How many books had such a vast space held? It was enough to confound the sharpest mind.

"What are they doing?"

Indigo was examining the opposite wall, which seemed to depict the inside of a library. Various beasts in multi-hued robes sat at long tables and benches beneath the domed roof, reading books of various sizes. Some studied maps; others browsed shelves or took notes with long tapered quills.

He saw the murals through her eyes, the activities depicted here as strange to her as they were wondrous to him.

"They're taking knowledge with them," he explained, pointing. "With Aktu's Language, they didn't have to memorize messages or songs or knowledge. They could simply copy it, then pass it on to others, or save it for themselves to relearn later."

"Were there ever any books about swordplay?" she asked.

"Lyusa said the Library of Elshon had mountains of books about every subject you could imagine. The stars, the weather, medicine, plants, history."

Brune shook dust from his coat. "Well, whatever this weapon is, I say we find it and give the Urzoks a thrashing they won't forget."

The bear was right. Time was not favoring them.

"If we want to cover all three levels in three days," Indigo pointed out, "we'll need to have a system. Make sure we look over every tile."

"Perhaps we should first walk through the entire palace," Theo suggested. "From the bottom up, and count how many chambers we need to cover."

The bear nodded. "A sound idea."

They descended to the lowest level, to the furthermost chamber, and worked their way up. Each level had a main hall large enough to seat at least two hundred souls, with six hallways each branching off to six chambers. Indigo used a knife to mark a spare torch she carried with her, making a slash for each chamber they counted.

By the time they had returned to the main chamber where they had started, both the princess and the bear looked grim.

"That's fifty-two rooms, if you count the hallways." Indigo frowned at the torch in her paws and put her knife away.

"We'll be lucky to cover it in six days, let alone three," Brune commented.

Theo said, "I want to walk through again."

"We all counted; it's fifty-two," Indigo said.

"It's not about the numbers." Theo glanced around him at the walls, then started his way back down. "It's about the art." At their questioning looks, he added, "Do you remember if any of the other walls showed word catching?"

They walked the old palace again. This time, they checked each and every wall for any depictions of books, paper, ink making, or the Library. Theo felt his excitement mount as they made their way up, until they were back in the main chamber.

"So this is the only hall with word catching." Brune gazed around them at the vast space. "What do you think that means?"

"It means that if there's a passage to the Library, it's likely in this main room." Theo lit any dormant torch he could find, until the great chamber was ablaze with firelight. All the paintings seemed to leap out at them in vibrant yellows and reds, kingfisher blues and purples. "Think about it. If you wanted to leave a clue as to where the entrance was, wouldn't it make sense to have it in the one room that referenced word catching?"

Indigo nodded. "Then let's start here."

She and the bear spread out to opposite ends of the hall, leaving Theo to study the walls in the center. He stepped over the odd remaining vine as he walked, his paws scouring the murals for any clue of where there might be a keyhole or a false wall. He felt and prodded, pushed and pulled. After a time, his paws tingled and grew raw from feeling every uneven tile, every raised bit of stone.

He stepped back, forcing himself to ignore his frustration. He surveyed the murals afresh, letting his eyes take in all the details about papermaking, bookselling, ink grinding. He looked back at the opposite wall, at the painting that seemed to show the inside of the Library with the endless shelves of books and maps, the calm, silent patrons bent over their tomes in their frozen quests for knowledge.

Where are you? Theo asked silently.

The Library had to be here somewhere. It had to.

CHAPTER 44

The forest seemed impossibly far now that they were outside Nyatha. Walls that had always been a barrier to freedom now seemed protective, reassuring even, compared to the wide, unfamiliar expanse of the fields beyond. Even with the full moon, the tree line bordering the patchwork of newly planted barley and rye around Nyatha looked dark and ominous from the open ground, rather than silver and beckoning, as it had from Hassah's window.

Pozzi saw Keeva shiver and flatten her ears to her head to keep warm. As Hassah's pets, they hadn't been let out at night since they'd arrived at Nyatha, which meant they were unused to the sounds and cold of night, and being naked didn't help.

They had stayed hidden in the wagon until they were past the gates of Nyatha and out on the road. For a long time, they didn't dare look over the lip of the wagon bed, and suffered the reek of the skins in silence. At last, Pozzi had peered over the edge and kept watch, trying to find a good place to jump out and hide. The road into and out of Nyatha's gate was too busy for a league or so, until they had turned a corner and Pozzi spotted the overturned crate. They waited for a lull in the traffic of ox carts and horses on the road, then Walnut had leapt first, followed by Keeva and Pozzi. They had dashed to the abandoned crate, no doubt fallen from one of the myriad supply wagons that traveled this route, and hidden there until nightfall, when all Urzoks were safely in their homes and the windows at Nyatha glowed and winked.

Only when the sun had disappeared, pulling the last of dusk with it, had they emerged and begun to backtrack around Nyatha toward the Redwood Forest.

"How much longer?" Walnut whispered. He kept sneaking glances back at Nyatha, in case the dogs were on their scent. Pozzi wondered how Hassah had explained the disappearance of her pets, and whether she would tell her father the truth. He didn't think so.

"We should reach it before the moon hits the treetops," Pozzi replied. He hoped that Argasar was still there, that he had kept the rabbits safe as promised. That he would keep them safe, show them how to survive in the forest. And then...and then what, exactly?

He didn't really want to think about what came after. Would they have to hide in the forest forever? They couldn't go home to Willago, for Willago was a burned-out shell, there was nothing there for them. They'd have to earn their freedom, and then see what the gods had in store. There was no other choice.

Pozzi's limbs started to go numb from the walking and the cold, and his breath was already labored. He'd never been terribly fit, but when had he gotten so useless? Keeva was feeling it as well, he could see, though she kept any complaints to herself. Walnut seemed the only one with unflagging energy, despite most of it being nervous.

They rested for a spell behind a tree stump that had evidently been so deep rooted the farmers here had given up claiming its space, leaving it to brood like a ghost. The rabbits ate a discarded apple core they had found by the side of the road. Pozzi gave up his share, insisting Keeva and Walnut have it. As soon as they finished, they struck out again, eager to reach the protection of the trees.

The deeper shadows of the arching redwood branches had barely touched their heads when Pozzi had the uncomfortable feeling they were being watched. Every paw fall and every breath sounded loud here. He tried to ignore how dry his throat was and be grateful that at least they weren't visible from Nyatha.

He was sure, however, that they were visible to someone in the shadows. But no matter how hard he listened, or which way he turned, he couldn't hear or see any threats. They struggled through thicker and thicker brush, trying to feel their way here where the moon's beams hardly penetrated.

Something landed on Pozzi's shoulder, and he jumped. A night beetle scuttled away, its iridescent underwings flashing briefly before it melted back into darkness.

He chuckled, more to cheer Keeva and Walnut than from any genuine mirth. "Been a pet so long, I'm afraid of bugs now."

But the expression on Walnut's face made the fur on Pozzi's neck twitch. And then he felt it—a rush of air above, like the sigh of some giant beast. What was most eerie was not the sensation, but that it was absolutely silent. Some primal instinct made Pozzi dive to ground and run on all fours as he never had.

A scream came, but it wasn't his, despite the searing pain that blossomed on his lower back above the tail. Something large and heavy landed behind him, so close he could hear the whisper of feathers. He scrambled for a weapon, anything, for the beast was almost on him. His paws found nothing but the ground, and this he grabbed. He twisted around and threw his pitiful collection of dirt and leaves into his attacker's face.

All he saw was orange. Fiery orange pools embedded in feathers. And then a beak. Sharp, open, lethal. Everything whittled into focus, and time slowed. Just enough so Pozzi could wonder at it all, could see that the next few moments were so beyond his control that it didn't make sense to be afraid.

Something smashed into his attacker's face, and the bird stumbled off him, stunned. Keeva, holding a thick branch in both paws, stood panting, trying to heft the weapon and deal another blow. Walnut rushed over to help, but Pozzi waved a paw at him.

"Get back, Walnut! Hide yourself!"

Pozzi pushed himself to his feet, then took the branch from Keeva. The bird's head snapped around, and its eyes landed on Walnut.

Pozzi had seen owls before, but never this close, and he had never had to fight one.

"Go!" Keeva shouted at the small rabbit. "Under there! Now!"

Walnut hesitated, and the owl attacked. The young rabbit dropped to the ground and began wriggling into the hollow under a tree root, while Pozzi swung the branch wildly. The blow landed, but the bird shrugged it off, intent on Walnut. The youngster had made it halfway into the hollow, his legs still exposed. The owl shot forward, fast as water, and Pozzi had a sudden insight to swing down instead of across, bringing the heavy branch into where he thought the owl's left leg would be.

He was rewarded with a reverberating crack as the branch broke in two, followed by a screech of pain from the bird. To his relief, Pozzi saw that Walnut had managed to pull his legs into the hollow. But relief was short-lived.

The beast whirled on Pozzi and Keeva, orange eyes fixed and unblinking. The bird spread its wings, and what little light was left from the moon was completely blocked out by the bird's impossible wingspan. It seemed to engulf the forest, stretch further than they could run. He heard Keeva breathe out a soft, despairing, "Oh!" and then the creature rushed them.

Pozzi curled himself tight around Keeva, putting his back to the beast. He prepared himself for the impact, the talons, but instead, heard a crashing of undergrowth, a snarl, and then a high-pitched scream.

The space around them filled with giant shadows—shadows

that growled and snapped and sent showers of feathers falling around them. Then all was quiet. Pozzi and Keeva clung to one another, frozen.

Around them, five wolves stood over the owl's inert carcass. Each wolf was tall, more than double Pozzi's height at the shoulder. In the dark, he could only make out their hulking gray shapes, but there was no mistaking the bright flash of teeth and their musky scent. And the smell of blood.

Pozzi pulled Keeva with him, prepared to flee.

"You came from Nyatha?" One of the wolves spoke.

Keeva recovered first. "Yes."

"We seek Argasar," Pozzi added. Wolves lived in packs. Perhaps these wolves knew Argasar.

The eyes around them didn't change, and Pozzi's throat tightened. What if they were rival packs?

"Come," the wolf who had spoken said, and the eyes retreated into the shadows. Pozzi heard the soft brush of the wolf's body against the undergrowth and gripped Keeva's paw in his. Walnut watched from his hollow, silent.

"The young one can come too," the wolf said. "You are safe with us."

After a moment, Pozzi nodded, and Walnut scrambled out of his hiding place, face still full of fear. The three rabbits followed the wolves ahead of them, their eyes adjusting to the heavy darkness.

They walked for what seemed an eternity, the forest warmer now that the branches blocked the wind. Whenever the rabbits thought they had lost their way, a pair of eyes would appear out of the night and guide them back in the right direction.

Gradually, the rustle of leaves and the creaking of branches above gave way to the sound of water. They emerged into a clearing near a thin, twisted brook. Here, where no trees blocked the moonlight, Pozzi saw signs of habitation. Burrows dug into trees, baskets and racks for drying food, even crude garden beds. He spotted the silhouette of a rabbit here and there on the periphery, like sentries. Keeva and Walnut stared, trying to absorb this.

"Argasar and the rabbits from Nyatha have been busy since the fire." The wolf who had first spoken indicated a space beneath a tangle of tree roots, covered with grass thatch. "This burrow is empty. You can sleep. Or bathe. Argasar will return in the morning."

Though Pozzi had an endless number of questions, he and Keeva and Walnut were nearly sleeping where they stood, not even caring that they still reeked from the cart. Keeva and Walnut were only too grateful to crawl into the shelter beneath the roots, but Pozzi forced himself to stay awake.

When the wolves had melted into the shadows, he checked that Keeva and Walnut were asleep, then ventured out. He spotted one of the rabbits he'd seen earlier standing near the fringes of the trees, and cautiously approached.

He could barely tell the rabbit's fur color, but he could see that he was solidly built.

"Pardon me askin', but—"

The sentry's head swung toward him, and Pozzi thought he saw teeth flash, though whether in a smile or a grimace he couldn't tell. "I know you. Aren't you the one who started the fire?"

Pozzi nodded. "What is this place?"

"Safe," the sentry said simply.

Pozzi tried a different tack. "Did Argasar lead you here?"

"Aye, we owe our hides to him. You too."

The sentry walked off, leaving Pozzi in no doubt that the conversation was over. As he wandered back to Keeva and Walnut, he thought about the sentry's words. Was this place safe? And if so, why did he still feel a pinprick of unease?

CHAPTER 45

$\mathcal{D}$awn slid on cold feet across the forest floor. Keeva woke, stretched, and rubbed at an ear with one paw. Pozzi knew he would never tire of that gesture, never want to wake up after Keeva and miss that ritual that she did each and every morning, without even realizing it. He watched her eyes open, the world come into focus. She burrowed her nose into Walnut's soft neck fur, and then she looked at Pozzi.

"You didn't sleep?"

"I just woke," Pozzi lied. Keeva raised her head, and Pozzi knew he hadn't fooled her. She looked outside their shelter, at kits scampering around, at rabbits returning with baskets of dandelions, wood sorrel, and clover.

"They all came from Nyatha?"

Pozzi shrugged. "I think so."

"I thought Argasar was supposed to be here?"

Pozzi had been both dreading and anticipating the wolf's presence.

"I am."

They nearly jumped at the voice, so close that they almost felt like Argasar was inside the warren. The great white timber wolf's head appeared in the entry, and Pozzi was glad they hadn't continued the conversation. How long had he been listening?

"Welcome, Pozzi. I'd hoped you'd come. We should probably talk."

Pozzi could only nod. For some reason his voice failed him.

Argasar motioned with his head. "Walk with me." He had a way of making commands sound like polite requests, Pozzi noticed.

Pozzi glanced at Keeva and the still sleeping Walnut, but Keeva motioned him away. "We'll be fine."

He stepped out of the root shelter and followed the wolf through dense brush and foliage, until they emerged onto a rock that commanded an enviable view of Nyatha. Pozzi could now see why Argasar had chosen this spot, not only because of its fresh water but also because of this barren rock that rose like a broken bone from the sprawling body of the forest.

"I was beginning to lose hope you'd come," Argasar admitted. A silence grew between them. "Captivity makes you forget the very smell of freedom. Do you taste it? Now that you're away from Nyatha?"

Pozzi almost felt more nervous than he had been in Hassah's household. There, he at least had known what to expect. Here, it seemed there was a whole new web of rules that he would have to unravel.

"You'll get used to freedom, the way you got used to captivity," the wolf said.

"Are we free?" At the wolf's look, Pozzi added, "I mean, why's everyone still here? So close to Nyatha?"

Argasar looked toward the fort, as if he could see into it. "Let me ask you something. Do you think the Urzoks can be defeated?"

Pozzi wasn't sure if this was a trick question. "I just want to see Keeva and Walnut safe."

"What if I told you there is no such thing as safe, or free," Argasar said, "unless every Urzok was dead?"

The rabbit stared into the wolf's eyes, unsure where this was going. Those eyes were flecked with dark amber. He noticed the scars across the wolf's lips. Some looked like knife wounds, while others looked self-inflicted, like Argasar had gnawed on something jagged for hours on end. And then he saw the brand, just inside the wolf's left ear.

Pozzi hadn't noticed it before, because he'd only seen the wolf at night and the brand could have been shadow. But now, Pozzi saw the crest clearly. Nyatha's coat of arms, a hand on a lion's head.

Catching Pozzi's stare, Argasar gave a mirthless grin. "Everyone here has one. I look forward to finding the Urzok that did it, and giving him a brand of his own."

"I'm sorry."

"I'd rather you be angry, Pozzi," the wolf said. "You understand, don't you, that none of us are safe as long as the Urzoks run this land?"

"You're finally free. Why would you take the fight back to them?" Pozzi couldn't fathom attacking the Urzoks. To escape was one thing, but to fight back? To invite Ghazan's full force? Perhaps Argasar had tasted too much victory.

"Because," Argasar growled, "they won't stop until they've taken everything from us. From you. From every tree, lake, and blade of grass that grows here. They've already taken everything I've ever had—I have nothing to lose and everything to gain."

Pozzi wasn't sure he understood Argasar's logic. "You could lose your life. Isn't that worth somethin'?"

The wolf stood, a humorless laugh rumbling in his throat. "The Urzoks taught me that my life's worth nothing."

"What's it you want from us?" He now knew what had bothered him last night when they had arrived at camp, that he hadn't figured out when he was half dead from exhaustion. Why hadn't the wolves and rabbits parted ways when they reached the forest? Famished wolves and available prey could not be friends for long.

"Your help," Argasar said. "I want your and your fellow rabbits' help."

"Our help? With what?"

"With the war."

"I don't follow."

"I want you to help us take Nyatha."

* * *

"YOU CAN'T GO BACK. Don't even think it."

Pozzi couldn't disagree with Keeva's statement. But he also wasn't sure what alternatives they had. They had been overjoyed to discover two rabbits from their hometown of Willago. Imma, one of Keeva's childhood friends, and Duggan, the Willago furniture carver's strapping black-and-gray-patched son. But they had also been devastated to learn about those they'd lost. Keeva's parents had gone to the cradles within the first week of arrival, along with every other Willago villager.

Their two friends bore brands as well, proving Argasar right. Everyone who'd fled Nyatha had the crest. Half of the rabbits had brands on their shoulders. Those who had been kept for fur had brands inside their ears, like Argasar's.

"How many are we?" Pozzi had asked.

Imma said, "Three hundred and forty-six, if you count the young ones. And then there are fifty-two wolves. Argasar's organized 'em into clans of ten, so there are five clans altogether."

"And what do they do for food?"

Imma smiled at his suspicions. "They hunt elsewhere. You know how many of us they've killed? None."

"No. One of 'em tried, remember," Duggan cut in.

Imma scoffed. "Argasar ripped out his throat, that's what he did."

Pozzi thought back to the night Argasar killed the sentry. "He killed a fellow wolf?"

"Wolf law, you see, is that the alpha can kill anyone who

defies him," Duggan explained, as a teacher would to an apprentice. He was busy fashioning digging sticks out of fir-tree branches. He already had a growing pile near him, and a group of young rabbits, Walnut included, sat helping him strip the offshoots and shave the bark.

"We all live by wolf law now?" Pozzi asked.

Imma shrugged. "Seems fair, don't it? Argasar and his wolves protect us, and in return, he asks for our help."

Pozzi shared a look with Keeva. "So y' know what he wants to do?"

Duggan paused in his carving and glanced up. "Aye. We've already started digging on a tunnel into Nyatha. We're taking the fight to the Urzoks. Going to kill every last one of 'em."

Imma's eyes narrowed. "I hope I'm there to see it."

"Every last one?" Pozzi repeated. "There are children in there."

A coldness settled on Imma's small brown features, and the corners of her blue-gray eyes crinkled. "Good."

With that, she stood and walked away.

Pozzi stared after her until Keeva touched his arm. "She had two kits while in Nyatha. They were both killed."

Duggan whittled away with harder strokes. "You won't find much sympathy for your little Urzok friends here, Pozzi. Almost every doe here has had children killed for their flesh, and every buck has seen a friend eaten, skinned, or both. Argasar says the good Urzoks are the dead ones. Can't say I disagree."

Pozzi was about to reply, but Keeva shot him a warning look. He let the protest die in his throat. Now was perhaps a bad time for reason. But where would this plan lead?

Duggan gave his spear a last hack and turned it around, examining the point. "Y' know, Pozzi, many of these here rabbits hated you when they found out you'd been coddled and fed while we were in the pens. But now, we see that Argasar's right. Your being kept as pampered pets has all fed into his great plan to take Nyatha."

"Is that why you are all still here?" Keeva asked.

Duggan nodded. "Waiting for you. You three are the key to Argasar's conquering Nyatha. And we're all to be part of his new pack. A new future without Urzoks, without farms, without slavery."

Their hope and confidence was contagious. So Pozzi didn't voice his thought. *At what price?*

CHAPTER 46

The wind this high was bone-chilling, summer or no. Irah's feathers made her impervious to the cold, but Orjo's fur was meant to withstand water, not needling air. The Proudfeather, perhaps sensing his discomfort, called back over her shoulder.

"Nearly there. The Dragon's Spine is just over that hill."

Orjo hadn't been to this coast in over a hundred years, but he remembered the wild, green waves that crashed against the ragged cliffs of the mainland. Several boat lengths out from those cliffs, a steep, narrow island rose from the foaming waters, like some submerged dragon's spine. Anyone trying to make the journey across the corridor of sea to that sliver of island would be dashed against the rocks, or sucked out by the merciless tide.

He'd be safe there. Away from the lost cause that was Manka-har, away from legendary libraries, from those who wanted him dead. Away from delusional dreamers like Theo. He wondered where the naive lad was now, and whether he had gotten himself killed yet. *Not that I care*, Orjo reminded himself. Soon, he'd be alone on his new island; the way he was meant to be.

All islands are connected underwater.

He batted away the unwelcome memory of the grandfather

rabbit's words. Old age was bad enough without having to hear voices. Or become sentimental. He tightened his grip on the Proudfeather and searched the horizon eagerly for signs of his destination.

Dragon's Spine. An apt name, not only for its shape, but also for the constant roar of sea against its sides. He'd have to get used to the sound.

"Here we are," Irah said, cresting the hill.

It was as imposing and harsh as he remembered. Waves battered the lower rocks before running in foamy rivulets down the jagged base of the island. The air smelled of salt and cold, and the few hardy scrubs that grew on the spine were bent double from wind more than age.

Irah circled the ridge of the spine, looking for a safe spot to land. She found a flat plateau just out of the wind and managed to negotiate the winds enough to come down on it. She sat down to let her passenger dismount. "How will you get back across the water?"

Orjo grunted as he slid down the bird's back and onto the plateau. "I don't plan to."

The bird's head feathers stood in surprise. "You want me to leave you here? You'll die."

The muskrat smirked. "I've made do in far worse places, lass. I'll build shelter and I'll fish for my food."

"I'm not talking about food and shelter," Irah replied. "I'm speaking of solitude. That would finish me off sooner than some bad weather or hunger."

Orjo snorted. "I've spent decades alone. You grow used to it."

The Proudfeather cocked her head. "But did you like it?"

"Of course," the muskrat insisted. And the Dragon's Spine was perfect. It was harsh, unyielding, and aloof. Like him. It had been here for thousands of years, and it would be here thousands more. How many times had he almost been killed over the last moons—mostly thanks to Theo? Here, he would have days of endless solitude. His infinite future on this island would be safe and undisturbed.

And boring.

He growled. Where had that thought come from? But it had come all the same, and he couldn't stop the next thought either. He hadn't felt this alive for a very long time. All those brushes with death since leaving his island had reminded him that he was still Orjo the Terrible. That he could still slay any bounty hunter, outwit any Urzok warlord, and even talk a Proudfeather into taking him wherever he wanted to go. Including this remote piece of Aktu-forsaken rock. He hated to admit it, but none of this would have happened if that rabbit hadn't come to his island. And if he dwelled on it too long, he'd be in danger of admitting something akin to fondness for that naïve lad.

The bird was looking at him askance, and he realized she had said something that he hadn't heard.

"What's that?"

"I said good luck. Aktu be with you."

Orjo watched the bird spread her wings, then disappear off the cliff.

He pondered what he was about to do and shook his head, incredulous at his own madness.

"Wait," he called.

The bird paused midair, then circled back up and landed on the ledge. "What now?"

"I need you to take me off this island."

CHAPTER 47

$\mathcal{A}$s the torches on the walls burned down to stumps, so did Theo's hope.

They were nearing the end of their third and last day, and Brune, Indigo, and Theo had found nothing to indicate an entrance to a secret library. They were dusty, sore, and red-eyed from lack of sleep. Their paws had also been rubbed raw running over the walls trying to detect any crack that might indicate a false door or a key space.

Indigo stepped back several paces from the mural and stood staring at the depiction of the Library, with a deep frown of concentration.

"What's wrong?" Theo asked, joining her.

"I don't know." She walked up and down the length of the wall that showed the inside of the Library, studying it. "I feel like we're overlooking something. Something obvious."

Brune sighed, rubbing grit from his eyes. "The only thing obvious to me is that this is like trying to find a snowflake in a snowball."

"Any progress?"

They turned to see Mercusa, Eluk, and Lyusa enter the

chamber, with another two Grodlyns bearing a tray with plates of spiced yamba and nut bread.

Brune glanced at Theo. "Some."

"But no library, I am guessing?" Eluk smirked.

"Not yet," Theo admitted.

"Then that's the end of it," the chamberlain said, firm.

"It seems the Library is not here." The queen looked at Theo. "I'm so sorry, Theo."

"We need some more time."

Eluk tucked his paws in his robe, his expression rigid. "We agreed. Three days and no more. I will see that your things are packed for you."

He turned and swept out. The two Grodlyns left the tray of food on the floor near them, then followed.

"We thought you could use a good meal after all this," the queen explained, indicating the tray with her tail.

Theo shook his head. "Thank you, Queen Mercusa, but I'm not hungry." He looked around him at the wall depicting the Library. "We are close. I know it. I can almost see it. The pillars, the room."

Brune took a chunk of nut bread from the tray and chewed. "It probably looks a lot like this place, I suppose." He waved one paw around, mouth full. "Large. Domed."

Theo froze, and then looked from the mural to the chamber pillars around them. A grin spread across his face. "Brune! You're right! Just like this!"

"Like what?" Lyusa asked, following Theo's gaze.

"Look at the mural!" Theo pointed, thoughts racing. "The pillars! The domed roof. The space. Look, look!" He ran to the painting of the pillars on the wall. "The details in the carving on the pillars, here—it's exactly the same as the ones in this chamber!" He turned to them. "This is the Library! We're standing right in it."

Mercusa cocked her head. "Don't the stories say the Library was buried?"

"Yes! And it was!"

"Buried beneath the new palace of Jaipri." Brune frowned. "But if this is the Library, where are the books?"

His question stumped Theo's momentum. "I don't know."

"Well, so many books couldn't have just disappeared into thin air," Indigo argued. "And we've been up and down this palace."

"That's true." Theo turned around, looking at all the walls, as if he could will their secrets from them. "We've found no books, but there must be a clue, a trace. As Indigo said, we must be overlooking something obvious. There must be some part of this we haven't…" His voice trailed off as he glanced up and caught sight of the ceiling.

Indigo followed his gaze up. "What?"

Theo turned, taking in the dome above them. A film of cobwebs and dust covered it, for no one had thought to clean anything so out of reach. But Theo could still clearly see the ornate painting there. A line of snakes tangled across the domed surface. There were hundreds of them, all multi-colored, knotted and coiled in an intricate pattern.

Theo turned around, looking at the ceiling from different angles.

"It's beautiful," Mercusa commented. "But what is it you see, Theo?"

"It's a message." He pointed at different snakes on the ceiling as he released the words. "'Those who know Her language will have Mankahar at their feet.'"

Indigo took a torch off the wall and lifted it to see better. "This is the Forbidden Language?"

Theo grinned. "Hidden as snakes in a painting! It's a trick of the eye. But the snakes form words, to anyone who cares to look."

Brune scratched one cheek thoughtfully. "It still doesn't tell us where the Library is."

"Mankahar at their feet," Theo repeated, thinking.

"The lower levels of the palace, perhaps?" Lyusa suggested.

Indigo shook her head. "We searched. There's nothing there."

"At their feet..." Theo looked down and began circling around the snake mosaic on the floor. It was comprised of eight great snakes, curled on themselves to form eight interlocking circles. Each snake was made up of dozens of green and gray tiles. Theo motioned at Indigo for the torch. He took it and knelt, bringing the light close to the floor. His fur stood up when he spotted first one tile with a different marking, then another, and another.

"Their scales are glyphs!" His voice shook with excitement, until he saw the blank stares around him. He tried to gain control of his rushing thoughts, his words. "Glyphs form words in the Forbidden Language, and each snake here is made up of little tiles. Each tile has a glyph carved into it."

He got on his knees and swept at the floor to see better. "See? Every snake has twenty-four tiles, with a different glyph on each one."

"So that means...?" Indigo prompted.

He paused. "I don't know."

"Maybe it says where the books are?" Brune bent down to examine the tiny tiles.

Theo looked at the glyphs, then shook his head in frustration. "It's nonsense. None of them are in an order that forms words. Not a single word."

"Sometimes when things don't make sense forward," Mercusa suggested, "you need to look at it backward."

Theo walked around again, following the tiles the other way. "You're right that it's a puzzle. But it's not backward." He looked back up at the ceiling. "Mankahar at their feet..."

"Maybe it's not a door at all? And we're just supposed to smash through it?" Brune sighed. "I miss my axe."

"Wait!" Theo counted the snakes again. "Mankahar at their feet...eight glyphs. Eight snakes." He turned to them, excited. "It's Mankahar!"

They looked at him, lost.

Lyusa cleared his throat. "Theo, you're the only omatje here."

The rabbit tried to gather his thoughts to explain as he pointed at the snakes on the ground. "In the Forbidden Language, the word Mankahar has exactly eight glyphs. There are eight snakes. So maybe if Mankahar is at our feet, then each snake holds one glyph that together makes Mankahar!"

He ran his paw over the snakes, searching. "Here! This is the only snake that has a tile with the glyph that Mankahar starts with, so…" He pressed on the tile, and it gave, remaining sunken. "Next glyph…"

He pressed down, one glyph on each serpent, until every serpent but one had a tile pushed in. He hovered over the last one, then pressed.

A deep, grinding of stone on stone sounded beneath them, like a giant gnashing his teeth. Everyone scrambled away, outside the mosaic ring of snakes, before silence descended again.

They stared, confused.

"I don't see a door," Indigo commented. "Do you?"

"No," Theo said, cautiously coming forward again.

"But something moved," Lyusa said. "Take care where you walk."

Theo examined the serpents again and cautiously stepped into the ring. Nothing happened.

Indigo joined him, running a boot over the tiles. "It was built a long time ago. Perhaps it's stuck."

"Then it just needs a little push."

"Wait, Brune!" But Theo's and Lyusa's warning came too late, as the bear brought his hind foot crashing down inside the ring of serpents.

As soon as the great giant's weight came on it, the stone circle flipped on some unseen axis, like a coin strung on a necklace. The bear fell through first, with Indigo and Theo falling on top of him.

Theo felt himself roll off the bear and onto a hard, dusty floor. He coughed as the stale air rushed into his throat. He looked up to see Queen Mercusa and Lyusa peering down from a short distance above, their faces full of concern.

"Brune!" Lyusa called. "Are you unharmed?"

"Surprised is all." The bear shook the dust from his coat and looked around. "What is this place?"

Theo stood and went to help Indigo up, but she was already on her feet. He turned to peer at the space around them, hidden in shadows. "It's like a tomb."

Indigo motioned toward Mercusa. "Your Majesty, would you mind giving us some light?"

Both serpents disappeared, then came back and lowered lit torches with their tails. Indigo took one, and Theo took the other.

They were in a small, hidden chamber, roughly twenty steps across and low-ceilinged enough that Brune had to stoop. The room was bare, and all the walls but one were painted white. Theo crossed to this wall, and held up his torch.

"By Aktu," Brune murmured as the three of them looked upon the sight.

The entire wall, floor to ceiling, burst with color that seemed as vibrant as the day it had been painted. Thick black lines divided the wall into three panels, with each panel containing a detailed painting, almost every inch covered with numerous beasts, activities, and depictions of war. Theo walked from one end to the other, staring at its depictions, then walked back again.

A soft thud sounded, and Theo turned to see Mercusa and her brother drop into the chamber.

"A secret vault," Lyusa commented. "I heard these were popular long ago, to store guarded treasure."

Mercusa slid closer, looking at the wall in wonder. "And is this what they were guarding? A painting?"

"It's a story," Theo said, softly.

Brune crossed his broad arms, looking over the images. "A story of what?"

"I don't know yet," Theo answered, "but look, it starts here. There's the number one. First, second, third."

"It looks like more drawings of the Library," Indigo observed, pointing at one panel. "There's a battle outside it here."

Theo stood at the square's first panel, gazing at the images as the others gathered around him. It depicted a walled city, the domed Library in the middle, with armed beasts at the ramparts. An invading force, led by an exaggerated tall figure in a red helmet, hurled fire and missiles from horseback. "It's a war, see? Those Urzoks are attacking the city, and the Library."

Lyusa nodded. "Most likely during the great Purges, when the first Urzok emperor ordered everything in the Forbidden Language destroyed."

"This must be the city of Elshon, where the Library was. And look here," Theo pointed to a grouping of serpents, in the lower left corner of the panel, that also formed words. "It says, 'He came.'"

Theo moved to the next panel. This one showed a defeated city, the walls and streets red with blood, buildings in ruins. The Urzok in the red helmet was placing a crown on a giant serpent's bowed head.

"They destroyed the city," Indigo said, looking at the image.

Theo searched, and this time, he found the serpents forming words in the top corner of the panel. "Here's more of the Forbidden Language."

"What does it say?" Indigo peered at where he was pointing.

"It says, 'He destroyed.'"

"Who is this he?" Indigo asked.

"I am guessing the first Urzok emperor," Lyusa said, tapping the red helmet with his tail. "He wears the crest of the empire."

"So the first Urzok emperor destroyed Elshon and everything in the Library," Mercusa concluded.

Brune studied the third panel. "If they destroyed it, what are they doing here?"

Theo walked over to stand next to the bear and took in the final panel. From the domed Library, Urzoks formed an assembly line. They were pushing carts full of goods out, and empty carts in. Groups of soldiers were shown loading the contents into great wagons drawn by teams of four horses, which snaked their way out of the smoldering city walls. Standing over them, on a rearing steed, was the Urzok in red, sword raised to the sky.

Theo located the last group of serpents forming words in the bottom right corner. "It says, 'He stole.'" He looked closer at the carts. "These are books. They loaded carts with books and took them away." His chest tightened as the enormity of the truth hit him. Theo looked at his friends' faces as they grappled with what this meant.

"So the shell of the Library itself is here in Jaipri," Mercusa said, "but the first Urzok emperor took everything in it?"

Theo was too stunned to even nod.

"Rot it," Brune growled. "There's only one place he would take it all."

"To the heart of the empire," Indigo said softly.

Theo nodded. "If we want to find the Library's books, we have to go to Kalyun-eh."

Just then, a roar shook the ceiling above them.

CHAPTER 48

When they emerged from the tunnels into the upper palace's outer corridor, they heard another boom, this time closer, and dirt showered down from the underground ceiling. They broke into a run as the shouts grew louder.

"Earthquake!"

Theo knew the panicked Grodlyns rushing past them were wrong. Earthquakes did not boom.

He turned to Indigo and Brune. "It can only be black snow."

"What's black snow?" Mercusa asked, concerned.

"Best if we act now and explain later, Your Majesty," Brune replied.

"We need to get everyone further underground, right now," Indigo urged.

"Commander Lyusa!" Ash emerged from a side corridor, coughing from the dust. "Upper tunnels have collapsed, I think all of our outer sentries have been killed or wounded."

Lyusa motioned with his tail. "The audience hall has the largest space with the strongest beams. We'll gather there. Mercusa, take Theo and Indigo down, tell everyone you meet to follow. Brune, my friend, I need you to come with me, if parts of Jaipri have collapsed, I could use your strength."

The bear and commander followed Ash, disappearing into the amassing throngs of confused Grodlyns and serpents.

"This way!" Mercusa commanded in a loud, yet calm voice. "Everyone to the audience hall! No rushing."

Another giant tremor shook the palace, sending up cries of fear, and this time, they heard the unmistakable crash of collapsing earth and timber. Screams echoed from the hallways next to them, followed by cries for help.

"You protect the queen!" Theo urged Indigo. "I'll be there soon."

"But—"

"You're best with a sword and with leading others, remember?" Theo argued. "The one thing I can do is help anyone hurt."

Indigo nodded, then followed Mercusa, who was still calling out to every able-bodied citizen to follow her.

Theo rushed toward the cries for help. He reached a busy intersection of tunnels where Grodlyns and serpents were gathering into a tide.

"Go to the audience chamber!" Theo shouted as loudly as he could against the din of rushing feet and panicked cries. But the hallways were becoming choked with dust and dirt that bloomed like a cloud, and his words were muffled by his coughing.

He stumbled upon a Grodlyn crushed under a beam, and bent to free him. But in the dusty haze, his paws touched the creature's neck, and the odd angle told him it was futile. He clapped a paw over his nose to ward against the dust, then felt his way along to the next victim crying for help.

Another great ripple shook the earth, accompanied by a crescendo of cracking tile and groaning wood somewhere nearby.

"Out and above ground!"

The voice was right next to him, and Theo grabbed hold of the speaker. In the gloom, he could just make out a Grodlyn, eyes narrowed in panic, fur dull beneath a layer of dust and blood.

"Go below!" Theo coughed. "Tell everyone to get below ground, to the audience chamber!"

The Grodlyn looked at him as if not understanding the words, and Theo noticed the trickle of blood coming from the Grodlyn's ears.

He pointed below them, then motioned for the Grodlyn to follow him. The little monkey pushed past him, however, and raced as fast as he could over the debris and up toward the palace exits.

He found the Grodlyn whose cries he had first followed, trapped beneath a pile of rubble from the ceiling. Another Grodlyn with rings in his ears ran up and began helping him. Together, he and Theo managed to push the rubble aside and pull the small trapped Grodlyn out to safety.

"You are thanked," the freed Grodlyn said, and both started toward the palace exits, the injured one limping in pain.

"No!" Theo grabbed the arm of the Grodlyn with the pierced ears. "We must go downward, to the audience chamber. Those are the queen's orders."

He pulled them along with him. When they reached Jaipri's royal hall, the area was already milling with high-ranking serpents and Grodlyns. Several torches had been lit, blazing over the assembled throng. He spotted a healer clearing a space for several injured nearby, and led the two Grodlyns from the hallway there.

"Wait here," Theo told the two Grodlyns. "Medicine and supplies will be coming soon."

They nodded and sank gratefully to the ground.

Theo looked around and saw Brune's conspicuous bulk standing next to Indigo near the throne area. She was deep in conversation with Lyusa and the queen. Eluk was on the queen's other side, scowling.

Theo made his way through the thickening crowd of Grod-lyns and serpents until he reached the throne.

"… why we're down here and not up there," Lyusa was saying.

"Because we'll be slaughtered," Indigo replied, curt.

"She's right," Theo said. "If it's what we think it is, we can't go anywhere near it. We have to stay here, beyond reach."

The chamberlain's face twisted at the sight of Theo. "You led Ornox here."

The name wrapped around Theo like a grip. The infamous warlord who had led the battle at Ralgayan. The one whose daughter took his grandfather, took his whole village.

"It's Ornox?"

Brune nodded, grim.

"If this is the black snow Brune has told us about," Lyusa said, "we cannot possibly fight him."

Dread settled in Theo's belly. How? How had the Urzoks come to possess black snow? Could Orjo have given it to them? He pushed this idea aside. They needed to focus on surviving, on saving every life they could.

"How many halls have collapsed?" Indigo asked.

"Eight so far," Lyusa said, "though a ninth is partially closed."

Brune frowned, ears flicking. "It seems to have stopped."

The queen nodded. "Perhaps they are showing us their strength before making demands."

"Should we send someone?" Lyusa asked.

His sister shook her head. "The Urzoks will send a messenger when they're good and ready. For now, we need to keep track of which passages out are still open to us, and which have fallen. We don't want to be buried alive."

* * *

As the queen predicted, the Urzoks sent the first messenger. Word spread that someone bearing the black and green colors of an envoy had arrived at Jaipri. When Theo, Indigo, and Brune

277

were summoned to the queen's private council chamber, they saw a thin man of medium build standing before Queen Mercusa, Lyusa, and Eluk.

At Theo and his companions' arrival the man turned and took in the three of them. His features were sharp, almost cutting. The rabbit had the uncomfortable feeling that the messenger's dark, narrow eyes could memorize every detail on sight, forgetting nothing.

"This is Yod of Vyad," Eluk said, indicating the messenger. "He speaks on behalf of Ornox."

Yod's eyes settled on Theo. "Are you the one they call Theo Griffinrider?"

Everyone's eyes turned to Theo. The only expression he could read clearly was Eluk's one of hostility. Theo was about to answer when Indigo silenced him with a paw on his chest.

"Why?" she asked.

"I am under strict orders." Yod's voice was soft, almost toneless. He reminded Theo of a spider, quiet and unobtrusive, but keeping track of every tremor in the web around him. "No discussion of terms unless I can confirm that Theo Griffinrider is here."

Brune took a menacing step forward, drawing a displeased look from Eluk. "And if he's not?"

"Then you have nothing of value to trade," Yod said, emotionless. "And my master destroys Jaipri." Seeing the look in Brune's eye, he added, "You may kill me, or not. It doesn't matter. My master will take my not returning as a sign that you turned down his offer."

Mercusa's tongue flicked out. "And what is his offer?"

"He retreats and leaves Jaipri intact. He ceases all use of his devastating powder."

"And in exchange?" the queen asked.

"In exchange, you turn over the Griffinrider." Yod turned back to Theo. "So I ask you, are you Theo Griffinrider?"

"Yes!" Eluk answered. "He is."

Lyusa and the queen shot him a disapproving glare.

"I need to hear the rabbit say it," Yod insisted.

Theo pushed aside his unease. "Yes."

Yod nodded. "Then Jaipri does have something to trade."

"You may be Urzok, but you must know Jaipri's sacred rules of neutrality." Mercusa's voice was chilly. "We do not send guests to their deaths, and we do not join sides in any war. Therefore, you are asking us to break a time-honored custom."

Yod bowed, though Theo doubted the man felt any genuine respect. "You'll have to decide what you value more, my lady. Your city and its inhabitants, or its time-honored customs."

Lyusa bared his fangs, but Mercusa laid her tail across his.

"You may go back to your master."

"Your reply?"

"I need time to consult with my advisors."

Yod bowed again. "You have until sunset. Your answer will determine whether you see the sunrise."

CHAPTER 49

Torches of yamba wood had been lit to signify the council was in session, and were almost as hot as the arguments that raged. The back and forth between Eluk, Brune, and the queen's advisors left barely any room for even Mercusa to interrupt.

Theo looked over the five key advisors in the queen's private council chamber. Lyusa, chief of arms, Eluk, chamberlain and chief of policy, and two other serpents and one Grodlyn that Theo did not know. One serpent was long, speckled in copper and black, while the other was a dull pewter color. The dull red Grodlyn with a knitted blue cap and several missing teeth said little, keeping his paws tucked in his blue robes.

"We have always been neutral; that is how we preserve peace," Pewter said. His voice sounded familiar, and Theo was transported back to the last time he was in Jaipri, when he had stumbled upon a meeting between Eluk and several serpent generals. A meeting where Eluk and his supporters had expressed their distrust of Theo and decided to search his belongings. Pewter had been one of those generals; Theo was now certain. Another foe, it seemed, when he desperately needed friends.

"I'm afraid the only peace the Urzoks are dealing is the kind that comes on a sword's end," Indigo argued.

Pewter gave her a hard stare.

"Brother, what are our options for fighting back?"

Lyusa flicked his tongue. "We don't know exactly how large Ornox's forces are. If it's a small force, we would have a chance. But this new weapon he has…"

"Suicide!" Eluk pronounced.

The queen turned to the serpent speckled in copper and black. A shaved jewel affixed to his head denoted high rank.

"What says my palace overseer? Do we have the supplies to withstand a siege?"

"Yes and no." Copper tapped the floor with his tail with each point he made. "First, it's mid-summer, and we don't have a full harvest, so food stores would only last a week. Maybe two. Second, the attacks contaminated our main-bore water supply. So sooner or later, we need to access the surface."

"How soon?" Lyusa asked.

"A day. Four. Hard to say. We don't yet have a total figure for all the wounded and dead. Our armory was also damaged in the attack, so we're short on weapons to defend ourselves."

"You see?" Eluk said. "We have no choice. We must meet Ornox's demands."

"And go against all that Jaipri stands for?" Lyusa shook his head. "What says our priest about that?"

The Grodlyn in the blue robe closed his eyes. "I have prayed to Aktu, but unfortunately, all roads are paved with sacrifice."

Eluk nodded. "It's just a question of whether we sacrifice a few or many! And for what? This lot came here to find a powerful weapon, and what did they find? Nothing. Instead, they lead a powerful enemy with a powerful weapon right to us! Aktu is punishing us for sheltering an omatje."

Theo started to say something, but Brune shot him a warning look. This was not the time to defend his taboo abilities.

"Perhaps we ask our guests to leave," Pewter suggested. "We

are neutral, but we are also not obliged to be a safe harbor. Ornox cannot punish us for that."

"Yes, he can," Indigo said.

"Ornox doesn't care about your rules of neutrality," Brune growled. "He just wants revenge. Ornox doesn't play diplomatic games."

"You're right," Theo said. Brune shot him another warning look, but the rabbit pressed on, amazed that he hadn't thought of this before. "And you know what that means? It means he's bluffing."

Everyone around the central hearth looked at him, waiting for him to explain this wild leap in logic.

"He has no more black snow!" Theo said. "Or if he does, he doesn't have much."

"How do you deduce that?" Pewter asked, clearly skeptical.

Indigo seemed to have followed Theo's thinking. "If Ornox had the means to destroy Jaipri, he would have done it already. That's his nature."

"If he's negotiating, it means he has no choice," Brune finished.

"That's a mighty big assumption, rabbit." Pewter looked unconvinced.

"Aye, one I'm not willing to gamble on," Copper agreed.

"Think about it." Indigo turned to the queen. "Why give you until sunset? Why not just destroy Jaipri and come in and take what he wants? He never negotiated with Ralgayan."

"And what if you're wrong?" Eluk snapped. He turned to the queen, pleading. "The rabbit is just trying to save his own skin. Understandable, but we cannot gamble Jaipri's entire future, all our lives, on calling a bluff."

"Although remember, they also have one thing we don't. Experience fighting Ornox," Lyusa pointed out. "They know him better than we do." He turned to his sister. "What say you, Mercusa?"

A silence fell, broken only by the popping of the fire in the central hearth, as everyone waited for Mercusa's decision.

"I do not like to break Jaipri's tradition for peace, but I also do not think our ancestors would expect us to simply turn a blind eye when we are being threatened." The queen looked at Brune, Theo, and Indigo. "We have not gone to war. War has come to us. We will not give you over to Ornox."

"Your Majesty, with all due respect, this is a mistake," Eluk hissed.

"Jaipri values neutrality," the queen said evenly. "But neither choice open to us is neutral. We must choose."

"Which is why—"

"Which is why," Mercusa interrupted firmly, "we will move all inhabitants down into the old palace, and Lyusa will ready our armed forces."

"What armed forces, Your Majesty?" Pewter protested. "Our forces have not been battle tested since Lyusa was molting his first skin. Which was before all our lifetimes!"

"Our forces are small and inexperienced," Lyusa agreed, seemingly unruffled by the insult. "But as the saying goes, even the smallest viper can bring down a tiger."

The queen nodded, and looked at each of her advisors in turn. "Let us show Ornox that serpents may be peace-loving, but we still have teeth."

Brune gave Theo an encouraging smile, but Theo couldn't quite share the bear's relief at the queen's words of support. Eluk's expression left him in no doubt that the queen's decision would not be popular.

CHAPTER 50

"*H*eave!"

A steady stream of Grodlyns hauled rubble from the palace's damaged halls to the two main tunnels leading to the surface. These, the council had decided, were the most likely routes through which the Urzoks would attack. Grodlyns dropped their cargo of rock and wood at the front before hurrying back to fetch more. Theo and Indigo helped Lyusa and his team supervise and stack the debris into a barricading wall.

If, as Theo thought, the Urzoks were bluffing, Ornox would have to invade the underground city, sending men deep into the tunnels. Lyusa's plan was to split his forces into two teams. One would remain in the underground city, and one would follow him out one of the myriad other exits and around the front. If the Urzoks met little resistance in the tunnels, Lyusa had argued, then they would advance deep into the heart of Jaipri until they met with these barricades. Lyusa could then enter the tunnel entrance from above ground and attack the enemy from behind. This would allow them to trap and kill Ornox's men in an enclosed space.

"Think we'll survive this?"

The princess put on an encouraging grin. "We survived

Ralgayan. And the odds were worse." At his expression she paused. "What's wrong? Besides the fact that Ornox might not be bluffing?"

"I just really thought it would be the other way around. That we would have the weapon and they would be under attack."

She put a paw on his shoulder. "You did what you could, the best you could."

"And it counted for nothing."

"No. It counts for everything. You didn't know whether you would find the Library, whether it would work, but you tried anyway." She looked around and lowered her voice so only he could hear. "Many in Mankahar, my queendom included, could have stopped the Urzoks, but didn't. You made the right choice to come, and so did I." She heaved a rock onto the wall. "Don't worry. We'll find the Library."

"Perhaps." He retrieved one of the broken beams from the pile behind him. "But I've been thinking. You should go back to the Order."

"Why?"

"Kalyun-eh is the capital. Going there will be dangerous."

Indigo worked her paws under a large piece of rock and motioned for him to pick up the other end. "Even more reason for me to go with you. I'm not letting you go alone."

They maneuvered the rock onto the wall, pausing to take a breath. "I'll have Brune," he reminded her.

"And me."

Theo frowned. "You have the strongest sense of duty of anyone I know."

"But?"

"But it's getting in the way of good sense."

She paused in picking up another rock, regarding him. "So now you feel I lack good sense?"

Theo knew he had touched a nerve, but for once, he didn't care. He had to make her see reason. "What if something happened to you? You have a queendom, a place in the Order."

"So do you."

"It's not the same."

"What's not the same?"

"It doesn't matter if things go wrong for me."

A dark look passed across her face, and she was silent, as if her thoughts were locked in her throat.

"That's one of the most naive things I've heard, even for you." She held up a paw to cut off his protest. "What about Brune? What about Mankahar? You think it wouldn't matter if everyone heard that the Griffinrider was captured, or dead? Not to mention how I would feel, because—"

She stopped, and Theo wondered if he was reading into her words.

His thoughts must have been plain on his face, for she cleared her throat and said softly, "What happens to you matters to me. A great deal."

They looked at each other, the air thick between them. Her eyes were full of a fierce tenderness, and for the first time, he clearly saw all his own emotions for her reflected back at him, warming him from the inside out. Had it always been there, invisible to him? Every doubt he had was magically washed away.

He leaned toward her.

"Theo!"

He turned.

Brune was next to them, and the sly look on his face let Theo know that he had overheard more than he was letting on. "The infirmary asked if you could help. They're more overrun than honeycomb on an anthill." He crossed his arms, squinting at them. "Everything all right between you two?"

Theo glanced at Indigo, the warmth in him like a fiery secret. "Never better."

Brune nodded. "Good. Then let's go."

"You're coming?" Theo asked, surprised.

The bear turned to make sure they were following. "Yes. And you too, Princess. From now on, the three of us stick together."

Theo and Indigo exchanged glances. "Did something happen?" she asked.

Brune stopped and turned around, his eyes darting to make sure no one could overhear. "I don't trust Eluk."

"Neither do I," Theo agreed. "But what do you think he'll do?"

"Don't know. But I don't see him around the queen as much as he usually is, and I saw him having what looked like a mighty secret conversation with that general who was in the council."

"The one with the pewter scales?" Theo felt a sliver of unease work its way into him.

Brune nodded.

"Neither of them liked the queen's decision," Indigo said. "But Mercusa was adamant Eluk would never betray Jaipri."

"But you're not convinced?" Theo asked Brune.

"My father always said a pound of caution prevents two pounds of regret." Brune looked at them both. "So I don't want either of you out of my sight. Agreed?"

Theo nodded. "We stay together."

* * *

THE INFIRMARY CONSISTED of three large rooms and bustled with healers trying to both manage the currently injured as well as prepare for the inevitable flood tide to come. Torches of willow and dried sage lined the walls, while a central fire pit held coals for heating water and medicine.

The head healer, a graying Grodlyn who kept his mane in check with a kerchief tied behind his head, seemed surprised to see all three of them, but hurriedly put them all to work in the furthest room, grinding and portioning what supplies of dried poppy sap they had in store.

"A short supply we have somehow," the head healer

explained. "This morning, more 'n three boxes were there, but in this commotion everything goes missing."

Theo knew why the healer was worried. The sleep-inducing pain reliever would be vitally precious come sunset, when the attack began.

Theo showed Indigo how to help him sort and pour the sap, while Brune helped other healers move heavy pots of water or furniture.

The two rabbits worked in silence next to each other, and Theo wondered at how he could feel at such peace when the enemy lay in wait outside, and he didn't even know if he would see sunrise. But right this moment, with the pestle in his paws and Indigo next to him, all the fears and regrets about his yesterdays and tomorrows magically faded to nothing. Even if he died with the dawn, he realized, this moment was happiness. And he didn't dare break it with words.

They were halfway through grinding the supply given them when Ash slid into the infirmary, eyes scanning. Finding Theo and Indigo, he made his way through the scurrying healers until he was before Theo's work table.

"The queen asks to speak with you," Ash said.

Brune lumbered over, hearing his words. "We'll be right there."

The serpent looked at him, frowning. "Her Majesty only mentioned Theo."

"Where he goes, we go." Indigo's tone was polite, but left no room for negotiation.

The serpent nodded. "Come with me."

They followed him out of the infirmary and into the corridor. A gong sounded, marking the hour. Sunset was not far. And with it, Ornox's forces.

They followed Ash down winding corridors and past throngs of rushing Grodlyns. Some were herding youngsters to safety below, others were bringing supplies up to the frontlines.

"The audience chamber is the other way," Indigo commented

when Ash led them through the dining hall to another corridor on the far side.

Ash didn't slow. "Mercusa and her advisors are spending the siege in her private quarters, away from the barricades."

They reached a side room entrance, where a team of six serpents stood guard.

The guards pushed the door open for them, and Ash led them into a chamber. The room was richly decorated in feathers of various hues, woven carpets, and curtains of silk. Behind one of these curtains, Theo could see an inner chamber.

Ash indicated the far room. "She's in there."

Theo led the way in, pushing the curtain aside as Indigo and Brune joined him. He found himself in a similarly decorated chamber and froze when he saw the figure waiting for them.

"Eluk?"

The chamberlain's look of satisfaction made Theo whirl around. Brune and Indigo had already turned to face the door, which was now blocked by the six large serpent guards, along with Ash and Pewter. The princess drew the short sword from her belt. The only weapon they had between the three of them.

Theo turned back to Eluk, dread growing.

"What is this?" Theo asked.

"Something I should have done when you first came to Jaipri." Eluk pulled a cloth kerchief from his pocket.

"Think this through, Chamberlain," Brune growled. "This is not serving the queen."

"You're right," the Grodlyn agreed. "This is serving Jaipri."

The guards lunged. Pewter sprang at Brune, who roared and grabbed the general beneath the head with both paws. Indigo dodged a blue-green serpent's jaws and cut a jagged mouth across his belly, making the giant snake writhe and hiss. Ash shot forward and wrapped himself around Theo, pinning the rabbit's arms and legs. Theo struggled, but felt the serpent tighten around him, and his breath leaked out of him.

Brune and Indigo fought, ferocious, spilling a good deal of

serpent's blood onto the floor. Pewter sank his fangs into Brune's shoulder, drawing a bellow from the giant. Another green-and-ginger serpent wrapped a burly tail around Brune's legs and pulled, bringing the bear crashing down. Ultimately, Brune and Indigo were forced to succumb to sheer numbers, the serpents crushing them in iron grips.

The blue-green serpent who had sampled Indigo's blade writhed in agony as he bled from his side. Pewter checked to make sure Brune was safely entwined in the green-and-ginger serpent's grip before letting go of Brune's shoulder.

"Aktu rot you, bear!" Pewter rasped through his bruised windpipe. Brune snarled and made as if to snap his jaws around Pewter's head, but the green-and-ginger serpent who held him coiled even tighter, forcing the bear to focus solely on breathing.

Eluk pulled a jar from his other pocket and used his teeth to uncork it. The familiar sweet smell of poppy, the same substance he had just been sorting in the infirmary, reached Theo's nose.

Eluk looked at Brune and Indigo. "My apologies, Princess, but plans sometimes don't unfold as we hope." He dabbed the cloth with the jar contents, then resealed the jar and pocketed it. "Goodbye, Theo Griffinrider."

The chamberlain stepped forward and pressed the cloth tightly to the rabbit's nose and mouth. Theo heard Indigo shout something and saw her green eyes full of alarm. Then the gagging smell of poppy stormed Theo's senses, pulling him away. Away to a place where pain, thought, and time dissolved into one another.

CHAPTER 51

When he woke up, he was in a sack, being dragged across rough ground that scraped his shoulder. He tried to move his limbs but felt unforgiving ropes around his wrists and legs. He tried to spit out the gag in his mouth, which still reeked of poppy.

He struggled. If he could get his feet under him, he could at least try to slow the steady drag, pause, drag, pause, of his captor. But his ropes, combined with the sluggish fog in his head from the poppy, made standing impossible, and he fell back onto something thick and cold that moved.

Someone yanked the sack so that he fell backward, off the thick body he'd stumbled on. "Stop! Let me walk at least!"

But no one answered.

He let himself be dragged again and tried to think.

Through the scratchy cloth, he could smell fresh damp air, hear the rustle of trees and the call of birds. As well as the tread of other feet. One set, from what he could tell. And the sound of leaves parting told Theo that several serpents were nearby. At least five. How far were they from Jaipri? Were Brune and Indigo nearby? Lyusa or someone else would surely notice his being gone and come searching. Where was Eluk taking him? Or having him taken?

The rustling of tree leaves changed, the sound deepening. Theo strained to hear through his sack, and after a few moments, realized it wasn't leaves at all—it was water. A river. Was this the river that Ash had brought them over? If so, they might not be far from Jaipri palace. But what were they doing at the river?

The neighing of horses and the clink of bridles made everything fall into place.

Ornox.

Eluk was defying Queen Mercusa and making a bargain with Ornox.

Theo had barely digested this before he was upended, sack and all, and he fell hard against the unforgiving ground. Although the sun was nearly set, the deep orange light was bright enough for Theo to hold up his bound wrists and shield his eyes.

He was indeed on the cliff by the river they had first crossed with Ash. In front of him, Eluk stood facing a line of Urzoks on horses, who blocked the way to the cliff's edge, and the river.

Theo took in Ash, Pewter, and the other Eluk supporters, who stood in a ring around their prisoner. Eluk's voice drew his attention back to the line of Urzoks.

"I come on behalf of Jaipri. We are here to accept Lord Ornox's offer."

The line of Urzoks parted in the middle, and Pewter butted Theo forward with his wide head. The rabbit stumbled past Ornox's men, followed by Eluk and his serpents.

Here, the cliff edge overlooked the rushing river, but the bridge was not in sight. Theo guessed they must be up or downriver from where they had crossed when they had arrived three days ago. Standing, his back to them against the sunset, was a towering Urzok in battle armor. Yod, the messenger who had delivered Ornox's demands, was watching from some distance away.

Eluk stood as tall as he could, but Theo could still hear the tremor of uncertainty in his voice. "Greetings, Lord Ornox. I am Eluk, Royal Chamberlain of Jaipri and a trusted member of her Majesty's council. I respectfully present you with what you asked for. The rabbit known as Theo, or the Griffinrider."

The figure turned, and for a split instant, Theo thought that time had played a trick, that he was somehow back at Ralgayan. That face, with its hard cheekbones, curved eyes, and hairline, was dead. Agacheta was dead. Theo had watched her die, yet here she was, standing here, older and scarred.

The figure walked forward and bent to examine Theo more closely. From this distance, Theo could see the hard, angular jawline and stubble, the thick eyebrows and downturned mouth that made this face more masculine than Agacheta's.

"This the one?"

The voice broke the spell completely. This was Ornox, the father, not Agacheta the daughter.

Yod nodded. "Yes, my lord. That is Theo Griffinrider."

Ornox straightened so that he towered once again over the rabbit. "You're small. Much smaller than I expected."

Eluk cleared his throat.

"Lord Ornox, do we have your solemn word that Jaipri will be left in peace?"

Ornox looked at Theo, then at the sun as it began its descent past the horizon. "You have my word. I will spare Jaipri."

Eluk bowed, relief and triumph in his face. "Then our business is done. I beg your leave." He turned and began leading Pewter, Ash, and the other serpents away.

"I never said I would spare you, however."

Eluk turned, confused. Pewter hissed as all the serpents coiled into defensive positions.

"I promised my soldiers they'd be well rewarded if victory

was ours," Ornox said smoothly, "and in Kalyun-eh, serpent steak is highly prized."

Theo watched Eluk's face turn from incredulity to disbelief, then to panic. The protest had barely formed from his mouth before the Urzoks descended as one, their swords flashing. The serpents tried to flee, but it was over almost before it began; the sound of Ash and Eluk's screams cut short as blades found their marks.

Theo closed his eyes. Eluk was no friend, but somehow, his slaughter made Theo feel in even greater danger.

"For one called the Griffinrider, you are very squeamish," the warlord said.

Theo opened his eyes. Several Urzok soldiers were hauling the giant bodies away. One of them picked up Eluk's bloodied corpse by the tail and tossed him over the edge of the cliff into the waters below. There wasn't even a splash. Theo felt sickened.

"You have no shortage of enemies, rabbit." Ornox clasped his hands behind the small of his back. "The empire wants to see you beheaded publicly. There are those who want your blood as it's rumored to reverse pacification. And even your own kind are too happy to betray you. Your death will be welcomed by all."

"If the emperor wants me publicly beheaded," Theo argued, "shouldn't you take me to Kalyun-eh?"

"I don't care what the emperor wants." Ornox pulled his sword, a long wicked blade as unyielding as fate. "I don't care about the Order, or this war you think you can win. What I do care about is my daughter."

Theo had been so focused on the blade that he didn't see Ornox's fist. It slammed into the side of his head, felling him like a hammer. Wet warmth flooded his mouth, and the rush of the river grew until it roared in his ears. He brought his bound paws to his jaw, which was already swelling.

He stumbled to his feet, forcing himself to ignore the hot pain in his head, and then sprinted. If he could take Ornox by surprise, he might be able to get around him and past the guards—

Ornox's fist found him again, and Theo felt his feet leave the ground. He landed nearer to the cliff edge, and this time, he realized the roar he was hearing was not the river, but the blood pounding in his skull. Just as he was getting his balance, he felt a hand on his shoulder, steadying him so that he wouldn't fall.

"There now, good thing I caught you."

He looked up, into Ornox's calm face, the dark eyes that stared into his.

"This is for Agacheta."

Something punched him, deep, cold, and hard. The rush of blood in his ears seemed to slow, just as the cliff and Ornox slid away from him. Whatever had hit him now ripped its way out of his chest, and there was nothing but pain. Pain and the vague realization that he was falling, detaching from everything physical and tangible.

As the hard, icy waters of the river below caught him, Theo couldn't tell whether he was seeing real stars or simply stars of agony.

The last thing he heard was a voice shouting, "Theo!" And that's when he knew he was dying, for the voice sounded like his grandfather, calling from the afterlife.

CHAPTER 52

Ornox watched the rabbit fall toward the turbulent water below.

"Theo!"

Ornox looked up.

Gliding over the river gorge was a large bird with a stone necklace, its crest feathers aglow in the dying sunlight. Astride the bird was an old rabbit with a severed ear.

For a moment, Oaks and Ornox locked eyes, one pair enraged, the other narrowed in disbelief.

Then the bird swooped down into the gorge, taking its rider downriver and out of sight around a bend.

Yod approached and peered over the cliff.

"Should we send men after them, my lord?"

Ornox shook his head. "They'll find nothing but a water-logged corpse."

Yod dipped his head. "There's a messenger come for you, my lord. A swift from Ghazan."

"Let him wait." He wanted to have this moment to himself, to stand on the edge of the cliff and feel the sword in his hand.

He looked out at the horizon, at the sun as its lingering glow finally surrendered to night. A full moon now hung low in the sky, red as heart's blood. A good omen, Ornox thought.

Blood for blood. A death for a death.

* * *

When he returned to the base camp upriver where they had left most of their horses and supplies, Ornox found a small swift circling above. The band around the bird's leg glinted melon green in the light from the cooking fires.

"My lord," the swift called out. "Ghazan sent word."

"Speak," Ornox told the bird.

"May I approach?" At Ornox's nod, the swift landed on his shoulder and cocked her head to the warlord's ear. Her voice was scratchy and parched. "Ghazan sends his greetings and says that his alchemist's efforts have borne fruit."

Ornox nodded. "Tell Ghazan we will return within the moon. I expect him to have it ready for testing then."

The swift bobbed her head. "Ornox will return within the moon. He expects it to be ready for testing then."

"You may leave."

The swift took to the air, her small, dark form disappearing into the night.

Ornox looked at his bloodied sword, which he still had not cleaned or sheathed. He touched the rabbit's blood, contemplative, then returned his sword to its scabbard and looked up at the night sky.

The crimson moon was even redder than before, and the stars were out, pure and hard in the cloudless sky. Ornox felt cleansed, in control. Something had changed, and he realized that it was the hole that Agacheta's death had torn in him. That hole felt smaller somehow. Not gone, but it did not burn white hot as before.

Ornox the grieving father was at rest. It was time to focus on the next phase of his life. Ornox, Emperor of Mankahar.

CHAPTER 53

The gray-and-black figure lay face down on the murky shore, wedged between two rocks where the water was too weak to dislodge this debris. Here, two thin islands forked the river into three, and this furthest offshoot was quiet and calm compared to its boisterous sibling which thundered past on the island's other side. Here, the reddish moonlit water flowed around and beneath the inert figure, gurgling to itself over the slick rocks and gnarled mangrove roots.

A scavenger bird landed softly on a nearby rock and cocked its head, assessing. It was about to reach out and peck the body when there came a screech from above, the flap of wings, and an irate voice.

"Get away! Get!"

The bird took flight, resentful, as Hygra landed in the water where the scavenger once stood. Father Oaks slid off the Proud-feather's back, not even waiting for her to kneel, and splashed his way through the shallows to the still figure, then gingerly rolled it onto its back.

The old rabbit's face seemed to crumple at the sight. "Oh, lad."

He took in the blood-caked wound in the chest, the scraped

gray-and-black face, the left eye swollen. The grandfather hooked his paws beneath his grandson's arms and pulled. Hygra came forward to help, and soon, they had the soaking limp rabbit on shore.

"There's much blood," Hygra said, grim.

"It's the moonlight," Father Oaks insisted gruffly. "A rose moon makes everythin' look red."

He rolled Theo onto his side and felt for a pulse at the neck. There was none. Determined, Father Oaks pushed hard on his grandson's back. Nothing.

"Come now, lad." The old rabbit rolled Theo back toward him and bent his ear to his grandson's chest. He pushed Theo once more onto his side, then pounded once, twice, against the younger rabbit's back.

A gush of mud and water flowed out of the rabbit's slack mouth, but otherwise, Theo didn't move.

"That's it, lad!" Energized, Father Oaks redoubled his efforts, pausing every once in a while to press his intact ear to the chest and listen for a heartbeat. He continued like this for some moments, but slowed as time after time, there was no response. At last, he stopped, panting, the truth seeming to creep on him.

"I am sorry," Hygra said sincerely.

Father Oaks simply sat, numb.

A splash in the water made them look over. Standing in the shallows was Hygra's daughter, with Orjo on her back.

"Irah!" The Proudfeather matriarch greeted her child with surprise.

"We spotted the soldiers," Irah said. "Overheard them saying Theo was killed and went into the river." She glanced at the figure. "It's true then?"

Orjo dismounted and walked over, gazing down at Theo's body.

"That's a heart wound," the muskrat said heavily.

"Like ye said, he's my grandson," Father Oaks replied, quiet.

"So he's mine t' bury. Go find yer island or whatever it is ye're lookin' fer."

The muskrat considered this, then said, "I have another suggestion."

The old rabbit sighed. "Don't take offense, rat, but I don't want yer help."

"I'm not talking about me," Orjo replied. "There is someone who might be able to bring Theo back."

Everyone turned toward the muskrat, incredulous.

"What are ye talkin' about?" Father Oaks tried to sense whether this was a cruel joke.

"Zo."

"Who is Zo?" Hygra asked.

"Zo of the Miraculous Cures."

The Proudfeathers looked at one another. "Never heard of him," Irah said.

"Her." Orjo bent down and slid his paws beneath Theo's back. "If anyone can bring back the dead, she can. Now lend me a paw." He looked to the Proudfeathers. "How fast can you fly?"

Irah looked at her mother, who hesitated. The sight of Father Oaks' imploring face seemed to tip the balance. "As fast as you need."

"Good," Orjo said. "Then we'd best stop wasting time talking."

Hygra knelt as Orjo and Father Oaks lifted Theo's body onto her back. The muskrat clambered up behind Theo, while Irah knelt and used her beak to help Father Oaks up.

"Hold on, lad," Father Oaks whispered to his grandson before the birds took to the air. They skimmed the forest trees and headed north, wings shining red in the blood moon's light.

CHAPTER 54

*I*ndigo was in a smoky warren, her skin prickling from the heat and the heady smell of rue. The wrinkled ink master had looked into her eyes and seen her future. But he stayed silent, unwilling to speak.

"Master of the ink, tell me." No one commanded the ink master, but she was to be queen. The queen of Alvareth. The ink master would tattoo her ears with his vision of her past, her future. Her destiny.

"I see an omatje," he said, as if the words were being forced from him. "One with immense power."

Excitement laced with fear swelled in her. "Yes. A muskrat." She swallowed. "Do I kill him?"

The ink master shook his grizzled head. "I cannot see if he is a muskrat. But you will not kill him."

Her heart dropped. "Then he shall kill me."

Again, the ink master shook his head. "I see you fighting to save this omatje."

"Why would I do that?"

"For love."

Indigo woke spluttering, the dream of her initiation day seared away like water spilled on a hot stone. She lashed out and found her paw gripped by a much larger, meatier one.

"You're safe, Princess."

The paw let go, and Indigo sat up to find herself on a pallet in Queen Mercusa's chambers. Brune's shoulder was bandaged, and behind him, the head Grodlyn from the infirmary was mixing a concoction of herbs in a bowl. The carpets, she noticed, had been taken away, leaving only small specks of blood visible along the edges of the room and on the walls.

"How's your head?" the bear asked.

She didn't care about her head. "Where's Theo?"

"Take it slowly. The healers say you had much too big a dose of that poppy sap."

Indigo's chest squeezed, as if she was still in the serpent's grip. The head healer came with the bowl and offered it. "Drink. Makes you sleep it does."

"I don't want to sleep," Indigo replied, firm. *If you want to rule, you'll need to be strong enough for truth.* "Where's Theo?"

Brune's eyes clouded. "He's gone."

Indigo waited for him to elaborate, to say he didn't mean Theo was dead. But the bear stayed silent, and she wondered if she was still dreaming. Hoped to Aktu that she was still dreaming.

"Eluk?" she asked.

Brune turned to the Grodlyn. "Please let the queen and her brother know that Princess Indigo has woken."

The Grodlyn nodded and retreated out the door. When they were alone, Brune turned back to her. He seemed older, eyes weary and dimmer than she remembered.

"Eluk took him to Ornox," Brune said, quiet. "We've also had news from birds that have been near the Urzok camps. They all say Theo was killed. By Ornox's own sword."

"Did you search the area?"

Brune nodded, pained. "Everything supports what the birds say. His body was swept away in the river."

Indigo sat very still, her mind and tongue numb. She shut her eyes to the hot tears that burned her lids, closed herself to the pain that threatened to shatter her.

"Princess! How do you feel?"

Indigo looked toward the door and saw Mercusa. The rabbit ground one paw against her eyes, determined to keep signs of shock and grief to herself. The queen slid silently up to the pallet and coiled her amber-and-wine-colored body next to Indigo.

"I assure you that everyone involved in Eluk's betrayal will be punished," Mercusa said. She turned to Brune. "I owe you both an apology on behalf of Jaipri. Eluk has been by my side since even before I became queen, and I have always trusted him. He has openly disagreed with me on many occasions, but never disobeyed me. I misjudged him this time."

And Theo paid the price, Indigo thought to herself.

The queen seemed to sense her thoughts, for the serpent's eyes lowered, as if steeling her will, before addressing them again.

"Eluk violated our laws on neutrality and brought shame to Jaipri. And there is no price we can pay to amend that. But the Urzoks are the ones who came and forced us to take sides." The queen glanced at Indigo, then turned to Brune, and her tone turned formal. "Ornox's demands and Eluk's actions have convinced my council that neutrality is no longer an option. Therefore, as Queen of Jaipri, I declare to you, Brune of Hegg, that Jaipri is no longer neutral. I pledge my queendom and my citizens to the Order and its cause to bring down the empire."

"Are you sure, Your Majesty?" Brune asked, surprised.

The queen nodded. "It is something we should have done when you first came to Jaipri."

Indigo knew Brune well enough to read the mixed expression on his face—gratitude for the queen's decision, but also sadness at the truth of her words. Winning Jaipri's alliance had cost Theo's life—for this possibility was beginning to harden into fact. She and Brune had gained thousands of allies, but lost the one they cared about most.

The one the ink master had foretold.
The omatje she loved.

CHAPTER 55

The bard's voice floated out the solar doors onto the balcony, where Dorgun, Emperor of Mankahar, stood watching the setting sun dye the clouds a raw pink.

The musician's voice rose, then dipped in the song's final verse, ending in a flurry of strums on the lute that was meant to be moving.

The silence stretched. Dorgun gazed motionless at the sun for a moment. Two. When he turned to face the bard, a youth dressed in bright mustard-hued robes over green leggings and polished boots, he saw a flushed face full of nervous pride. Standing at attention but at a discrete distance was a retinue of servants.

Seeing the emperor's expression, the youth's confidence faltered. "Your Eminence?"

"Hm."

"What... Did it please you, Your Eminence?"

"Did what please me?"

The youth looked unsure. The emperor could tell he was gauging if Dorgun had had a lapse of wits due to his age. "Did the song please you?"

"Your stopping pleased me greatly."

The emperor motioned for his servants to show the bard out, then turned back to the balcony as the youth left.

How hard was it to commission a bard these days? Someone who could compose a popular song that would drown out the drivel of this nursery rhyme about the Griffinrider? About the Order, who had already taken the city of New Hegg and seemed to be gaining ground in the north? But all the bards could come up with were insipid, lukewarm tunes that flattered his ego and compared the empire to a mighty mountain that would never fall. He was old, and his body was not the one he had fifty summers ago, but despite the rumors circulating at court, he knew he wasn't cloudy in the head. Not in the least. He knew songs like these would never sway the people. He needed a musician who could wield words and music like a weapon. Disseminate a song like pacification powder, where everyone who heard it thought what he wanted them to think, what he wanted them to feel.

Where were the bards of old like Calgornan? He scowled, wistful. Calgornan could have composed the proper song in his sleep.

"Your Eminence."

The voice made him turn back to the room. His three remaining advisors, now that Brel was dead, stood in their robes just inside the entry.

"May we approach?" The tallest and eldest of the three, Haegon, had taken to speaking for them since Brel's body had been discovered in the Stone Forest and brought back to the capital. The emperor's blood still boiled at the thought of Ornox's brazen act. Did Ornox think he could go unpunished, cutting down the empire's highest-ranked advisor?

"You have news?"

The three prostrated themselves before him, then stood. "Word is that Ornox of Vyad has killed the one called Theo Griffinrider."

The emperor digested this. "Does he have the body?"

"Our sources say it was washed away in a river in Jaipri."

"And Ornox is headed for Kalyun-eh?"

"Most likely. He will want to be rewarded for the kill. Pardoned for Brel's death." The second advisor, Unndoran, had a luxurious beard that he groomed with care, possibly to make up for his bald head. The third advisor, Pridan, nodded but stayed silent, as was his habit.

Unndoran spoke reason. But if so, why let the proof of his victory disappear into a river? Unless the warlord had no intention of currying favor with his emperor. Which meant he didn't care for his emperor's good will. Which meant Ornox had very different plans.

Dorgun made a sign of dismissal. The three advisors bowed and retreated. The emperor watched until night had drowned out the outlines of his capital before he left the audience hall for his private chambers in the castle's central well.

Perched atop a pyramid in the innermost courtyard of the Kalyun-eh fortress, the royal chambers had a carved-stone staircase that led from an expansive balcony down the pyramid side to the courtyard. Two wide overhead hallways, with no windows but a dozen evenly spaced arrow slits, connected the chambers atop the pyramid to the castle's second level.

Dorgun now walked through the eastern hallway and into his expansive royal chambers, which consisted of a foyer, a middle private-dining area, and then a suite of sleeping and bath chambers. Once inside his foyer, he dismissed all his servants and waited for the mahogany doors to shut behind them. He then continued through to the bedchamber, where he pulled up the rug that covered most of his floor. Beneath it was a circular mosaic of interlocking serpents, as wide as his arm span.

The emperor pushed his silk sleeves aside and knelt, his age-stiffened fingers finding the tiles of their own accord. It was a familiar ritual, pressing the tiles with their individual glyphs in a code that only he knew. The tiles pressed down easily, and he heard the grinding of the stone lock opening.

He pushed down on one side of the circular mosaic, and the disc turned sideways on a metal axis, revealing a staircase that wound down into the pyramid below. With the pyramid walls several stones thick, no one could guess that the inside was hollow. Or that it descended deep beyond the castle floor.

Dorgun took a lamp from his bed chamber and walked carefully down the narrow steps until he was standing in a vast underground cavern that had six archways leading to further chambers beyond. Each room was lined with shelves, and all the shelves were filled end to end with books of every size and color.

In the middle of the chamber, in a place of pride on a square altar, was a crimson war helmet. The emperor placed his hand on it, feeling the familiar gouges that told of ancient battles.

"Good evening, Grandfather Dakus." He enjoyed saying the name of the first emperor. His ancestor from generations past.

The emperor made his way along the shelves, searching with his one good eye. He finally found what he was looking for and pulled out a thick, black bound volume with red-and-gold lettering.

"*War Songs by Calgornan.*" Dorgun ran his finger over the lettering, releasing the words as he went. He tucked the book under his arm and proceeded back toward his bed chamber, singing quietly.

> *War, war, war*
> *I hear it on the tide*
> *The scream of a thousand bow strings*
> *Will sing men to sleep tonight*
>
> *Come with your horn and swords*
> *I'll bring my wine and chords*
> *And we'll see who bleeds the more*

War, war, war,
I hear it on the tide...

He was still humming as he pushed the stone disc back into place, once again entombing his library, and all the secrets of Elshon, in airless dark.

Thanks for reading! Join my reader list to find out about the next book in the series, and receive:

* subscriber only bonus scenes from *Theo and the Secret of Elshon,* told from Princess Indigo's perspective;

* the prequel to *The Book of Theo* series, *The Queen and the Dagger;* plus

* reader exclusives, like previews to the first few chapters of upcoming books. JOIN NOW at www.melanieansley.com

If you enjoyed *Theo and the Secret of Elshon,* please consider leaving a review on Amazon and Goodreads. You'll be ensuring many more adventures follow in the *Book of Theo* series.

ACKNOWLEDGMENTS

Writing a book is a marathon, and wouldn't be possible without the help of all the champions cheering along the way.

Thanks to everyone who read the first book and kept asking about the sequel—Cecilia Sutton, Kristine Hall, Vicky Auyeung and numerous others, I can't thank you enough for the unflagging support.

Thank you to Sue, who was always willing to lend an eye to covers or offer an opinion when I couldn't see the forest for the trees, but first and foremost for being the best sister ever. Thanks to Monika Zec for her work on the cover, as well as my editor, Shelley Holloway, for helping me clean up the manuscript. To my ARC team (Maya Reid, Terry Kaye, Kendra Munger, Cecilia Sutton, Kristine Hall, Vanessa Church, and many others), thanks for helping spread the word even before the race started.

To Artemis and Evander, thanks for reminding me every day how important stories, and storytelling, are; that they are a necessity, not a luxury. And thank you to my partner in life and crime, Sam, who graciously read through more drafts of this book than is humanely reasonable.

ABOUT THE AUTHOR

Melanie was born in Canada but raised in China, and now lives in Ballarat, Australia with her husband and two children. She loves to read, write, and laugh. She also makes movies.

facebook.com/melanieansleyauthor
twitter.com/writingrooster
bookbub.com/profile/melanie-ansley

www.ingramcontent.com/pod-product-compliance
Lightning Source LLC
Chambersburg PA
CBHW010509100726
47902CB00011B/2140